Losing to Win

Also by Michele Grant

The Montgomery Series

Heard It All Before

Pretty Boy Problems

Any Man I Want

Sweet Little Lies

Losing to Win

Crush (with Cydney Rax and Lutishia Lovely)

Published by Kensington Publishing Corp.

Losing to Win

MICHELE GRANT

Dafina
Books

KENSINGTON PUBLISHING CORP.
http://www.kensingtonbooks.com

DAFINA BOOKS are published by

Kensington Publishing Corp.
119 West 40th Street
New York, NY 10018

All Kensington Titles, Imprints, and Distributed Lines are available at special quantity discounts for bulk purchases for sales promotions, premiums, fund-raising, and educational or institutional use. Special book excerpts or customized printings can also be created to fit specific needs. For details, write or phone the office of the Kensington special sales manager: Kensington Publishing Corp., 119 West 40th Street, New York, NY 10018, attn: Special Sales Department, Phone: 1-800-221-2647.

Dafina and the Dafina logo Reg. U.S. Pat. & TM Off.

ISBN-13: 978-0-7582-8964-3
ISBN-10: 0-7582-8964-2
First Kensington Trade Edition: October 2013
First Kensington Mass Market Edition: September 2015

eISBN-13: 978-1-4967-0151-0
eISBN-10: 1-4967-0151-8
Kensington Electronic Edition: September 2015

10 9 8 7 6 5 4 3 2 1

Printed in the United States of America

For Nellie Mae: true Southern belle; accomplished scholar; AKA card shark; crossword wizard; hat-wearing, shoe-matching, Bible-quoting Sunday-school teacher; mentor; wife; mother; and grandmother . . . Making bougie look good at eighty years old.

She gave me my first true love of books and reading.

Love you, Mom!

ACKNOWLEDGMENTS

A special thanks to all those clubs, organziations, and groups that embrace "my kind" of writing: Romance Writers of America, RT Book Reviews, OOSA Book Club, Black Pearls Keepin It REAL book club, Reads4Pleasure.com, UrbanReviewsonline.com, the Black Novelists Co-op, the wonderful folks from Black 'n Bougie, and so many more I'm sure I'm forgetting to mention.

I appreciate you!

1

I knew it was about to get a whole lot worse

Carissa—Monday, May 23—8:46 a.m.

"Can you tell us what you're thinking right now, Carissa Wayne? At this very moment?" The host chirped at me in his overly perky voice and a hush fell across the large room as the eager audience awaited my answer.

Standing on stage in front of the student assembly, teachers, and administrators of the Havenwood Academy while my friends, family, and townspeople eyed me with varied degrees of awe and apprehension was surreal. Having three cameras, four spotlights, and two microphones directed solely at me was discomforting. My answer to Jim Swindle, the aptly named host and ringleader of this debacle, was real.

"I'm wondering if your expense account will

cover my bail money," I announced without blinking.

The audience tittered and Jim held his smile in place. "Bail money? For what?"

Quietly, without the slightest bit of humor, I deadpanned my answer. "Someone is going to have to die for this."

Everyone, with the exception of my family, dissolved into laughter. My family, at least, had the good sense to know I wasn't joking. Upon further review, death was actually too good for whoever conspired to set me up like this.

It was the last day of school at Havenwood, an exclusive private school for grades 4–12 in Belle Haven, a small but modern outer suburb just to the north and east of New Orleans, Louisiana. As was tradition at Havenwood, everyone—including the staff—came dressed casually to clear out classrooms and lockers in preparation for summer. Any summer classes or programs were administered from an annex location. The main campus of Havenwood went dark from June to late August. This was the *only* reason I was in public rocking chocolate brown, wide-leg yoga capris that sagged in the back and a slouchy pink T-shirt that read "Girl Power—Get Into It!" My hair was snatched back in an unfortunate ponytail and my lips were adorned with nothing more than mint-flavored Carmex. My face was absent of even the tiniest speck of makeup. I had only expected to run into one or two students and then head home to start my re-coup. from the grueling school year. Teaching high school sophomores AP English Literature was a job that necessitated a three-month-long break. And a subscription to the Wine-of-the-Month Club. But that's not the point. The point was . . . I had not been expecting to socialize, let alone face this ambush.

And really? There was no other word for it. One moment I was wiping down my desk with lemon-scented Pledge; the next I responded to an overhead announcement requesting my presence in the auditorium. When I walked in, I attempted to take a seat at the back. I was called to the stage by Principal Garrett. As I walked down the aisle, I saw quite a number of townspeople not affiliated with the school seated in the audience. It wasn't until I noticed my mother, sister, and two cousins alongside my best friends Taylor and Mac all seated in the front row that I knew something was up. Not one of them would meet my eyes. Nor had any of them warned me about this. Traitors.

Even then I was still naive enough to think I was winning some sort of Teacher of the Year award. But oh, my entire damn, no. They had something else in store for me. I climbed the stairs and headed toward the middle of the stage. I tried to walk with some dignity in my run-down Reeboks and prayed that my butt wasn't jiggling too much. Again, these are things I would not have had to worry about if I was in my usual armor of tailored classics made of structured fabrics with Spanx holding everything in underneath. As I arrived at the podium, bright lights suddenly shone on me and a microphone was shoved in my face.

"Carissa Melody Wayne, your friends and family nominated you and you've been chosen to appear on *Losing to Win!*"

I blinked rapidly against the glare and cluelessly asked, "What is *Losing to Win?*"

The host shifted in his navy blue sport coat and looked astonished. "It's a competitive weight-loss reality show! Have you never seen it?"

"No, never," I snapped while trying to understand exactly what was going on.

The host shook his head in dismay. "You've seriously never watched the show?"

"Dude, don't be insulted. I don't watch any reality shows. I teach literature. My taste runs more toward history, documentaries, AMC, PBS; that sort of thing."

This seemed to stun Jim quiet long enough for me to absorb what he had to say.

"Wait a minute—did you say a competitive *weight-loss* show?!" No way would my people set me up to talk about how much weight I'd gained. Would they?

Swindle found his plastic smile again. "Well, you have to admit you could stand to lose a few, Carissa."

My jaw dropped as the audience gave a collective "Ooooo" sound. No he didn't!

"Carissa, here is a picture of you from your high school yearbook." This time the audience reaction was a breathy "Whoooaa" sound.

I turned in dismay as the wall behind me showed a gigantic picture of me doing the splits in the air in my size 4 Belle Haven High cheerleader uniform. Now dammit, that was just mean. Battling through my emotions, I tried to look at myself objectively. I had the same thick shoulder-length sandy brown hair that curled easily around my face. Okay, maybe now it was shot through with a gray streak here and there and didn't currently look its best scraped back in a brown scrunchy. My skin was the same shade of café au lait. My caramel-hued eyes were still wide, oval with a tilt at the end, decent lashes even without any cosmetic assistance. My lips were still somewhere between lush and full. My jaw was still a curved oval. A little more fleshy but oval. My complexion was still clear and wrinkle free. I was still five foot five with long legs, generous cleavage, and a short waist. I'd still maintained my cute. My cute had developed a few more pronounced curves here and there.

That's where the similarities between me and the smiling girl from fifteen years ago ended. Young Carissa was ready to take on the world and thought it was hers for the taking. She was 108 pounds of lean, muscled, go-get-'em. I, on the other hand, weighed at least fifty more pounds. I was far more fluffy than lean these days. My cleavage had moved past generous to cup-runneth-over a few years back. My biggest muscle was my brain and my get-up-and-go had gotten up and fled without a backward glance years ago. Life had kicked me in the ass and I hadn't quite struggled back into fighting shape yet.

I folded my arms and glared at Jim Swindle with his perfectly coifed blond hair, gleaming white teeth, and carrot-toned tan. "Yes, so I see."

"Would you say you've put on some weight since then?"

I glared harder. "Clear-ly," I bit out.

"Some of your friends and family are caring and concerned enough that they thought you needed this push."

"Is that what we're calling it? 'Caring and concerned'? Okay then." I sent a laser beam side eye toward the front row where said friends and family shifted uneasily.

"Carissa, about how much did you weigh in that picture?"

"Somewhere between 105 and 110, why?"

"It just so happens we replaced a section of the stage with a built-in scale and you are standing on it. How much do you think you weigh now?"

I flushed hot and then cold and then hot again. I looked to the side for an opportunity to escape. Someone had to be kidding me with this! I could only assume that someone among friends and fam was getting quite the check from this stunt. But this kind of humiliation could not be smoothed over with a payday. I was standing in front of an auditorium of people plus cameras struggling not to cry. The best I could come up with was a shrug and a shake of my head. I knew I was overweight; I had no idea by how much. Nor did I care to know.

"We're going to put your weight up on the screen, if you don't mind," Jim said in that annoyingly cheerful voice.

"And if I do mind?" I asked, still hoping to make this all go away.

"I'm afraid we're going to do it anyway," he replied gleefully. "Are you ready?"

I just shook my head and quickly swiveled toward the screen. One beat, two beat, three beats . . .

and there it was. 188. One hundred and eighty-eight pounds?! Gasps rolled through the audience.

I blinked twice and the offending number in bold black font was still there. "What?! That can't be right."

"I'm afraid that is your current weight, Miss Wayne."

All I could do was stand there in shocked denial. There was no way I had gained over seventy pounds in fifteen years. No. Possible. Way. This day sucked. And since I couldn't figure out how it could possibly suck more, I turned back around to see what was next.

That's when he asked me how I was feeling and I told him someone needed to die. When the audience settled back down, he continued.

"All jokes aside—here's the deal. You and five other contestants will compete for around four months. You'll be given a trainer, a nutritionist, and a workout partner. Not only do you earn money for each weight milestone you achieve, you earn money and points for winning competitions, for challenges, and in other ways we'll reveal along the way. At the end, if you and your partner have the highest point total combined with the greatest weight loss, you split one million dollars!"

Half a million dollars? That was at least pause worthy. "Besides this humiliation, what's the catch?" I asked sardonically.

"The catch is that your entire life for the next few months is going to be filmed. If you agree to do the show, you get a check for ten thousand dollars today. Because your community and your family and friends have been so outgoing and welcoming, we're going to base the show here in your hometown of Belle Haven, Louisiana!"

It was beginning to come clear to me now. This assembly of half the town, the nervous but eager smiles of everyone around me: my decision was about more than me. If I agreed to this craptastic nonsense, the town, the school, and everyone around gained from it. If I refused, the lights and the cameras and the revenue packed up and went elsewhere.

Jim turned toward the cameras. "This small town in the storm-ravaged Gulf area of Louisiana is one of the many areas suffering through the economic downtown. With the combination of Hurricane Katrina, the oil spill, and the recession, areas like these have struggled to regain their way of life. In our own small way, *Losing to Win* partners with the cities where we host our shows. Not only by spending our time and money here, but also by showcasing the community and hopefully bringing some tourist attraction. We've spoken to your local government about ways to support Belle Haven industries. We will patronize restaurants that work with local sustainable foods, and of course our cast and crew will stay here for the majority of the filming of the show. Just one of the many ways that our network invests in small-town America." He completed his spiel and turned back toward me. "So what do you say, Carissa, wouldn't you like to give a little something back to the city that you love?"

Nothing like having epic guilt heaped upon your head in front of town and family. "I take it I have to decide right now in front of everybody with the cameras rolling?" I asked rhetorically. I already knew the answer. That was the whole reason behind the staged ambush: to put me in a position where I couldn't say no without looking selfish. Someone was going to pay and pay dearly for this when all was said and done. I raised my head up, threw my shoulders back, and looked directly into the cameras. "Fine, I'll do it."

The place erupted into cheers and whistles while I struggled not to shoot the finger at everybody. I was the one standing on stage looking my absolute worst discussing things that were best kept between me and my physician.

"That's great, Carissa! You've made a great decision. Would you like to meet the other contestants and your partner?" Swindle smiled extra wide. So wide, I was struck with a wave of dread. He was up to something. As bad as these fifteen minutes on stage had already been, I knew it was about to get a whole lot worse.

I closed my eyes, took a bracing breath, and smiled. "The faster we do it, the faster we're done. Bring it on."

Underneath the heavy stage makeup, Jim's eyes lit up with approval. With a nod, he turned toward the left wing of the stage. "Up first is a housewife from Maine who went to Belle Haven High School with you. She says the two of you competed for everything back in the day, from prom queen to head cheerleader. She's determined to win this time. Please welcome—"

"Suzette Pinchot," I muttered under my breath as Jim announced her as Suzette Pinchot-Allendale.

My high school nemesis. To say we were competitive was an understatement. There wasn't anything I wanted that Suzette had not attempted to take, break, or steal. The only reason she married Jerome Allendale was because I started a rumor that I liked him. Even though nothing could make this moment suck less, it was some consolation that when Suzette walked out on stage, she had clearly put on more weight than I had. She was virtually unrecognizable as the curvy Creole siren she used to be. Her once lustrous black curls were frizzy and hanging in her face. She and I eyed each other from a distance and exchanged the briefest of nods.

"The next contestant hasn't been back to Belle Haven in over twenty years, though he remembers it fondly. He used to pull Carissa's pigtails and call her 'Kissa Wayne.' Please welcome Xavier James to the show."

I could only weakly wave at XJ. I hadn't seen him since middle school. He still had the playful smile and laughing eyes, but I wouldn't have known him. He was bald, short, and nearing three hundred pounds, unless I missed my guess.

"This next contestant says she knows many of Carissa's secrets from college but is sworn to secrecy through their bonds of sisterhood. Let's see how long that lasts! Niecy Tibbs, come on out!"

My eyes went wide as my line sister from Howard strolled out on the stage. She was one of my best friends from college, though we didn't see each other often. She had stayed in DC when I moved back home after college. Niecy had been a size 22 for as long as I'd known her and was, as she said with two snaps, "Fabu-lustrous, darling!" With a squeal, I ran over to her and gave her a hug. It was great to see a friendly face. "What in the world are you doing here?" I asked under my breath.

"Thought I'd spend the summer hanging out with you; obviously skipped some of the fine print."

"Oh damn," I commiserated.

"You got that right. We'll talk later; you're in for a ride," she murmured as the host pointed me back to my spot on the stage.

I rolled my eyes and walked back near my assigned spot, avoiding the area where I knew the scale was hidden. No need to step on that again if I could help it.

"Next up, another blast from your past. This man said he tried courting you in graduate school, but you only saw him as a friend. He's here to change all that. Jordy Little, come on out." My study partner from grad school, a generally nice, light-skinned guy with whom I had zero chemistry came out on stage. He was handsome, congenial, and completely nonconfrontational. Jordy looked pretty much the same. A shade over six foot, curly dark brown hair a touch too long, and a paunch belly that had grown into more of a spare tire since I'd seen him last. He sent a grin my way and stepped next to Niecy.

I smiled back at him before I turned to the camera and put my hands on my hips. "Jim, what is this? '*This Is Your Life*, Carissa Wayne'?"

The audience laughed and Jim gave me another insincere toothy grin. "Well, we have to keep it interesting. You would know that if you ever watched the show."

"Oooooo" from the audience again. I decided

to play along so we could get this over with. I nodded with false cheer. "You got me on that one, Jim." I scanned the stage. "We're one contestant short and do I get to pick my partner?" I was picking Niecy. Hands down. No contest.

But Jim was already shaking his head and giving me the look that meant more shiggity was up his overstarched sleeve. "We've already picked someone for you. It's someone you know well. Someone we all know well. Born right here. The pride of Belle Haven."

I went completely still. They couldn't . . . they wouldn't . . .

"Your former high school sweetheart. The man you referred to as 'the love of your life' not so very long ago. Your former fiancé, in fact. Former homecoming king, former Heisman runner-up, and former All-Pro NFL wide receiver, known as the Bayou Blue Streak. The one, the only Malachi Knight."

Strolling onto the stage with that familiar rolling gait was the *former* love of my life. Though heavier than I'd ever seen him, he still possessed more charisma, star power, and magnetism than one man needed. As the audience roared and clapped, I saw him flash the smile that sold Gatorade, gym shoes, and thousands of *Sports Illustrated* copies. I'd heard about his career-ending knee injury two years ago, but at that time we were way past the point of solicitous phone calls or e-mails. When the last words you say to somebody are, "I hope that football keeps you warm at night," you're not entitled to call when that career ends abruptly.

Mal was the color of burnished walnut with jet black wavy hair and features that whispered of both Indian and African heritage. He was the classic kind of Sidney Poitier/Denzel Washington handsome with personality to spare. He was the kind of guy that men wanted to have a drink with and women wanted to get naked with. He was That Guy. Always had been and he knew it.

I noticed he had let his hair grow past his customary low cut and it was trending toward curly. At six foot four he carried his weight well, but I could tell he was at least thirty to forty pounds over his normal weight. It didn't detract from his overall attractiveness. I found that patently unfair, adding insult to injury. As he walked toward me, his dark chocolate eyes raked over me from the tip of my head to the toe of my shoe. That look used to make me melt; now it made me more irritated than I already was. He raised a brow as I glared at him. This was definitely not how I wanted to look and act when our paths crossed again. We had studiously avoided crossing each other's paths for years. My dream of meeting up with him while looking fabulous with my gorgeous rich husband on my arm was shot all to hell and back. I was not at my best. Oh, whatever, this was what it was. I raised my chin up a notch and raised my brow to match.

He stopped in front of me and said one word. "Rissa." His voice was still a deep rumble of Southern goodness.

"Mal," I responded, not giving an inch.

"This should be interesting," he acknowledged.

"No doubt," I snapped out shortly

We both knew instinctively that Jim, the cameras, and the audience were looking for us to create some kind of dramatic, messy scene. We weren't going to give it to them. We turned in silence to look at Jim.

"That's all you two have to say to each other?" Jim prodded.

"Yep," Malachi answered.

"I'm good," I responded.

With a deep sigh, Jim continued, "Niecy and Jordy will be partners. Suzette and Xavier will be partners. Of course, Malachi and Carissa will be working together. Tonight you can eat what you want, drink what you want, sleep where you want. But tomorrow . . ." He paused dramatically. "Let the games begin! You are the season six contestants on *Losing to Win!*"

As the audience applause rolled again, a petite blonde came bounding out on stage and made a slashing motion with her hand. "And cut! We got it! It's going to be perfect. Great work, everybody!"

She bounced over to me. "Carissa, I'm Bliss, and I'm the producer and director of the show, great to meet you. Sorry about all the shock and awe, but it makes for great TV, don't you think?" She continued on without waiting for my response. "Since you were the last person added, you still need to go over your contracts and get your check. My production assistant, Ren, will be by to get you squared away. Also, Marcy, our associate producer, will meet up with you and Malachi tonight to review the taping schedule. We can do it separately or together, doesn't matter. You'll meet your training team in the morning. Okay? You good? All set? Okay. Call me if you need me, Ren has the phone list." Before waiting for an answer to any of her statements, she bounced away.

"Bliss, Ren, Marcy?" I repeated with a glance at Malachi.

He smirked. "We should have expected no less."

"I wasn't expecting anything at all."

"So it seems. But here we are. Welcome to Hollywood . . . South Bayou Edition."

I started to grin back and then I remembered that he was the man who broke me. My face settled into a neutral mask. "This day continues to suck," I said and turned away. He reached out to touch my arm and a treacherous sizzle shot through my veins. We both froze in place. I dropped my eyes down to his hand and looked up at him with a raised eyebrow. He raised one in return.

"We're in this together, Cari."

"I've heard that before from you. This time I'm smart enough not to believe it."

With a sigh, Mal leaned down and said quietly into my ear, "We need to talk. We can get through this together."

I snatched my arm away. "*Together*? That's rich, coming from you. But you are right about one thing. We do need to talk. Fortunately for you, I have people higher up on my list to deal with right now." I stalked a few feet away before pausing. It was better to get this over with sooner rather than later. "I'll be home this afternoon. Come see me and we'll talk. I bought the old Somers house."

He looked at me in bemusement. "So you

really did it, huh? Moved back home, bought the house . . . the whole nine?"

My mouth twisted. "There are a few pieces to the puzzle still missing." I marched down the stairs with my head held high and approached my back-stabbing family.

"Carissa Melody Wayne," Malachi called out.

Since the whole auditorium fell silent to listen, I answered him. "Malachi Henry Knight?"

"It's good to see you, even under these circumstances."

"I wish I could say the same." I pointed to my family and toward the side exit door in an unmistakable gesture. I reached the door first and held it open as they filed past one at a time, heads down and wordlessly. After the last one exited, I looked over my shoulder to find Mal standing in the same spot watching me. I felt no remorse for stepping outside and letting the door slam closed behind me with a loud reverberating bang.

2

What is a shebacle?

Carissa—Monday, May 23—9:34 a.m.

I pasted what I hoped passed for a smile on my face. Nodding at the fine folks of Belle Haven, I marched my family toward the tiny closet I called my office on the Havenwood campus. Across the main pavilion, up a short flight of stairs, and down a hallway, we progressed in charged silence. Reaching the office, I stomped toward my desk and took two deep breaths. Relax. Relate. Release. Woo and sah.

When I thought I could speak without screeching, I twirled to glare meaningfully at the assembled motley crew of co-conspirators. In the front of the group huddled on the opposite wall was my older sister, Ruby Ann. She stood in all her five-foot-ten, size-16 Creole glory rocking a bright paisley maxidress with her ebony hair streaming down her back in waves. Right next to her in a dramatic

hot-pink suit, looking half her age, was her partner
in crime, my mother, Eloise.

Behind them hid my cousin Sharon, whom we
all called "Sugar," and her brother "Middle Mike"
(aptly named so as not to be confused with his father, "Big Mike," or his younger cousin on my
dad's side, "Little Mike"). Sugar barely reached
five foot tall and looked like a light wind could
bowl her over. She was olive skinned with short
curly hair and wide expressive eyes. She appeared
almost doll-like. When she opened her mouth,
however, all similarity to sweetness and light fled.
Sugar swore like a sailor and had colorful (if not
lewd) commentary for all occasions.

Mike was her complete opposite in every way.
He topped six foot, possessed skin the color of
deep mahogany, and weighed in at over two hundred and fifty pounds, yet he spoke quietly and politely in a gentle Southern drawl. He never had an
unkind word to say about anyone. I couldn't imagine how he'd gotten embroiled in this plot.

Even farther away, the only two looking the least
bit chagrined were my best friends from childhood, Taylor Rhone and Mac Bisset. I should have
known something was up from the looks of them.
Taylor was an artist. She was the kind of girl who
never met a headband and ratty jeans she didn't
love, yet here she was dressed to the nines in a silky
wrap dress with dangly earrings and wedge sandals.
Her hazelnut-hued skin gleamed and I detected
mascara on her lashes. Her normally untamed curly
fro was pulled into a complicated upsweep. Mac
was a contractor and real estate developer in a company he ran with his brother, Burke. He stood five

foot ten, a light-skinned, whip-thin guy, not the least bit aware of his attractiveness. And he generally spent his days in cargo pants and faded T-shirts. Today he was in a perfectly pressed and tailored linen suit that I'd never seen him wear before.

I shook my head at the lot of them. "Look at y'all, all dandied up for TV. Some Hollywood folks wave a few dollars at you and you throw me under the bus? No warning, no nothing? Really?! I mean, look at me!" I held my hands out to the side, took another deep breath, and exhaled shakily. I felt more than a little bit betrayed.

"Cari, baby . . . now listen," my mother, the normally sensible Eloise Wayne, started in. When I held up my hand and sent her a look she had used on me countless times, she subsided.

"Mom, no. I don't care what they promised all of you; this was too much. That . . . shebacle you just witnessed is going to be televised nationally! People I've never met know how much I weigh! And Mal?! After all I've been through to get over him? There's no excuse for this. None. What. So. Ever. Someone better start explaining. And I mean right the hell now." I ended my mini-rant by crossing my arms and tapping my foot.

Sugar slapped her hands on her nonexistent hips and stepped forward on her five-inch stilettos. "Before we start yammering on, I got one quick question for you, Carissa Melody."

"What?" I frowned at her.

"What is a shebacle?"

"Oh. It's a combination of bullshiggity and debacle."

Middle Mike covered up a laugh with a cough and turned his head to the side.

Ruby Ann spoke up. "You hate us all you want. You'll get over it. You always do." I tried to interrupt and she put her hand up. "Nuh-uh, you wanted an explanation. You gotta let me get through it." She paused and I shrugged to indicate that she could continue. "All right, then. This here is a win-win for everybody. So what you got a little embarrassed, Rissa. It's not like you don't know you could stand to lose a pound or two. Before you start squawking again, listen: these Hollywood folks are going to be here for at least three months or so, not counting postproduction. This town needs that cash influx, not to mention the exposure."

Taylor added, "As you know, we're a distant suburb of New Orleans; people may or may not find us even when they are looking. This is not just a few dollars, Ris. This show can single-handedly revitalize the Belle Haven economy. You know how tough it's been around here since the flood, the oil spill, and the economy crashing. This is an opportunity to get people into Ruby Ann's restaurant, Sugar's bed-and-breakfast, my gallery. Mac might actually have a few people hand over cash for their house repairs instead of paying him with gumbo and homemade biscuits."

"Great. So everyone profits from my humiliation?" I was far from mollified.

My mother stepped right in front of me. "Carissa Melody Wayne. How many times have you said you wished you could do something more to boost the economy around here?"

"Yeah, but—"

"But nothing. This is something more. So what if you have to run on a treadmill thingy for the world to see and actually spend some time with the man you used to adore? Who cares what the rest of the world thinks? You have always carried yourself with class and dignity. A few cameras are not going to change that."

I sighed. My mother had a way of breaking things down in such simplistic terms that I felt foolish for bringing it up in the first place. And then I remembered standing on that damn scale with my weight flashing on a huge screen and bright lights blinding me. And I asked the one question I really needed an answer to. "What about Dad?"

Eloise's face took on the resigned, pinched look associated with any mention of her ex-husband. "What about him?"

"C'mon, Mom! Cameras, publicity, money? How long until he rolls back into town from whatever misadventure he's been on and makes this situation even worse than it already is?" My father, Stacy Wayne, known to all as "Blue," was the quintessential rolling stone. Blue was a talented musician and entertainer but a lousy father and husband. He wanted to be wherever the action was and the spotlight shone brightest, preferably on him. He met my mother when she was singing and playing piano in a New Orleans lounge. One year later they were married with Ruby Ann on the way.

The first time Blue Wayne was forced to come home to a tired wife and a screaming baby, he announced that he was going out for formula. He didn't come back for three years. Swearing to do right by Eloise, he talked his way back in. A year after that, I arrived. Six months later a talent scout offered Blue an opportunity to do session work in Nashville. He was packed and gone before sunset. The first time I spent more than twenty-four hours in a row with him, I was three years old. And I could count on one hand the number of times we'd spent significant quality time together since.

His visits home had been both infrequent and insincere. Finally, one hot summer night when he was sneaking out the back door with his suitcase, his guitar, and that month's rent money, my mother decided she'd had enough. She told him to leave an address where she could forward the divorce papers and bolted the normally unlocked door behind him. I was five years old at the time.

Since then, Blue tended to visit when his funds got low or he was looking for some sort of an ego stroke. Most of the town thought that Blue had hit the big time in Nashville, playing on records for B. B. King and Bobby Bland. What they didn't know was that he usually spent more than he made. Blue Wayne spent the majority of his adult life on the road playing gig after gig just to make ends meet. As far as I knew, he'd never remarried, owned a home, or settled down. Just imagining his reaction to actual Hollywood camera crews in Belle Haven and an opportunity for a payday was enough to make me want to scrap the whole thing.

Eloise tilted her chin upward with dignity. "Don't you worry about Stacy Wayne. If he shows up, I'm ready for him."

Ruby Ann and I exchanged glances. That could mean anything. And none of it good. I changed the subject. "Fine. But really *no* one could tell me? I look a hot mess and I would have appreciated a little heads-up before seeing Mal again." What I really could've used was a four-day head start to get the hell out of town, but that was neither here nor there.

Mac shot me a look. "Say I came to you two days ago and told you about all this? Where would you be right now?"

"As far away as my Visa balance would allow," I snapped.

"I believe you answered your own question," Mac finished.

Ruby Ann rolled her eyes. "It's a few months of your life. Suck it up."

Middle Mike added quietly, "Sorry, cuz. We couldn't think of any other way. You didn't do bad up there, though."

I shrugged. "What options did I have?" They all fell silent. I shook my head. "Well, what's next? I'm sure you all have plotted and schemed how you want the next few months to go? I assume visits to each of your establishments with camera crews following? Basically be a walking commercial for the great town of Belle Haven?"

Sugar clapped her hands. "See now? That's the kind of love I'm looking for."

They all looked at me expectantly. After a deep sigh, I gave in. "Fine."

A collective sigh of relief was heard.

Taylor stepped forward and gave me a hug. "Sorry about springing Mal on you. But maybe this is for the best. Give you a chance to get some closure. Put the past in the past?"

My mother snorted. "Or to pick things back up again and put them right, if you ask me."

I crossed my arms and tapped my foot. "Respectfully, Mama—did I ask you?" Sometimes my mother drove me crazy with her unsolicited remarks.

"No." Eloise sniffed and smoothed her hands down her silk and linen suit. "But I'm telling it anyway."

"Mama, don't start in on her," Ruby Ann admonished, with another roll of the eyes.

"Since when is telling the truth not allowed? Carissa Melody Wayne and Malachi Henry Knight belong together. Everybody in this town has known that since they were in junior high school!"

"I don't think Malachi got that memo, Mother," I said in a quiet voice that indicated I was done talking about it. In fact, the whole wretched morning was starting to catch up with me.

Mac caught my eye and nodded. "Why don't we clear out and let you, uh . . . marinate on the morning?"

The door to the office swung open and a tall skinny kid with thick-rimmed glasses, skinny jeans, and a nervous expression stepped inside. "Hey, Carissa, I'm Ren, your production assistant. Is now a good time?"

"For what?" I said in not my friendliest tone.

"Er. Uh. Well. To go over your paperwork and the filming schedule?"

This was it. I was about to sign my life away . . . literally for the foreseeable future. Opening up parts of my life I had no interest in dissecting on film. For all to see. It was a nightmare. Ren slid a folder in front of me with the *Losing to Win* logo on it. Flipping it open, the first thing I noticed was a check made out to me in the amount of ten thousand dollars. I picked up the check and studied it. It was drawn from a local bank. With this check, I could afford to pay Mac to finish the upgrades on my house and maybe get Ruby Ann the new grill top she wanted for her restaurant. With a few more checks, I could restore the backyard jungle into presentable gardens. Buy my mama the grand piano she'd always wanted. Maybe I'd finally lease some space for the youth center I was to open someday. I could set aside a nest egg. I could travel.

Suddenly, I got it. My miserable existence for the next few months equated to business and money for my hometown and those I cared about. It was a chance to get out from under, a chance to get ahead. This is what they called "taking one for the team," and I could walk away in a better place physically and financially. I mean, how bad could it really be? I closed my eyes briefly and nodded slowly.

"Sure, Ren. Now's a great time. Come on in." I pretended not to see the relieved looks my friends and family exchanged as they filed out the door.

3

This could be my shot

Malachi—Monday, May 23—9:27 a.m.

It took over an hour to extricate myself from all the Belle Haven well-wishers who wanted to chat me up, relive old times, thank me for doing the show, and generally just have a moment of my time. Then there was the matter of a short meeting with Pierre, my best friend and agent. Pierre Picard had been a business marketing major at LSU, one year ahead of me when I showed up on campus. Originally from Beaumont, Texas, his family had deep roots in Cajun country. Pierre was also popular on campus, tall and good-looking in an old-school Billy Dee Williams kind of Idris Elba way. He was heavily into student politics and president of his fraternity. While most people on campus were kissing up and trying to be my friend, Pierre just nodded an acknowledgment and kept moving. We met the first time Carissa came to campus. I was running late, and by the time I caught up with her, she was sitting in the lobby of my dorm talking to Pierre as if they'd known each other forever. I gave him my best "mess with my woman and answer to me" look. He just laughed, thanked Carissa for a pleasant conversation, and walked away. For some reason, that impressed me. I sought him out, realized he was probably about the most business-savvy guy I'd ever met, and asked him to be my agent on the spot. He not only became my advocate in all things business but a good friend to me as well. He was the one who approached me with the idea to do the show, and though it was unconventional, I could definitely see using this as a vehicle to get back to where I wanted to be.

By the time I turned onto Climbing Rose Lane, I was still struggling to digest all that had happened in the past few weeks.

Regardless of some current opinions, I wasn't a bad guy. Really. I was just a guy who had lost his way and was trying to get back on track. Everything in my world was up in the air. It was good to pull into the driveway and see that some things stayed just as you'd expect.

My childhood home had looked the same for as long as I could remember. It was a tidy-looking, blue double-gallery-style house with wraparound porches on both stories. Painted iron railings of stark white adorned the house. Large windows facing north and south gleamed as though freshly cleaned. The stucco and brick structure had outlasted many a storm and attempts at destruction by me and my younger brother, Meshach. The house still stood as a stately and serene haven in front of the rolling acres behind it.

I rolled to a stop at the curve in the paved portico of my parents' home to see my father sitting on the aged walnut rocker on the front porch. Before I'd climbed out of the rental SUV, my mother stepped outside to join him. My parents were good, Southern, salt-of-the-earth, shoot-straight people. No matter how famous, wealthy, or worldly I became, they stayed the same: rock solid, rooted in Christian values, tolerant, full of unconditional love and steady advice.

Henry and Valentine Knight looked at me with equal parts love and censure. My father was about five foot nine and my mother stood five foot seven in heels. They were both slight and slender. Where he was light, she was dark. They complemented each other in every way. He liked to say she was the cookies to his cream, both in looks and personality. Henry once shared with me that he still woke up every day tickled to be married to the woman of his dreams.

They said I was a throwback to my grandfather, a Chickasaw warrior who stood well over six foot tall in his prime. My father, a mostly retired small-town doctor, had taken to dressing in dark jeans and a button-down denim shirt with lace-up boots. My mother, a fully retired schoolteacher, was dressed per usual: as if she expected a tea party to commence at any minute. Today's pleated silk dress was in a soft shade of green. Pearls winked at her neck and ears.

"Boy, what the hell was you thinkin'? Settin' that gal up like this?" My father's distinctive drawl reached me before he did.

I put my hands up. "I had no idea they were going to spring it on her like that, Dad. Believe me, the last place I want to be is in Carissa Wayne's doghouse."

"You mean farther into the doghouse, don't you, son?" My mother laughed as I picked her up and spun her around, kissing her noisily on the cheek. She patted her short curly hair as I set her down.

Henry cackled gleefully when I picked him up and gave him the same treatment. "What's farther out than the doghouse, Malachi? The outhouse?" He slapped me on the back a few times and I set him down with a grin.

"Maybe under the house, I don't know," I sheepishly acknowledged. "But Ms. Wayne clearly has nothing good to say about or to me. Did you see how she looked at me when I walked out on that stage? Whew. That death glare she sent me clearly broadcasted her wish that I was anywhere but near her and preferably six feet under."

"Whose fault is that, son?" my parents asked at the same time.

"Don't double-team me. The fault is probably 70 percent on my side and 30 percent on hers."

"You gonna fix it this time?" Valentine asked with a raised brow as we walked into the house.

I followed her into the huge, recently renovated kitchen and sat down at the granite island. She handed me a glass of iced tea and I took a deep sip while I thought about Carissa and trying to "fix" the situation. Nothing quite like cool, sweet minty tea in the South. It was simple and expected. Unlike the issues between me and my former intended.

The rift between me and Carissa was multifaceted and complex in nature. It wasn't easily categorized as "we didn't want the same things"; it was a complete breakdown of communication, goals, and trust. It was messy and I had enough on my plate without diving into messy right now. When I'd said it was 70 percent my fault, that might have been too conservative. I still didn't fully understand what I'd done to make her leave, but the fact that she had left without a backward glance didn't sit well with me. Yeah, it was messy and nothing I cared to share with my parents. "I don't know, Ma. One: I'm not sure if I *can* fix it after all this time. Two: It might be best to leave that water under the bridge. And three: She won't want me to even try and repair our problems if things work out the way I think they will."

My parents exchanged glances and sat down across from me awaiting an explanation.

"You both know when I got injured, I wasn't ready to quit." An understatement if ever there was one. My entire life up until two years ago had been about the chase of a Super Bowl ring. Until that point, I was a Pro Bowl wide receiver for one of the league's elite teams. I was one of those guys who had played football since the age of six and been successful at every level. I won a high school state championship followed by an easy leap to a Division 1A college with a full scholarship. My sophomore team was the one that brought the Rose Bowl trophy back to Louisiana. I was runner up in the Heisman Trophy balloting in my junior year; supposedly I was a shoo-in to win it the following year, but I opted to leave and take my chances in the NFL.

Chosen as the only first-round draft pick of the Houston Stars, it was a challenge to find myself on an expansion team that wasn't supposed to go far. I was single minded in my pursuit of greatness. I wanted to break all the records, sign the most endorsements, and get my name mentioned with the greats. If I neglected Carissa or took her for granted along the way, well, I figured that's what it took to be great. She knew I loved her and that if I kept pushing the wedding date back, it had nothing to do with how I felt about her. I thought she and I had all the time in the world to be together, but the shelf life of an NFL athlete is short. It took eight years to get there, but the high-powered Houston Stars offense had arrived at the conference championship game only to come up three yards short of the Super Bowl in the last forty seconds.

The whole team imploded in the aftermath. My quarterback left, the running back quit to find himself, the coaches were fired, and a front-office shuffle began. The team was just pulling back together during a preseason game when The Incident happened. The details are hotly debated to this day. I believe I was the victim of a cheap-shot defensive back; others say I landed wrong. Either way, I tore both my MCL and my ACL. All of the specialists said it was a career-ending injury. I never announced my retirement; I just faded out of the spotlight. I isolated myself, packed on weight, and basically wallowed in self-pity for about a year. The only person I reached out to was Carissa. And by that time, she wasn't having it or hearing it. Not from me.

One night, after refusing to sign a fan's T-shirt, I overheard him calling me a "fat washed-up coulda-been" and it hurt. Insults that ring a little true often do. So I started rehabbing and getting myself together, making plans for the future. According to the specialist, the knee was at 95 percent. I had less than forty pounds left to lose.

I looked across at my parents and made my announcement. "I know the show is kinda stupid, but it accomplishes a few things for me. I want to use the exposure to show the league that I can come back. This could be my shot. I'm thirty-three years old. Most receivers are hanging up their cleats by now. I want one last shot at that ring. I want to go back."

"To the NFL?" my father asked with a small smile on his face.

"Yes, why are you smiling like that?"

He shrugged. "What took you so long?"

I threw my head back and laughed. "I could never surprise you. I needed to be mentally and physically ready. I needed to make sure I could make a real run at it without making a fool of myself. When I was sitting on my sofa well over three hundred pounds, I wasn't ready. I talked to Pierre; he says the Stars will give me a walk-on tryout whenever I'm ready. We're shooting for mid-August." Pierre wouldn't let me take this shot if he didn't think I could do it. He had stood beside me when no one else but my family could stand listening to me.

Valentine came around and took my big hand in between her softer, smaller ones. "Mal, we only want you to be happy. If trying to play again makes you happy, so be it. But son, wasn't your NFL lifestyle one of the reasons you and Carissa split?"

I was not getting into that aspect of our breakup with my mother. Not today, not ever. "Like I said, Mom: I don't know if I can fix things with Cari."

She squeezed my hands. "Since you were a teenager, you've talked about two things you wanted in life. One was to win a Super Bowl and the other was to marry Rissa Wayne. And I gotta say, it doesn't sound to me like you're 100 percent ready to give up either dream yet. Don't lose one holding on to the other."

Not knowing what else to say, I nodded and changed the subject. "Are you two ready for the bright lights of Hollywood to shine down on Climbing Rose Lane?"

My father sucked his teeth in disgust. "Boy, this is some damn foolishness you've dragged us into this time. Some woman came around and asked if I was going to need extra time for makeup on shooting days. Do I look like the kind of man who will allow them to put makeup on me?"

I smothered a chuckle. "No, sir, you surely don't."

My mom nodded her approval. "I think it will be good for the town. Goodness knows we could use the revenue."

"That's the other reason I agreed to do it.

Doesn't hurt to give a little something back to Belle Haven. This town has been good to me. If having Hollywood folks following us around for a few months brings in a few dollars, the better for it."

Dad looked skeptical and shrugged. "I certainly hope this all works out, Mal. For you, Carissa, and the town."

"Me too, Dad." More important, I hope it doesn't all blow up on a nationally televised stage. Even at our best, Carissa and I were a combustible combination. Add in lights, cameras, and action, and it could go thermonuclear in no time. "Me too."

4

A brain in her head, ambition in her soul, and far more self-respect . . .

Carissa—Monday, May 23—2:46 p.m.

It had been a few hours, sixteen phone calls, half a sandwich, and a generous glass of wine since I'd been ambushed onstage at Havenwood. In that time, I'd spoken to family, friends, the mayor, half the town council, and almost everyone I'd ever passed on the streets of Belle Haven. My home phone was unplugged and I became really comfortable letting my cell phone calls go to voice mail. That "ignore" feature was a miracle of modern science.

I sat at my kitchen table and enjoyed the relative calm before the upcoming storm. The past few hours should have acted as a cooling-off period, soothing my nerves and giving me some perspective. But it was not enough time to prepare myself for the imminent arrival of Malachi Knight.

Malachi Henry Knight. The only man I'd ever really loved and the only one who I'd thought really loved me back, ever since I was fifteen years old. We had broken up and gotten back together more times that I cared to admit. At last count, maybe . . . eight times? Not sure; some of the break-ups were just breaks. There was one semester where we were sort of broken up until he realized that meant I could see other people too. He showed up on the Howard campus during pledge week and announced in the middle of the quad, "This is my woman. Touch her, and me and my boys are coming for that ass." That took care of me seeing other people for a while. The men at Howard were brave—bold, even—but not stupid. Who wanted to take on the front line of the LSU Tigers because of one semi-cute ex-cheerleader? Malachi 1, Men of Howard 0.

Think the ladies of LSU afforded me the same respect? Hell no. For as long as Mal and I had been together, there was always a contingent of thirsty-assed women trying to get a long good sip of Knight water. For a little while, we'd had an unspoken rule: As long as we were apart and his "extracurricular activity" was not in my face and I didn't hear about it, so be it. I wasn't naive enough to believe that Malachi was staying faithful and true to me while he was in Baton Rouge and I was in DC, but later, when I packed up and moved to Houston, I expected—no, I demanded—a cease and desist of all nefarious shenanigans with other women.

To this day, I don't know for sure if he cheated. But he damn sure didn't act like a man with a fiancée. And that was just problem number one. Number two was his tunnel vision about winning a Super Bowl. Nothing was as important—not me, not our wedding (that kept getting postponed), not our future, nothing. Number three was the fact that he didn't want me to work because that would "look bad" to his teammates. And number four, the killer, was what fame, stardom, and the NFL lifestyle had done to Mal. He became a persona—no longer my sweet best friend Mal, but "MALACHI KNIGHT, NFL Superstar!" His very presence was punctuated by exclamation points. There was nowhere we could go and nothing we could do without people wanting to be dazzled by him, and he was happy to oblige. This still could have been okay; I could have worked around it . . . except that he started believing his own press. When he was on that field, he was larger-than-life Number 84. When he was at home, I needed him to be just my man. But he couldn't or wouldn't be just Mal. He didn't know how or he didn't like to turn it off, at times treating me like more of an accessory than a future life mate. As he grew, I shrank.

Living together was a period of adjustment for both of us. But I wanted and needed a life outside of being the future Mrs. Number 84. He wanted and needed me to be the obedient little woman who didn't make waves, ask questions, or slow his roll. I put up with it for five years, telling myself that this was what it took to be with him. And wasn't it worth anything to be with Mal?

I'd known Mal almost all of my life and had loved him since high school, before I even knew what love was. In spite of any other ambitions I had for myself, my primary life goal had been marrying Malachi Knight, having two or three kids, and living happily ever after. Through all the suspected other women, the neglect, and the attitude, I still believed in my heart of hearts that he was worth it. This was Mal, after all. The guy who'd held me when I cried over my father's callous indifference, encouraged me to go to Howard when I would've followed him to LSU, and been my best friend for as long as I could remember. All of my best memories to that point were wrapped up in Mal. No matter how unhappy I was, I knew that one day our life was going to turn back into the fairy tale we were destined to live. I was proven wrong when it all came to a head the night after his first playoff win.

I was waiting for Mal in the players' parking lot beside his new Mercedes. We had plans to meet Taylor and Mac as well as Ruby and her husband, Renard, at our favorite little Cajun spot near the Galleria. They had all come to town for the game. I was so excited about the win and proud of his performance that night. He'd caught ten passes for over one hundred yards and scored twice. It was a career night. I didn't mind waiting because I was positive he was swarmed with press. Mal was worth the inconvenience and the wait.

The sun had set and a breeze had kicked in from the east when I realized that it was getting late. The parking lot emptied out one car at a time and still I stood waiting on him. Finally, I sent a text. Hey All Star, I'm waiting. You almost done?

He sent a text back almost immediately. Went out with some of the guys. C U L8R.

I stood there staring at the phone in disbelief. He knew we had my friends and family in town but chose to go hang out with some teammates without letting me know? Really? I decided to give him the benefit of the doubt. I texted back. We have plans with Belle Haven peeps. Meet us at the restaurant?

He wrote back. Can C them anytime. Make my excuses.

I pressed the icon to dial him. I needed to hear this from his voice. The phone rang twice and then went to voice mail. Since he had texted me less than thirty seconds before, I knew this meant he'd hit the IGNORE button. I dialed three more times and the same thing happened. I leaned against the car and let that sink in. The love of my life, my future husband, my MAN had hit the IGNORE button so he could hang out with guys he saw every day.

I sent a text. R U srsly not answering?

Ris, can't argue now. This is important.

So is this.

We just won.

I know. I was right here supporting U and watching U like always. R U coming?

I'm not coming.

Wow.

Grow up & live outside my shadow 4 1 nt.

Something inside of me cracked right at that

moment. Broke everything I thought and believed into jagged pieces inside of me. He wanted me to live outside his shadow? I never asked to be *in* it. *This* was what our life was going to be about? I sat around looking cute, waiting for him to come home, and planning for a wedding that never happened while he hung out with his boys and did God knew what?

Okay, I reasoned, maybe I should have made my growing unease and displeasure clear a long time ago. Maybe I shouldn't have let it get this far. But enough was enough. I worshipped him and he disrespected me? Hell no. He may have been MALACHI KNIGHT, but I was Carissa Wayne, by God. Former valedictorian, prom queen, and winner of the Beleiux County Fair Beauty Pageant for three years in a row. I was a beautiful, degreed black woman with a brain in her head, ambition in her soul, and far more self-respect than my day-to-day existence reflected. I was not one of Malachi Knight's damn groupies. What I was, as of that very moment? Done.

"Are you okay, Mrs. Knight?" the security guard called out and headed toward me. He was ready to go home and I was holding him up. I waved at him to let him know I was okay and dug in my purse for the keys to Mal's car. Mrs. Knight, my ass, I thought angrily. I drove to the restaurant on emotional autopilot. My friends and family took one look at my face when I entered the dining area and it was instantly evident to them that something had gone wrong.

"Where's Mal?" Ruby asked with alarm, searching the space behind me for my absent fiancé.

I laughed shortly. "Out with the boys, I guess. He says he wants me to stand outside of his shadow for one night."

Taylor gasped. "The hell?"

Mac sucked his teeth. "That boy has lost his damn mind."

Ruby went right to the heart of the matter. "What do you want to do, Rissa?"

What did I want? That was a damn good question. I took a deep breath and really thought about it for a second. Immediately, the answers popped into my mind. "I want to leave Mal. I want to go home. I want to go back to school. I want to go back to being about the business of Carissa Wayne and I want to do it tonight. Right now."

They all exchanged glances as if they had known this moment was coming. Renard was the first to stand up. "Let's go get started."

Four hours later, when Malachi strolled into our Tuscan-style, six-thousand-square-foot home in Hunters Creek Village, I'd already sent six suitcases and four boxes ahead with Ruby. Two additional suitcases were in the trunk of the car. I'd turned down Mac, Taylor, and Renard's offer to stick around and kick Malachi's ass. I was sitting in the den in the dark with my overnight bag and my purse.

"Mal," I said quietly from the plush navy wingback chair I'd lovingly designed and custom ordered for this room.

He spun around at my voice. "Hey babe. What are you doing up? You didn't have to wait up for me."

"Yeah. I got that. I wasn't waiting up. I was waiting to leave."

His brows shot up. "Leave?" He spotted the suitcase at my feet. "Where are you headed? It's the playoffs!"

If I'd had any doubts about leaving, that did it. "It's the playoffs for you. For me, it's just another long lonely winter."

He rolled his eyes. "Oh, here we go. Here's the 'how Mal done Rissa wrong' song."

"Nope, no tunes left to sing. I'm going home."

"To Belle Haven?"

I stood up. "Yes."

"For how long?"

I slid off the seven-carat, emerald-cut canary diamond ring I had never liked and set it on the coffee table. "Forever, I guess."

"Just like that? After all this time? 'Cause I wouldn't hang out with your crew tonight?"

"Mal, if you really think I'm leaving because you were an insensitive ass *tonight*, you are further out of touch than I thought."

"Come on, Rissa. I've had a long day. Let's get some sleep and talk about it in the morning." His eyes searched mine and he held his hand out, expecting me to take his in acquiescence.

I slapped my hand down on the arm of the chair in exasperation. He still didn't get it. "What happened to the guy who refused to let us go to sleep angry with each other? What happened to the guy who drove all night to come see me and make sure I was okay because I was a little homesick? What happened to the guy who said he was happiest when I was happy? Where has that guy gone? Where was he tonight?"

"Babe, I'm right here. I love you. You know

me." He lowered his voice and stepped toward me.
It was his BCTB (Baby Come To Bed) voice. It usually worked on me. A few words in that voice, a kiss
here, a touch there, and I generally melted like
butter. Not this time. The stakes were too high.
Enough was enough.

"Malachi. Don't. You're not hearing me! You've
become someone I don't know, don't like very
much, and can't remember why I loved. You've
taken me for granted and I allowed you to. We've
been engaged for six years. Six years!? That's ridiculous. I gave up my life, my career, and, well . . . me!
I've been trying to be someone that I thought you
wanted and it turns out that you don't really care
that much about who I am. I'm like your car or
this house or one of your big shiny watches. If this
is how you love me, I do not want it. It's enough.
I'm done."

Something in my rant finally registered with
him and he understood how serious the situation
was. He clicked on one of the floor lamps and took
a second to really look at me. Astonished, he
blurted out, "You're seriously walking out now.
Tonight. With everything I have going on?"

"Okay. You still don't get it. For once, Mal, it's
not about you. It's not about the playoffs. I'm
done and I'm leaving. Oh, and I'm taking the new
Benz. I've earned it."

He assessed me silently as if to see whether I
was sticking to my guns or backing down. "You're
going to regret this."

I smiled humorlessly, stood up, and picked up
my overnight bag. "No, I won't. Or hell, maybe I
will. Either way, it's done. I've spent enough time

regretting decisions. You, however? You're going to miss the hell out of me, Malachi Knight. I'm sorry I won't be around to see you figure out that football is not your whole life; it's just the way you pay for the rest of it."

"Football is everything. You never understood that for me."

"I know you better than you know yourself. You never understood that football is for now. Marriage and family is forever. I want the forever. I wanted it with you. It's what you promised me and I shouldn't have to beg for pieces of it."

He raised his hands in agitation. "No one is stopping you from having your perfect forever! You can have all of it. We'll get married, have kids, you can teach, buy that old house in Belle Haven you've always wanted. We'll do all of it. Just give me a little more time," he argued.

His actions had spoken louder than these words I'd heard before. "You've had plenty of time and it hasn't helped. You realize you didn't answer my phone calls tonight? That's what we've become. What I am to you. I've become so disposable to you that you can hit the IGNORE button three times in a row, knowing you left me standing in a dark parking lot waiting on you. And for what?"

He smacked his thigh in frustration. "What was the big damn deal? You were safe. I was hanging out with some of the guys; we were talking football."

"Good for you. I hope that football keeps you warm at night," I snarled.

"I don't think my nights will be that chilly. I

doubt I'll have a problem with that," he said in a silky voice that set my teeth on edge.

"Oh yeah? Thanks for making this easier." I decided I needed to just walk away, before we got really nasty with each other and said things we could never take back. Without another word, I turned and walked away from the only man I'd ever loved. I remember walking out to the garage and willing him to come after me. I remember sitting in the car and taking my time putting my key in the ignition and starting the engine. I even backed out slowly thinking he would come after me and fix this. Sitting behind the house, I saw the upstairs lights go out. That was that. I drove away without another look back.

I was jolted out of my morose walk down memory lane by the sound of a car pulling into the driveway. I glanced at the clock on the wall. It was past three p.m. Looking out the window, I saw Mal climb out of a blue SUV and stand staring at the bright red Benz that I still drove. The license plate no longer said "1Knight," but everything else about that car was in the same pristine condition as the day I drove it home from Houston. Like I said, I'd earned it.

Before he could catch me looking, I checked him out. Dammit, he still had that sexy thing going on. He looked good—a little heavier but good. He was in a blue T-shirt with khaki cargo pants. He'd always reminded me of a jungle cat, all coiled energy and deceptive nonchalance. Dangerous and compelling, with the ability to pounce at any time. I was in no mood to be prey to his predator.

With a sigh, I pushed away from the table and looked down. I had changed out of that tragic outfit that was destined to appear on TV. I was in a flattering teal peasant shirt with a colorful broomstick skirt. My hair, though not fully recovered, was down in waves and held off my face with a decorative scarf. I had on bright dangly earrings and cute sandals. I was not sure when and where the cameras would be rolling, but I was determined not to be caught looking quite that raggedy again. It was one thing to be overweight, another to be a sloppy mess about it.

Glancing out the window again, I saw Mal walking around to the back of the property. What was he doing? With no small irritation, I walked through the shotgun-style house to the back patio. Pushing the door open, I leaned out. "Are you casing the joint?"

He was kneeling near the entrance to my gazebo where my roses grew. He looked up from the fragrant blooms. "Are these my mother's roses?"

"Yes." Val Knight was a renowned gardener. Just because her son had turned into an idiot was no reason I couldn't stay friendly with her. Two summers ago when I'd bought the house, she came over with some bare root roses from her garden. They were the first things I planted in the yard. The rest of the backyard might have morphed into an overgrown jungle, but my rose garden around the newly painted gazebo was perfection. There was charm and fragrance and color in abundance.

He stood slowly, brushing off his pants. "So you still speak to my mother."

I nodded. "Your father and Meshach as well."

"Just me that you ignore?"

"Did you have something you wanted to say?"

"Maybe I did. Maybe I do."

"I've been right here, if you were really looking."

"Maybe I wasn't ready to have this conversation. You're grown up, you could've called me."

"Phone works both ways, Mal."

"Are you being evasive?"

I smiled evilly. "I learned from the best."

He crossed his arms with a sigh. "Okay, let's have it out."

"Have it out?"

He dropped his arms and strolled toward the porch. "Clearly you have some issues to work through. Some beef with me. Let's work it out before the cameras start rolling."

I laughed. "I don't have any issues. I said what needed to be said five years ago. If you'd like to discuss this show you've hoodwinked me into doing, then by all means. Please come in."

"Hoodwinked? Really? So you're still just the victim and I'm the evil puppet master, huh?"

"Mal, seriously. You don't have that kind of power over me anymore. Clearly, you want to do this show for some reason and I'm your ticket to making it work. So if you want to make nice, now's your time to do it."

He brushed against me as he entered the house and looked down as he walked past. "Oh, I think we have quite a bit of unfinished business,

Ris. And one thing I've always been good at? Making nice."

Watching him walk into my home as if he owned it gave me a moment of unease. Was I really ready to take on Mal Knight?

"Scared?" he teased as he stood in my kitchen looking around.

"Cautious. There's a difference." I straightened my shoulders and slammed the door shut behind me before heading toward him.

5

Can we get past it?

I caught the bottled water Carissa tossed my way and decided not to wonder if she was aiming at my head. I began to study the house she'd made her own. When we were seventeen, driving past this place to get to the lake, she declared her intention to buy this house and bring it back to life. It had belonged to the Somers family, who had helped found Belle Haven in the 1800s. The last surviving Somers had moved away years ago and the house had stood in decay until Carissa bought it a few years ago.

It was a tall, skinny house with the traditional shotgun style on the ground floor, which meant you walked through each room to get to the next. There had been additions and a second floor added over the years and I found myself curious to see how she'd fixed them up. The kitchen was an eclectic mix of old South and classy, sleek contemporary. Much like the owner. The subtle blend of colorful vintage pieces and classic mission-style pieces suited the bright, sun-filled space.

Swinging my gaze back to her, I took my time studying the new Carissa Wayne. Even with the extra weight, she was a beautiful woman. Her face was traditionally lovely: high cheekbones, arched brows over wide oval eyes, and a pink-tinted, bow-shaped mouth that I still had a dream or two about. Her hair was the same silky fall of tawny curls I'd sunk my hands into countless times. She was a bit more round here and there but no less attractive in my eyes. She was lush, curvy, and had clearly grown into a confident, independent woman with no tolerance for nonsense. I still wanted her and I had no idea what to do with that. I held back a sigh. In that instant, I recognized what I'd lost. The weight of my arrogant insensitivity weighed on my conscience.

I didn't have to be told that I'd messed up with her. The thing about Rissa? She was the best person I had ever known. Her heart was the biggest and best part of her. The bitter taste of regret burned in my throat and I swigged some water to choke it down. Maybe this was why I hadn't wanted to see her, hadn't sought her out. I wasn't ready to admit I'd let a good thing go bad.

The fact of the matter was, I had been an idiot. If I could go back and do it again, I would marry Carissa right out of college and encourage her to do whatever the hell she wanted. I would listen instead of dismiss. I would pay attention to things both on and off the field. But from the look on her face, she wasn't trying to hear it. I didn't know whether I was more irritated with her or myself at that moment.

"So . . ." she said, watching me watch her.

"So . . ." I replied, "catch me up. What did you do after you drove away in my brand-new car and left me all alone?" The minute I said it, I knew it was the wrong thing to say. I guess I was still mad that she'd actually left me. Not that I blamed her; I deserved it. But I'd wanted her to stay and fight for me.

Her jaw set and she put her bottle of water down on the quartz countertop with a loud snap. "Really, that's how you remember it and that's truly how you want to play this right now?"

I put my hands up. "Sorry. It came out wrong. I just . . . Look, there's no way we're going to live in each other's back pockets on camera for the next few months without getting some closure about the past. Can we talk about it?"

She sat down on a wooden barstool, crossed her arms, and gestured me onto the stool across from her. When I settled in, she started talking. "After I pushed past the fact that you weren't coming for me, that you didn't care enough to fight for what we had—"

"Wait a minute, I was supposed to come after you? You weren't supposed to leave!"

"You checked out way before I left," she accused.

"But you actually left," I tossed back.

She flung her hands up. "After five years of crap, I wasn't supposed to leave?"

"I wasn't that bad for all five years." I hedged, "I will admit my head got a little big."

"A little?!" she interrupted.

"Okay, more than a little, and I lost my way there for a minute. I got caught up in the life. You could've talked to me. You should've made me see instead of just running away."

Her voice was pain laced when she spoke quietly. "I tried, Mal. I tried and I tried. You didn't listen. You wouldn't listen to me!"

I sat back in defeat. It was worse than I thought. "Wanna hear something funny in a sad way?"

"Sure, I could use a chuckle right now."

"Well, I actually thought I'd outgrown you," I said regretfully.

"Outgrown me? In what damn way? You shoved me in the dark, shoveled shit on my head, and wouldn't let me grow! How was that supposed to work out?"

I'd never heard her talk to me in that tone of voice. It was full of disapproval, disgust, and distrust. "I made some mistakes."

"On that we agree. Anyway, after I got over it—"

Wait. "You're over it? You're over me?"

"Mal, you want to hear this or not?"

I motioned for her to continue, while tucking that question away for a later time.

"I moved back to Belle Haven and into a room at the Idlewild, Sugar's place. As easy as it would have been to live at home or with my friends, I needed to be on my own. When I said I needed to get back to the business of being Carissa Wayne, I also needed to find out who that was and what that meant. In a very short time, I applied to the graduate program at Tulane. I worked part time at a charter school in New Orleans while I got my master's degree in secondary education and teaching. When I graduated, I was offered a position at Havenwood. I took the job, bought the house. Mac and I have been fixing it up ever since. And here we are."

I asked a question that had been dancing around in the corners of my mind. "So you and Mac?"

"Me and Mac, what?" She arched a brow.

"I always had a feeling he wanted to hook up with you."

Her head reared back as she crowed with laughter. "This is one of your problems, Mal. You see things that aren't there. If anything, he's half in love with Taylor and hasn't realized it."

My eyes traced the line of her neck and the curve of her shoulder. Her shirt slid down her arm, revealing a bright pink bra strap. I was nostalgic for the days when I could just reach out and touch what intrigued me. A part of me would always look at her as mine. Slowly, I lifted my eyes back to her face. "Oh. Does that mean there's no husband, fiancé, man?"

"What's it to you?" She glowered.

"I'm just asking, Ris."

Her spine snapped straight and her voice was clipped when she answered. "The answer is no, not that it's any of your damn business. Where's the next future Mrs. Mal Knight?"

"There is no such woman." I hadn't dated seriously after Carissa bailed. I didn't have any interest in starting anything serious, so my encounters were mostly casual and short, cards on the table up front, no strings and no drama.

"Mal Knight without a woman? That's got to be a first." Her voice was waspish.

I sighed. "This isn't going to work if you hate me, Ris."

"I don't hate you, Mal," she said tiredly.

I asked the tough question. "What do you feel?"

She waggled her shoulders up and down in a shrug. "Can't say I like you very much, but other than that, I don't have strong feelings one way or the other."

"You used to love me," I reminded her.

"*You* used to love *me*," she countered.

"Can you tell me what you used to love about me?"

"What do you mean?" She looked confused.

"Well, you were one of the few who loved me with or without a football in my hands. I just wondered why."

"If you really want to know . . . I thought you were sweet."

"Sweet?" I frowned.

"Yes, sweet."

"Not hot, sexy, manly?"

She grinned. "You were that too, but underneath all the macho jock bullshit you were a nice Southern gentleman. You protected your own, you put others first, you cared about things. You loved your family, you were kind to children, you were good with your hands, and you accepted me as I was—no conditions. You were driven, but it was a healthy ambition and I admired that about you. You were there for me, you listened to me, you made me feel cherished and important. You were . . . everything."

Her tone clearly said I wasn't any of those things anymore, in her opinion. "I was all of that, huh?"

"You were. Until you weren't." She crossed her arms and met my gaze directly.

"Why didn't you tell me?"

"Mal, for the last time, I did. Over and over again. You quit listening."

"You should've made me listen."

"When was the last time anyone made Malachi Knight do anything?"

She had a point. Not knowing what else to say, I sighed again. "I'm sorry. I should've done a lot of things differently and I definitely should've come after you when you left. Will you accept my apology?"

She looked as stunned hearing it as I was saying it. Finally she relaxed and beamed. "I accept your apology."

"Seriously? Just like that? And you forgive me?"

"Not just like that, but what's the use of holding on to it all, right? Give me a little time to get my head around it, okay? It's a lot of baggage to let go all at once. I mean, yesterday at this time, I was hoping never to see you again. And here you are, in my kitchen."

"You know, it's the 'what could have been' that haunts me," I admitted. What if I'd done things differently, what if she'd stayed, what if I hadn't gotten hurt, what if we'd had the wedding and the kids. What if I'd gone after her at any time over the last five years? What if, what if, what if?"

She slashed her hand through the air. "Well, stop it, because you can't live life looking backward."

A hopeful thought took seed in my brain. "Can we be friends again, at least? I miss my friend."

She eyed me skeptically as if wondering what my angle was. Finally she shrugged. "I'll try."

"Fair enough. What do you think? Can we get past it?" I wondered out loud.

Tentatively she started to speak, then stopped. Then she asked, "If I ask you something, Mal, will you answer me honestly?"

"Yes." I vowed that no matter what she asked, I'd be honest.

"Did you cheat on me?"

Ah shit. I took a deep gulp of water. Knowing my next question was telling in and of itself, I asked, "When, specifically?"

Her stare was a rich brown laser beam of accusation. She rolled her eyes and crossed her arms tighter against her chest. "Not while we lived apart. I understood our unspoken agreement. I'm asking about after college, when I moved to Houston. Were you cheating?"

That, I could answer unequivocally while looking directly into her eyes. "No."

She looked unconvinced to say the least. "Hmm."

"Swear to God, Rissa. When you were living with me, I never slept with another woman. I flirted, I teased, I was probably way more friendly than I needed to be, but I did not cheat." I paused a beat and then added, "Not sure if you recall, but you and I were fairly energetic in that department."

She flushed and squirmed on the seat. "I recall."

"One area where we had no problem was in making that physical connection." My voice went a little deeper as I allowed myself to dwell on it. "We were explosive together."

"Um-hmm." She cleared her throat and fidgeted a little bit more.

I hid my grin. She remembered as well. "Even when things were bad in other areas, we were always in tune with each other in the bedroom . . . and the living room . . . and the garage . . . oh my God, that one time in the press box, " I teased.

"I said I recall." It was her turn to take a deep sip of water. Her neck was a little red. Nice to know that part of our chemistry was still there just beneath the surface.

"Even when I wasn't what you needed emotionally, I could always reach you on that physical plane. You know, there were times when I was supposed to be on the field or in a meeting and I'd be distracted by the thought of getting back to you so I could get inside of you—it was all I could think about. Because once I was there, deep and warm with you wrapped around me, I was Superman."

"Oh," she said with an unfocused stare into space.

I leaned toward her and continued, "Between what you and I had going on and my dedication—"

"Obsession."

"—obsession with football, I had no time or interest in other women."

"The groupies, Mal."

"I kept them around for appearances' sake.

Sounds weak as hell, but it's true. I swear to you, Carissa Melody Wayne, on my mother: I did not cheat. I was an asshole, not a scoundrel."

She considered for a moment and then nodded.

"Anything else?"

She took a deep breath and it was her turn to look me squarely in the eye. "When are you going back?"

"Where? To Houston?"

She rolled her eyes again. "To the NFL, Mal. When's your tryout?"

I shouldn't have been surprised that she'd connected the dots, but I was. "How did you know?"

"I know you, Mal. And at your core, you're a football player. You can't help but give it one more try. You haven't given up the dream yet."

She always understood me better than most. "My tryout's in August."

"Good luck," she said simply and slid off the stool to place her empty bottle in a recycling container in the pantry.

"Do you mean it?" After everything we'd been and done to each other, I still wanted her approval. She was Carissa. It was as simple and as complicated as that.

"I do. I know how bad you want it. I hope you get a chance to win the ring."

I'd gotten this far; I decided to wade in a little deeper. "What will this do to us?"

She spun around quickly. "Us? What us? What are we?"

I stood up and walked toward her. "I don't

know what we are exactly, but I don't think we're done."

"My life is here. With the money from this ridiculous show, I'm going to start that college prep and mentoring program for teens. I'm going to fix up this house, finish the garden. I'm going to help Ruby expand the restaurant. I'm going to—"

"I got it. You have plans. Right here. Plans that don't include me anymore." I took a step closer. "What if I wanted to be part of those plans?" I put my hands on her shoulders and drew her against me. She was stiff, but she wasn't pushing me away. After a few minutes, I felt her relax and lean into me.

"In what way, exactly?"

"I don't know, Carissa. But what if I wanted back in your life, in some form or capacity. What would you say to that?"

"I'd say it's going to be some time before I allow myself to care about what you want again."

That stung, but I wrapped my arms around her and held tight. "Okay, what about what you want? Have you missed me at all? Just a little bit? Maybe at night sometimes when you're listening to Maxwell before you go to sleep? You still do that?"

She leaned back and looked up at me. "What are you doing, Mal?"

"Testing something. I'm curious. I wonder . . . Just let me check something right quick, okay?" Before she could answer, I leaned down and covered her lips with mine. I pressed once and then twice before coaxing her mouth open. We both groaned as our tongues meshed together. It was like coming home after a long journey and finding it better than you remember. We slowly rediscovered the licks and laps that took our breath away. I'd forgotten how small she was against me. How soft. God, she smelled good. She felt good. Her perfect lips and tongue teased mine and awakened sensations long dormant. We slid into each other with comfort, delight, and hunger. Everything was familiar, yet different. One thing hadn't changed: one taste of Carissa Wayne and I wanted more. I wanted everything she had to give.

Her arms slid around my middle and up my back as I pulled her even closer. Christ, it was like she was made to fit perfectly in my arms. Had it always felt this way . . . so destined? God, she smelled good, like vanilla and flowers. Pressed against me, she felt amazing. Why had I ever let this go?

Without breaking the kiss, I backed her against the counter and slid my hand down her side, curving around her rear and down her thigh. I cupped the back of her knees and lifted her up. She wrapped those long legs around me as I set her down on the counter so we fit even tighter together. I couldn't resist grinding against her once just to see how that felt again. Perfection.

Her head fell back. "Malachi."

"Right here, babe." I kissed a trail down her jaw and along her neck, resting my lips against the fluttering pulse at the base and licking lightly. She shuddered in my arms.

"What are we doing?" she whispered before wrapping her arms around my neck and kissing me with more heat and passion than I remembered. I was seconds from going up in flames and taking her right there on the kitchen counter.

"That's what we're wondering," a deep male voice said from behind us.

With a groan, I recognized my brother's voice. Sighing with regret, I leaned back and tilted my head to the side. Taylor; Mac; his brother, Burke; and my brother, Meshach, all stood in the arched doorway to the kitchen with varying expressions of amusement and dismay.

Meshach glanced at his watch. "Took you two almost eight hours to start groping each other like you're back under the bleachers in high school after a pep rally. Some things never change."

I looked back at Carissa to gauge her reaction. To my relief, she had her hand clapped over her mouth and a few giggles escaped. "Jesus, I can NOT be trusted around you. Stay at least five paces back!" She pushed me away and hopped down from the counter. "So, beyond the entertainment, what are y'all doing here?"

Burke walked over and gave Carissa a hug. "Good to see you, girl. We're here to take you out for your last supper."

6

You don't know the half

We were settled in the long booth along the back wall of Ruby's restaurant. I was huddled at the far end closest to the kitchen with Taylor and Mac on one side and Niecy and Sugar on the other. Filling out the long table were Burke, Pierre, Renard, Meshach, and Malachi. One table over sat three contestants—XJ, Jordan, and Suzette—with the show producer, Bliss, and the associate producer, Marcy. I had been introduced to Jerry, one of the cameramen, when I came in. He was seated with Ren and some other staff near the front of the restaurant. If nothing else, this show was already good for business. Ruby's hadn't been this packed on a Monday evening for quite some time.

I finished scanning the other tables while studiously avoiding any type of eye contact with Malachi. I wasn't ready to deal with the implications of my little kitchen relapse just yet. When I drew my attention back to Mac and Tay, I found them eyeing me with equal parts exasperation and humor. I guessed I was going to have to deal with it.

I exhaled deeply. "I know, I know. You don't have to say it," I said, shaking my head before letting it fall into my hands. I massaged my scalp as if willing some sense to appear there. "Believe me, I know. It was just . . ."

"Inevitable?" Taylor suggested, rolling her eyes.

"Stupid?" Mac added with a smirk.

I held up my hands. "Spur of the moment," I amended.

"What are you going to do, Rissa?" Niecy asked quietly.

"What I always do."

"Run in the other direction?" Mac said.

"No!" I frowned; did they really think I ran when things got tough? "I'm going to pretend it's all okay until it really is."

"Avoidance." Tay nodded. "I guess that works."

I raised my brows. "You two would know."

"Beg pardon?"

"Beg away. Are we going to pretend that you two aren't circling each other like prey?" It had long been my opinion that the two of them were perfect for each other but did nothing about it for fear of ruining the friendship, or some such other random reason. But the air around the two of them was constantly charged and uneasy like a storm waiting to break.

Taylor glared at me. "Don't deflect. If we hadn't walked in, you were a scant good minutes from a horizontal mambo with your ex-fiancé. Talk about two people circling each other."

I might as well own up to it. "Clearly there's unfinished business there. Maybe it's physical, maybe it's nostalgia, maybe it's more. But I've learned my lesson. I don't have to give in to it; I've been down that road and nothing has really changed. You two, however . . ."

"Hey Rissa." Jordan came over from the other table and squatted down next to me. "I haven't had a second to talk to you since this whole thing started."

Jordan Little had been the first person to greet me at Tulane registration. He was a North Carolina guy, a Southern gent with a sharp sense of humor and steel-trap mind. He'd been in a master's program for behavioral psychology, so some of our classes overlapped. We became fast friends and study buddies. Soon after graduation, we lost touch with the exception of Facebook updates and holiday cards. Last I heard he had a practice in child psychology and was married and living in Atlanta.

I scooted down and patted the spot beside me, inviting him to sit. I teased, "Hey there, Jordy, how did they get you to agree to this nonsense?"

"Girl, someone's paying me to spend the summer losing weight—something I was going to do for free—and I get to hang around my fave person from grad school in her hometown? I was all in." His eyes twinkled as he flashed a wide grin.

"Jordy, this is Mac Bisset and Taylor Rhone. My two best friends in the world, whether they like it or not. This is Niecy, my girl from undergrad, and this is my cousin Sharon. We all call her Sugar. I couldn't tell you why."

"Because I'm so damn sweet," Sugar snarled with a smirk.

"Right. Everyone, this is Jordan Little. Jordy got me through many a late-night study session. He was a saint to put up with me."

He snorted with a mischievous smile. "Is that what you thought? That I was saintly?" He laughed. "I was trying to figure out how to talk you into bed."

I was stunned. "What?! You never said anything or made a move."

"Apparently my moves were too subtle." He met my eyes and grinned in a charming way I hadn't noticed before.

"Apparently." I'd had no clue, never thought of him in anything but a platonic way.

"Yeah, well, you were pretty messed up over"— he hitched his chin down the table toward Malachi— "you know. I was biding my time. But now I'm here; you're here. Everyone's grown. Am I being less subtle?"

I goggled at him in amazement. "Um. What happened to your wife?"

"Aw, well . . . Like Scarlett O'Hara, she's gone with the wind. Met some exotic brother from Haiti and took off for parts unknown." He fluttered his hands in a flying gesture.

I put my hand on his arm. "I'm sorry, Jordy. I didn't know."

He gave a self-deprecating shrug. "Water. Bridges.

Spilt milk. All of that. Thankfully, I'm over it. Life goes on. What about you? You still waiting for the Bayou Blue Streak to catch a clue and do right?"

Taylor and Mac burst into laughter. Mac slapped Jordy on the back. "I like this guy."

I nodded in agreement. "Me too. And no, I'm not waiting for Malachi to turn into someone different. Me and this town are still just a speed bump on his way to bigger and better things."

Taylor shook her head. "Is he going back to the NFL?"

"He's got a tryout in three months."

Ruby walked over at that moment. "Who has a tryout? Mal?"

"Yep."

"Some things don't change." She sucked her teeth.

"You don't know the half," Mac muttered and I shot him a look.

"Jordy, the food's here! You betta come get it before it's gone," Suzette screeched out from the other table, while sending me a look that all but screamed for my imminent demise.

Jordy leaned in. "What the hell is that woman's story and why does she hate you so?"

"There was some *Mean Girl*–type drama back in high school; she's still not over it," I whispered.

"Whoa. Stuck in high school over a decade later. All right, then." He ran a hand across my shoulder as he moved away. "Love to spend some time with you while I'm here, girl. If you'd like." His hand lingered, one finger slightly grazing my collarbone in a blatant caress.

It wasn't at all unpleasant. In fact, it was quite a

nice surprise. Hmm. I hadn't seen that one coming. I met his eyes and raised a brow. He was interested, he was serious, and he wasn't hiding it. The idea intrigued me. Someone who put their cards on the table? No games? Tempting. "I don't see why not," I answered in a slightly breathy voice.

"Good. That's real good. I'll talk to you later." With a last smile in my direction and a nod to the rest of the table, Jordan walked away.

"Um, Miss Thing?" Ruby asked, sliding into the seat Jordan had vacated. "What was that?"

Taylor had jokes. "At last count, that would be Guy Number Two who hit on Carissa Melody today."

Mac added, "In the last two hours. In front of witnesses."

Sugar leaned in. "What? Rissa's getting her groove back?"

"You do know no one really says that anymore, right?" I informed her.

"I know when you're avoiding a question, cuz," Sugar said with a gleam in her eye.

"Do tell?" Ruby nudged my arm. "You 'bout ready to give up your dry spell?"

Taylor cackled. "She has been keeping the goodies on lock for a while now."

"You're a fine one to talk," I countered.

"We're talking about you and your epic dry spell, ma'am."

I rolled my eyes. "Could we all lower our voices? I see no need to discuss my self-imposed celibacy with this entire restaurant."

"Did someone over there say 'celibate'? Did I hear that right?" Bliss, the producer who could apparently lip-read, squeaked from across the room. The entire restaurant fell silent and eyes swung toward our end of the table.

I quickly pointed at Taylor. "She's not getting any. It's tragic. We're going to work on that." I ignored the kick in the shins she sent my way as I smiled innocently. "Who's ready to order? This being my last supper and all."

Laughter rippled through the space and most of the patrons went back to minding their own business. I glanced up to catch Malachi cheesing with all of his teeth at me. Last damn thing I needed him to overhear.

"Problem?" he mouthed.

"Not at all," I mouthed back with a "shoo-fly-don't-bother-me" wave of my hand. I determinedly turned my head.

Ruby whistled. "You and Mal? You and Jordy? Are you about to turn our wholesome town show into some hot mess TV? Love triangles and relationship drama?"

I closed my eyes. "God, I hope not. Can I get the catfish platter with a mixed green salad and the bread pudding for dessert? Oh, and wine. Lots and lots of wine."

Ruby stood up as her waitstaff came over to get the rest of the dinner orders. "Girl, I hope you know what you're doing."

"I don't have a clue. But you guys got me into this; I expect you to help me navigate whatever comes next."

Niecy smiled. "We got you, girl. I mean, how much drama could one former prom queen generate?"

"Well, now you've jinxed it," I moaned. Before the words had completely dissolved, Suzette got up and walked over to me.

"Can we talk for a minute? Alone without your cheerleaders," she snapped out with way more hostility than I could understand.

"Why must she always be so nasty?" Taylor muttered.

I raised up my hands to quash anything before it started. I didn't like Suzette, but Taylor absolutely couldn't stand her. Said she wouldn't know a genuine act if it was stamped and tattooed on her ass. "Sure." I got up and walked to Ruby's office in the back. After she followed me in, I shut the door. "What's up?"

"I just want you to know that I'm not going to be putting up with your shit this time around." Her dark eyes snapped with barely restrained acrimony.

"What shit? This time? Huh? I beg your pardon?" My eyebrows jumped up as I had no idea what she was talking about.

"In the sixth grade we were both up for the lead role in *Our Town* and you stole it from me. Don't think I don't know how you really won those pageants. I'm sick of being your understudy because you cheat and lie to get what you want."

"Sixth grade and pageants, huh? Still hanging onto that. And yet, here you are in a supporting role in a show about me."

"You like to act like you're the favorite daughter of Belle Haven and whatever, but I'm not going to let you treat me any old way on this show. I am a grown woman with talents and accomplishments of my own that I can showcase, thank you very much."

"Suzette, contrary to your beliefs, I had no idea you were coming back to town. I had no idea that this show was going to happen. Feel free to showcase whatever the hell you'd like. I have no intention of treating anyone poorly. If anything, you and I have had misunderstandings in the past, and while I'm sorry for those, I'm willing to let all that go so we can get through this show with some class."

"You're a two-faced attention ho and I just wanted to let you know where I stand."

So much for class. "Attention ho?" I took a deep breath and let it out. I wasn't going there with her tonight. "Whatever, Suzette. Why don't we just stay out of each other's way as much as possible? As soon as the show's done we can go back to ignoring each other, how's that?"

"Suits me just fine. Just because you lost your man and got fat doesn't mean we're here to kiss your ass."

I shook my head in confusion. She wasn't exactly a featherweight herself, but slinging mud wouldn't get us out of this room any faster. "I'm certainly not here to tell you what to kiss. You enjoy your dinner." I swung the door open and headed back to the table.

"I see you still think you get the last word," she hissed as she walked past.

I sat down at the table and took a generous sip of my drink. "As God is my witness, I promise we'll try and get through this with some dignity."

"And thinner thighs. All this bullshit is only worth it if we net thinner thighs out of the deal, right?" Niecy asked as I raised the glass Ruby had just refilled. "To thinner thighs!"

As glasses were raised, I met Jordy's glance. He tipped his glass in my direction. At the end of the table, Mal raised his water glass and sent me a smile chock full of prurient intent. Uh-oh. I might be in some trouble here. I drank deeply from the glass again and turned my attention back to Taylor and Mac, where all was safe and drama free.

7

Already a pain in the ass

"Good morning, Mr. Knight," a strange male voice said from the door of my bedroom. Not the best way to wake up.

I opened up one eye and glanced first at the clock: 4:15 a.m.? Seriously? I turned my gaze toward the voice. In the doorway stood a tall skinny twenty something in a "Barack the Vote" T-shirt and jeans. Even more alarming was the burly guy standing next to him dressed all in black and carrying a camera on his shoulder. The red light was on. Next to him stood a kid barely out of high school holding up a huge pole with a fuzzy microphone on the end also pointed in my direction. As I came to partial wakefulness, I recalled that the producer was Ren, the cameraman was Jerry, and the kid with the mic was DeMarcus. Knowing this did not explain what they were doing in my bedroom at the crack of dawn o'clock.

"Are we filming?" I rasped while looking down to make sure I'd actually worn something resembling pajamas to bed. I was in a Houston Stars T-shirt and loose cotton shorts. "You know, for some reason when you said we'd start first thing in the morning? I assumed that meant eight or nine?"

"We want to grab some Day One shots and get each contestant used to having us around," Ren explained helpfully with a little too much cheer for this early in the morning.

"I see. Well, good morning, world. Hope you're getting more sleep than I am." I blinked and smiled into the camera as I sat up in bed. Hey, this face had sold its fair share of sports drinks and gym shoes not so long ago. I could still turn it on when I had to. However, there was one thing I needed to address. "Could a brother tip to the restroom without witnesses, please? The camera needs to know boundaries."

"Yes, of course. Sorry." The red light went off. "When you come back, make sure you pack a bag for the next month."

"Say what now?" I paused on my way to the closet. "Where are we going?"

"Oh, I thought they told you. All of the contestants are moving on campus. To the Havenwood Academy dormitory."

Pretty sure I'd missed that in the fine print. "Why?"

"It was decided that having everyone in one

place is easier for filming and adds to the overall team experience."

"Uh-huh. Does Rissa know about this?"

"Um, I think she's being told this morning."

I snorted. "Good luck with that." I pulled some underwear, socks, sweats, and Nikes out of the closet before heading to the bathroom. "Why 4:15 in the morning?"

"We wanted to catch everyone while they were still sleeping so the first reactions are all honest."

"Brilliant," I agreed with a saccharine smile, closing the door firmly behind me. Reaching in to turn on the shower, I shook my head. What exactly had I gotten myself into? I definitely missed the part of the contract where they could barge into my house before dawn and start filming. The only saving grace was that this was a rental property on loan from Burke and Mac's company, Bisset Custom Homes. Maybe they'd pick up free publicity from the impromptu early morning footage. I was enjoying the house, it was spacious and well laid out. Pity I was headed for a high school dorm room. Just another sacrifice for the greater good.

And really, that was the whole point of doing this ridiculous reality show: publicity for everybody. Some for me, some for the town, and some (albeit unwanted) for Carissa. I slid under the heated spray and searched for the body wash. I was in the middle of sudsing and rinsing when a knock came at the bathroom door. Before I could answer, the door swung open. I looked incredulously at it.

The skinny producer stuck his head in. "Sorry, dude. Your cell phone is ringing. The display says it's Carissa. We thought you'd like to take it."

I stepped out and wrapped a towel around my waist before I snatched the phone from Ren. I saw Jerry standing behind him with the camera on his shoulder and red light on. Intrusive much? I frowned. "Dude, not on camera." I swung the door shut with a loud click and answered the phone. "Rissa, is everything okay?"

"Not so much. I assume you also have a camera in your face at this ungodly hour in the damn morning?" She sounded irritated, agitated, and unrested. Her Southern accent was more pronounced this early. Her voice sounded like spiced whiskey. I had to concentrate on what she'd just asked me.

"I just slammed the bathroom door shut on it. Even I have my limits."

"Did you know about this dormitory situation?"

"I did not." I dropped the towel and pulled on a pair of black boxer briefs. Turning sideways, I checked myself out in the mirror. The last forty pounds were not going easy. I was still a ways from football shape. I shifted the phone to my other hand and popped the top on the lotion. Just because it was early as hell was no excuse to be ashy.

"Mal, if I ask you something, will you answer me honestly?"

The fact that she felt she even had to ask told me how far into disrepair our relationship had truly fallen. "I will."

"If I back out of this thing, will you be okay? I mean, for your comeback and everything? I don't want to mess you up, but I'm not so sure I'm feeling this."

I closed my eyes. I knew she wasn't comfortable with this. But I didn't realize she was absolutely hating it. We were only on Day One. If she wanted out, I couldn't stand in her way. I'd done enough. "Ris, if you want out, walk away. I'll back you up. It's not a problem. Really."

She expelled a deep breath. "What about your tryout?"

I stepped into thin black sweatpants and pulled an LSU T-shirt over my head before I answered. "Babe, they'll either give me a shot or they won't. You've given up enough for me. If you're this unhappy before we even get started on Day One, it's not worth it. I'll make it work."

"Thanks, Mal. I'm tempted. So very, very tempted. But too many people are counting on me, counting on this show—the money, the exposure. I can't back out now. Promise me we are not going to do anything cringe worthy in front of America?"

Might as well speak true. "Not sure I can keep that promise. Even at our best, we could get a little rowdy together."

She huffed out a laugh. "Look at you being all honest this early in the morning."

I sat down on the toilet seat to pull on my socks. "Too damn early to sugarcoat."

She sighed. "This is already a pain in the ass."

"A huge pain in the ass."

"Okay, I'll quit whining. See you at the dorm."

For some reason, I wasn't ready to stop talking to her. "Ris?"

"Yeah?" she answered tentatively.

"Are we friends again?"

She stayed silent a long time. "Sure, Mal. We're friends."

"With benefits?" I couldn't help but add.

She choked on a soft laugh. "Don't push it."

I grinned. "Can't blame a brother for trying."

"Sure I can."

I'd gotten this far, so I decided to push a little more. "Do we need to talk about what almost happened yesterday?"

"No, we absolutely do not."

I laughed. "Denial?"

"Refusal."

"At least admit we have a few loose ends to tie up."

"Probably more than a few. You are right about one thing, though."

"What's that?"

"It's way too early for this." She hung up abruptly.

I grinned again and slid the phone into my side pocket. I swung the door open to find Ren outside the door and DeMarcus next to him. "Did you seriously just tape a closed-door conversation from outside the bathroom door?"

He nodded unapologetically.

"So not cool. We're going to have to set some boundaries."

"You did agree in your contract to be on film 24-7," Ren reminded me.

"I'm very positive I excluded some things such as"—I gestured to the room behind me as I stepped into the hallway—"bathroom time. Let's try and maintain some of the mystery, shall we?" I glowered down at him with my best "I'm a football player and will hurt you" glare.

"Sorry, sir." The glare still worked.

"You don't have to 'sir' me, just show some basic decency or this is not going to go well for any of us. Speaking of which, walking into the bathroom—in fact, any room—without waiting for permission: that's not going to happen again. Got it?"

"Yes, si—Mr. Knight."

I rolled my eyes as we walked past the kitchen. "I can be Mal. Truly. I assume breakfast is out of the question?"

"We have breakfast set up at the dorm."

The dorm. Jesus, it was like a bad training camp flashback all over again. I quickly went into the closet and put together a variety of clothes, shoes, and toiletries for a few weeks. After years of weekly travel, I had the art of packing down to a science. I was rolling a tie and sliding it inside a shoe as my phone rang again.

"You're popular this morning," Ren said and motioned to Jerry to roll again.

I flashed my trademark "don't you want to get like me" smile. "I'm popular every morning." I thumbed on the phone. "This is Mal."

"On camera already?" Pierre's cultured tones flowed across the line.

I glanced up at the camera. "As a matter of fact, I'm staring into the red light as we speak."

"Ah, well. I'll keep it short. You talk to Cari this morning?"

"Yes. Why?"

"She called me to go over the terms of her

agreement. I got the impression she was looking for an escape loophole."

"You got the right impression, but she decided to stick it out for now."

"Okay, good. I think this is going to be a great experience for both of you."

"Are you matchmaking?" Underneath the Italian suits, Pierre was a romantic Southern gentleman at heart.

"Do I need to be?" When he started answering questions with questions, it meant Pierre had something else to say.

"Go ahead and say what you gotta say."

"You're better with her."

I frowned. "Wait a minute, now." Not only did I not agree with that assessment, I didn't appreciate it, not one bit.

"You don't have to like it for it to be true. Sorry, but you're a better athlete and a better person when she's around. This is not only your last chance at the NFL, this is your last chance with Cari. I'm telling you not to blow either one." His voice was crisp, as if he wanted to be clear that this was not a topic he considered to be up for discussion.

I shared my major concern with him. "What if I can't have both at the same time? I don't even know if it's possible."

"Well, my friend, only you can make that decision, but I'll tell you this: you have many business ventures to keep you challenged professionally. There is only one Carissa Melody Wayne."

"Noted." I was done talking about something I had no control over today.

Briskly, Pierre continued. "All right, then. I'll be on set later this week. Unless you need me sooner."

"It's been a while since I was your only client and needed my hand held," I teased.

He laughed. "My first and best, though. Stay outta trouble, Mal."

"Trouble? Who, me? I'm always good." I hung up as he snorted a response. Putting one last pair of socks in the bag, I zipped it closed and looked around for the matching laptop case. Striding past the camera, I couldn't imagine that the people of America would be interested in watching me packing a cell phone charger and iPad. But hey, whatever. Tossing in my MacBook Pro and a few peripherals, I scanned the room to see if there was anything else I couldn't live without for a few weeks. Satisfied I had the necessities, I set the laptop case on top of the rolling bag and turned toward the door.

"Everyone ready?" I asked with feigned cheer as I snatched up the car keys. "Let's get this party started."

8

Bad jou jou

"I thought this was going to suck and it really does. And by 'this' I do mean this whole reality show experience," I stated flatly while staring into the camera. Niecy was seated beside me. We were perched in the "confessional," a small room they had set up with a sofa, a backdrop, and a candid camera so that contestants could plunk down and give their recaps of the action taking place. We were dressed in skintight forest green yoga capri pants and truly unflattering electric blue tank tops that read *Losing to Win* across the chest. Both Niecy and I were well-endowed in that area, so the letters were stretched and appeared to be screaming in frustration. Not a good look. In fact, the entire town was peppered in the blue and green *Losing to Win* logo. Good for the town, bad for us.

Niecy was a natural-born diva from Savannah,

Georgia. She ran a successful lifestyle and beauty blog. She believed that a Southern lady was never fully dressed unless her hair was done, her lipstick was fresh, and her earrings dangled. Though Niecy was a solid size 22, she was curved in all the right places and thought it was unladylike for a woman to jiggle in public. She was the kind of woman who was referred to as striking. Statuesque, great bone structure, a smile she kept perfectly white, and full lips generally painted with a shade of mauve pink lip gloss from Lancôme. She had flawless skin the color of toasted wheat and thick hair she wore in long spiral twists that fell past her shoulders. Usually.

Today, we both had sad ponytails that may have been cute several hours ago but had long since lost the sexy. On top of that, the hairstyles were magnifying every feature of our makeup-less faces. Who looks fresh when sweaty and sleep deprived? Neither of us, unfortunately. This was, I could truthfully say, the first time I'd seen Niecy sans some semblance of war paint. Truly, this experience just kept getting better. Yes, I was leaning heavily on snark and sarcasm to make it through.

So far today, I'd been yanked out of bed at 4:00 a.m., moved into a dorm room with Mal as my suite mate, and been asked a series of what I considered to be very personal questions with a camera in my face and a fuzzy microphone hovering over my head.

Jordy and Suzette had the suite across the hall. Niecy and XJ were down the hall. No one was pleased with our accommodations. We were grown folks with real estate of our own, living in housing meant for teenagers. Skinny teenagers at that.

We were introduced to our nutritionist, Hannah, who spent what seemed like hours discussing the evils of processed foods, sugars, and fat grams. White foods were apparently the devil. White breads, rices, potatoes: all sent by Lucifer to keep jiggly junk in our trunk.

From there we met with the three trainers attached to the show. Jacob, Darcy, and Paul were the perkiest damn skinny people I'd ever met. They took fitness—oh, I'm sorry, "total wellness"—very seriously. They used words like "amped" and "super-fun" in real sentences. On purpose. This was my life now. Marcy, Darcy, Bliss, Ren—it was a bit much.

Having met our fitness team, we each sat down with our team and came up with a goal weight. Their goals and my goals were not the same but I wasn't in the mood to argue. We also came up with a projected plan of how much I needed to lose weekly and monthly.

Then we had been given three bites of granola, a piece of turkey sausage, and a small bowl of fruit for breakfast. No coffee. No tea. Carrot-ginger juice, which I hated at first sip.

"Niecy, what has been your favorite part of the day so far?" Marcy, the associate producer, asked from off camera.

Niecy and I exchanged glances before she answered with considerable sass. "Could there be anything more fun than being squeezed into spandex and weighed on camera?" We snickered at the remembered humiliation because at this point, what else could we do but laugh? Along the way, between housing and granola, we had been introduced to what they called the "weigh-in ceremony." Yes, the reality was as much fun as you'd think. We were lined up in front of the panel and, of course, the omnipresent cameras. The panel consisted of Jim, the trainers, the nutritionists, and a guest judge. We were spared a guest judge today but had that to look forward to in the weeks to come. When your name was called, you stepped forward onto the invisible scale. On the huge screen behind the panel, they flashed your starting weight, your current weight, and your goal weight. This went into a formula with your age and created a point total that would be deducted from your final score. Since the person with the highest point total won, you clearly wanted this number to be low. The more weight you lost, the better your chances to win. Good times.

"What about you, Carissa? What's been your favorite moment so far?"

"Oh, the two straight hours of cardio—for sure. Nothing says summertime fun like an hour of the elliptical machine followed by bicycling and treadmill."

"How are you feeling?"

I spoke the answer that popped in my head. "My thighs are still quivering and I truly believe the only reason thighs should quiver is if multiple orgasms are imminent."

"Rissa!" Niecy barked out a laugh and nudged me with her shoulder. "You realize you just said that on camera."

"Oh, shit." I kept forgetting that I shouldn't put quite so much real into this reality show. "Can you edit out the orgasm part?"

Marcy shook her head, eyes twinkling. "I think you can count on that making the final cut."

I closed my eyes. "My mother is going to see that. Think before I speak. Got it." I opened my eyes and smiled. "Anything else, or can Niecy and I go munch on the seaweed and celery we're no doubt getting for lunch?"

"One last thing. What are your thoughts about the rooming situation?" Marcy asked.

Niecy piped up, "We didn't live in the dorms after freshman year when we were in college, so you can imagine how excited we are to live in one now."

I nodded with much attitude. "And having us share suites with our partners? Nice. I see you all have this rigged for maximum dramatic potential."

Clearly Marcy was on a fishing expedition. "Does it bother you being in close quarters with Malachi, your ex-fiancé?"

I shot her a look. "You know, you could stand to be a wee bit more subtle. I'm not taking the bait. Whose idea was it for partners to share suites?"

Marcy smiled. "We thought that would foster solidarity between the teams."

"You thought it would cause more drama," Niecy corrected.

Sensing she'd gotten all she was going to get from us, Marcy signaled the cameras off. "Thanks, ladies, lunch is being served in the cafeteria and

then you have your first competition this afternoon."

"Oh, goodie." Niecy smirked. "I can't wait."

As I lay face down in a shallow pond of what I
hoped was just mud, I again wondered how my life
had come to this. Raising my face and arms toward
the heavens, I railed. "Seriously, Jesus? What did I
do to deserve this? I'm a good Southern Christian
lady. I attend church on Sundays. I may have com-
mitted an illicit deed or two in my past, and I'm
partial to many adult beverages, but really?! If you
just let me get through this with a sliver of dignity
left, I will swear off Bienville sauce and fruity mar-
tinis except on Mardi Gras. I'll endeavor to do the
right thing for the rest of my days. I'm begging,
here."

The entire cast, crew, and slew of onlookers
dissolved into laughter at my dramatics. Malachi,
who had finished the course minutes ago, jogged
back across the obstacle course from hell. He
leaned down and extended a hand.

"Babe, you were supposed to leap over the
rock, tip across the logs, and then jump over the
swampy area. Jump o-ver." He motioned with his
whole body. "O-ver."

I shot him a look of regal disdain as I grasped
his hand. "You think I meant to land face first in
this muck? Like I'm already not glam enough for
TV? Is that what you really think, Mal?"

"Um . . ." As he pulled me up, I saw the smirk
on his face and couldn't resist. With the little dex-
terity I had left, I yanked him off balance and slid

a foot behind the knee that wasn't surgically repaired. I didn't play fair, but I didn't fight dirty either.

He went down like a fir tree at Christmastime. What I hadn't calculated was his considerable weight landing directly on top of me and both of us winding up splattered with the swampy mess. And there we were in a bit of a compromising situation in front of town and television. Filthy. In more ways than one.

Mal stared down at me and his eyes narrowed before he flung his head back and roared with laughter. I snickered and then joined him, giggling helplessly. I put a hand on his chest and rolled so that he was in the mud and tried to lift myself off of him. His hands gripped my hips and held me in place. Straddling the ex for all the world to see? Awesome. My life was so much win right now.

"Carissa, if you wanted to get down and dirty? All you had to do was ask. I would have preferred that you'd picked a less public place to show me what you had in mind, though." His bad-boy grin was in full effect.

I scooped up a handful of muck in one fist while sliding the other up his chest with an innocent smile on my face. His brows raised as I leaned over him. When my lips were a breath away from his, I took the fistful of mud and smashed it into the top of his head.

"Just a little something to cool you down, Malachi," I announced before jumping up to run the rest of the obstacle course.

"Woman!" he bellowed, climbing out of the muck.

I was already gone. I scaled the rock wall like my life depended it. I looked over my shoulder once and ran for the finish line with all the adrenaline my thirty-something, oft-neglected body had left.

Mal caught up with me just after I crossed the finish line, my hands raised in victory. His arms came around me and he swung me around. I looked up at his handsome, mud-streaked face and blinked with fake innocence. "We finished."

"Yes. In third place and muddy as hell. You know how much I hate to lose."

I rolled my eyes and patted his filthy face. "Yes, your aversion to losing is something I know well. But Mal, there's always tomorrow. I promise to do better tomorrow."

"Actually, you two have a chance to make up the points you lost right now!" Jim Swindle's overly cheerful voice cut in loudly.

I really had to remember that cameras were pointed at me 24-7. With a sigh, I turned toward Jim. All the other contestants were lined up beneath the *Losing to Win* banner. They were staring at Mal and me with undisguised amusement. I decided to ignore them for now. "How would we do that, Jim?"

"Well, you two can decide to accept the blind challenge. If you accept it and complete it, you automatically take the lead."

"What's the challenge?" I asked suspiciously.

Jim gave me a pitying look. "Well, now—that's

why we call it a blind challenge. You have to agree sight unseen."

"We'll do it," Mal announced.

"Wait a minute, Big Baller, you do *not* get to decide for the both of us. You've done that before and that did not turn out well," I sniped.

He glared down at me. "Actually, you made a pretty big decision for the both of us a few years back and that didn't turn out so well either."

"Turned out just fine."

"Says who?"

"I say. That's who."

"And you'd be wrong. Again. Not that you'd ever deign to admit it," he snapped.

"We are so not going there. I'm not going to eat goats' balls or roach intestines just because you hate to lose." I crossed my arms and matched him glare for glare.

"Um, I don't think roaches have intestines, Rissa," Jordy called out, breaking the tension. Everyone dissolved into laughter as Jim stepped toward us.

"That's an entirely different reality show," he said, shaking his head. "Believe me, the last thing we'd have you do on *Losing to Win* is any kind of eating challenge."

Realizing Mal and I were still toe to toe, I took a step back. "Oh. Good point." I thought for a minute. "You know what? I'm dressed like this, have been dipped in mud, and smell like a swamp. I'm sweating what's left of my pleasing personality away in this hot-ass Louisiana sun, I've eaten the equivalent of a side salad all today, and I'm stuck being roomies with my ex. How much further downhill could it go from here? Bring it on, Jim."

In my peripheral vision, I saw Bliss hopping up and down with unmitigated glee. Dammit. I was in for it now. Whatevs. Like the true Southern Belle I was, I squared my shoulders, stuck my chest out, sucked in my stomach, raised my face to the camera, and flashed the smile that had won me Junior Miss Belle Haven more years ago then we need to count. "Whatcha got?"

Mal slid back to stand next to me and squeezed my shoulder. I looked up at him. He was staring down at me with a mix of admiration, pride, and pleasure. "You heard the lady, Mr. Swindle. Bring it."

Jim smiled wide, almost blinding us with his teeth. "Carissa Wayne and Malachi Knight, you will be playing 'truth or dare' tonight! We'll prepare the questions and the dares. You'll have to complete five rounds. If you forfeit or walk away, you stay in last place. If you complete all five rounds to the judges' satisfaction, you move to first place and you win this week's cash prize."

I rolled my eyes for the umpteenth time that day. "What are we? Back in junior high again?"

"Who are the judges?" Mal asked.

I nodded. "Oh, good question, Mal."

Jim bared his Zoom-whitened teeth again in his Hollywood version of a smile and pointed. "Your fellow contestants."

"Yes!" Suzette said with a pump of her fist. Even though she looked like holy hell and basically had had Jordy carry her through the obstacle course, she seemed to be enjoying my abject humiliation and discomfort with genuine giddiness.

XJ, who had stayed pretty quiet all day, just shook his head. "Wow, this is not your day, Cari."

"Tell me about it," I agreed. I caught Niecy's eye and glared at her. "This is all your damn fault!"

She blinked twice. "Beg pardon? How do you figure? What did I do?"

"All that snarky attitude you were giving the camera in the confessional earlier. The bounce-back bad jou jou landed on me."

She laughed and shrugged her shoulders. "Better you than me."

"Jou jou?" Jim asked uncertainly. "What is jou jou?"

This time my grin was wide as I walked past him toward the refreshment table. "Yes, Jim, le jou jou: the Louisiana equivalent of karma. Something you should worry about . . . a lot." I grabbed a bottle of water and emptied it over my head. Looking over my shoulder, I asked, "Is it time for our next two bites of food yet?"

9

You have exactly what you wanted

Malachi—Tuesday, May 24—8:00 p.m.

We were all gathered in the third floor common room, really just a lounge with some televisions, tables, couches, and a refrigerator full of zero-calorie, sugar-free drinks. At some point this evening, XJ found out that most of the rooms had hidden cameras and mics. Ever since learning that little tidbit, we'd ceased to relax completely. Tense is too polite a word to describe the atmosphere in the lounge. It had been a long day; people were tired, irritated, sore, and hungry. Not the best combination.

Carissa sat next to me on the long, low couch with legs crossed, arms crossed, and a "can we do this already" look on her face. She was wearing a brightly colored V-neck top and some knee-length pants with sandals. Her hair was done up and she had makeup on. She looked nice. I had changed into jeans and a polo shirt.

XJ and Niecy lounged on the sofa across from us. Both looked as if they could fall asleep at any moment. Jordan was sitting on the edge of the chair on the other side of Carissa. Suzette was the only one who was buzzing with energy. She was pacing back and forth, clearly looking forward to Carissa's continued discomfort.

I remembered Suzette from back in the day. During her junior high and high school glory days, over one hundred pounds ago, she had been—at least in looks alone—the prettiest girl in Belle Haven. She was that classic Louisiana mix of African, French, Indian, and Spanish heritage that manifested in creamy skin; long, wavy hair; and curves for days. Suzette was one of those cute girls who knew she was cute and she was particularly skilled at using that cute to get what she wanted. I couldn't even count the number of times she had theoretically tossed her panties in my face. She kept offering; I kept turning her down. No doubt that contributed to her violent dislike of Carissa. Even though we ran in the same circles, I never had the slightest interest in Suzette. Especially not after hooking up with Carissa.

From the minute Carissa and I met at age thirteen, it was always her. I'm not saying there weren't a few instances where I'd strayed along the way, but at the end of the day, I always knew that I wanted Carissa Melody Wayne to be mine. And I'd blown it. So far, this competition wasn't helping the state of whatever relationship we had left.

"You guys ready?!" Bliss bounded into the room with various crew members billowing in behind her. I exchanged a glance with Carissa and we both rolled our eyes. The whole "truth or dare" concept was on some epic bullshit level, but if it got us back on top, I figured it was worth it.

Jim walked in the room just as the crew set up backdrops and lighting. He was handed a microphone, which he clipped onto his lapel before turning to face the room. The additional lighting turned on and Bliss counted down. "We're live in 3–2–1 . . ."

"Good evening, contestants," Jim chirped enthusiastically. "How was the first day for everyone?"

He was met with stares and outright glares. He laughed. "Okay, it was a tough day. I get it, but tonight will be fun. We're here to play a game. Who's with me?"

Suzette smiled. "I'm ready. Let's go!"

Beckoning her closer to him, Jim waved some index cards at all of us. "All right, then. How about if we go over the rules again and then Suzette will kick off the game for us!"

I personally hated how dude sounded like he ended all of his sentences with an exclamation point, but whatever. If this was how they wanted to play this TV thing, it was just a means to an end. I caught Carissa's eye and we nodded. We were on the same page, whatever they threw at us—we were going to handle it.

"Okay, this is 'truth or dare.' We're playing five rounds. Each round you are allowed to hear the question first, then you have to choose to answer the question with the truth or take the dare. You cannot do all truths or all dares. If you don't answer and you don't take the dare, you have one opportunity to pass the dare to one other contestant. You can only pass the dare once. If you refuse to answer and don't take the dare OR your other contestants are dissatisfied with your answer or your completion of the dare, you forfeit the game and stay in last place. If you complete all five rounds successfully, you move into first place. First place means you win the bonus money for today's challenge; you win points toward your final score. In the overall scope, if you get first place three times, you not only get bonus points but immunity from an upcoming challenge. Any questions?"

Why they were determined to complicate a simple game confused me. As with most games, the person with the most points at the end of the game won. Every challenge you won brought you closer to winning the whole game. I spoke up. "We win, we rock. We lose, we suck. Got it."

Jim nodded. "Basically, yes. Ready for the first round? Let's go. Suzette, please read the first question aloud."

She snatched the card, read the question, and her eyes started to gleam. "Both of you must answer this question truthfully or accept the dare. The first question to you is: Who broke off the engagement?"

I drew in a quick breath. Aw, hell. They were going straight for the dirt. I guess I should have expected it, but I didn't. I thought they'd ask some crazy questions about our sex life or my life as a football player, but this was just some *National Enquirer*–type bullshit. I looked at Carissa and she looked resigned. Clearly, she had been expecting something like this.

"Well?" Suzette crowed. "Are you going to tell the truth or take the dare?"

I leaned into Carissa. "What do you want to do?"

"I'm sure as hell not taking the dare. They clearly have this rigged to make us as uncomfortable as possible. Let's just tell the truth and be closer to being done."

Sitting back with my arms crossed, I answered the question. "Carissa broke off the engagement."

"Seriously?" Suzette asked in disbelief.

Jim took the index card from her. "Carissa, is that the truth?"

"That is the truth."

"Why?" Suzette asked.

Both Cari and I sat mutely staring her down, though I was sorely tempted to tell her it was none of her damn business.

"We're not required to answer follow-up questions, are we, Jim?" Carissa asked, her foot tapping the air in irritation.

"No, you are not. Are the judges satisfied with the answer?"

Everyone but Suzette nodded.

"Next question. Jordan, you have the honor of asking it."

Jordy stood up and took the card. He read the question and shot me an apologetic look. "Okay, the next question. Were either of you ever unfaithful to the other during the course of your relationship?"

What the hell were these questions? I felt myself getting irritated. I braced myself and prepared to tell the truth. This would suck, since I was trying to get back into the NFL and get back my endorsement deals, and being known as a former philanderer would not help me along. But sometimes a man had to do what he had to do. I had wanted this show; I wanted first place; this was the cost. Carissa put a hand on my thigh. I met her eyes. She shook her head.

"Let's take the dare."

"Really?"

She nodded shortly. "Really."

I turned to Jordan. "We'll take the dare."

He flipped the card and shook his head. "One of you has to kiss someone else in the group."

"So we are back in junior high." Carissa rolled her eyes. "Why don't we just break out spin the bottle and be done with it."

Jim smiled insincerely. "First you have to decide which one of you will do the kissing and then the panel will decide who you get to kiss."

Suzette was practically vibrating with excitement. Oh hell no. I sent Carissa a pleading look. Grabbing her hand, I murmured into her ear, "I promise to write a check toward that teen program you want to start if you take this one. Please do not let that woman get her lips near me."

Carissa giggled. "Does big strong Malachi Knight need Carissa Wayne to save the day?"

To hear her laugh like that with me again was worth anything. I dropped my voice. "Girl, whatever you want—it's yours. Name it."

The awareness that was never far from the surface flared up between us. Her eyes met mine again as she took in the heat of my regard. "I just might hold you to it, you know."

"You can hold me to anything. Please do," I said huskily, letting her take that any way she wanted. Damn, I'd missed talking to her, being around her, getting inside her. Shifting closer, I reached over and took her hand in mine. "Any damn time."

Jim cleared his throat. "Um, Carissa? Mal? The kiss?"

Carissa sent me a slow smile and answered, "I'll do it."

"Judges, who should Cari kiss?" Jim continued brightly. "We're open-minded here. It can be a man or a woman."

I laughed when I saw the dismay that crossed Suzette's face. Then I frowned when I saw the anticipation on Jordan's face. XJ was looking kinda eager too. I agreed with Carissa; I was ready to be done with this.

XJ, Suzette, Jordan, and Niecy huddled together for a few minutes before turning as one to Jim. Suzette stepped forward with a smirk that spelled trouble. "We chose Jordy. Jordy will be kissing Carissa."

Jim nodded. "On the lips, count to five, that's it."

My eyes narrowed when I saw the look that passed between Jordy and Carissa. Was there a story here I wasn't aware of? Jordan extended his hand to Carissa. When she put her hand in his, I tensed. Then I forced myself to relax. I knew they were hoping for a big reaction from me and I wasn't going to give it to them.

No. I wasn't. Not even when Jordan pulled my

woman (yes, my woman) close and slid one hand behind her neck and one around her waist. Tilting her head up, he approached this kiss like a man who had been waiting for this moment for a long, long time and meant to enjoy every second.

And even though I really wanted to swing the dude, I held it back as he slid first lips then tongue across Carissa's lips. The lips that I firmly believed belonged to me and me alone and always would. When he slipped in between those lips, I held back. But when he pulled her tighter and took an extra taste and groaned into her mouth? And she wasn't backing away? Aw hell no. I stood up and took a step forward.

I don't know if she sensed me behind her or was already wrapping it up, but Carissa eased back, took a deep breath, shared another of those unfathomable looks with Jordan, and turned toward everyone else. "We good?"

Niecy's brows went up. "Uh, yeah, girl. You good?"

Carissa just shook her head and sat back down on the couch. "Next question."

I remained standing with my arms folded across my chest. I sent Jordan a look. He looked back without blinking. This was going to be a problem. I'd had about enough of this bullshit.

Jim cleared his throat. "All right, then, let's continue." He looked at me nervously and shuffled the index cards.

The next two questions were fairly tame in comparison to the first two. I answered a question about my knee. Carissa answered a question about her students. We answered the final question about whether we thought we'd ever get back together differently. I said, "Time will tell." She said, "Right now I can't fathom how."

We stared at each other. My eyes fell to her lips, still slightly swollen from kissing another man. The urge to wipe off all traces of his kiss and imprint mine instead was almost overwhelming. The one thing I knew for sure was that Carissa and I weren't finished. Not by a long shot. There was still that certain something that drew us together against all practical odds.

"Guys." Marcy's voice cut into our staring contest. "You won the challenge. Can we get you in the confessional for five minutes before we wrap?"

"Do we have a choice?" we said at the same time.

"Not really."

"Well, then." I grabbed Carissa's hand and pulled her forward. "Let's see what there is to confess this evening."

"Did you and Jordy have some kind of a thing I don't know about?" I asked the minute we sat down in the small room. Because, the kind of familiarity they just displayed? Not a new thing. Something was going on and I wanted to know what the hell it was.

Carissa looked at me skeptically. "Are you crazy? No, we did not. You do realize everything we're saying is being filmed, right?"

"I don't care. What was that?" Film or no film, I wanted answers.

"What was *what*?" She raised her hands in confusion.

"That kiss!"

"It was just a kiss."

"It wasn't *just* a kiss. That was a serious kiss. Like something y'all had done before. Let me ask you something."

"Might as well." She shot me a look warning me not to say anything too crazy.

I ignored it. "Did you wanna skip the question on infidelity for my sake or yours?" Not until I saw her with Jordy did I wonder if maybe she had a few things to hide as well.

She gasped. "You have GOT to be kidding me."

"I don't know, Cari. That's why I'm asking."

"Right now, with the film rolling? Excellent, Mal. You know damn good and well I never cheated on you. It wouldn't have occurred to me. If you take a minute to think about what you're saying, you'll understand how hard I'm trying not to slap you silly right now."

One look at her balled-up fists and the fire in her eyes shooting angry daggers at me and I knew I was wrong. I kept putting the wrong foot forward with her. "Okay, Cari. Okay. I'm sorry. My only excuse is that I still consider you mine on some level and that kiss threw me."

She shrugged. "I'm not yours and it was just a kiss."

"You liked it," I accused.

"Are you seriously jealous right now?"

"I am. Do you not recall that you almost slept with me yesterday?"

"Malachi!" She pointed. "One: Cameras! Two: That is NOT what happened. Three: Are you kidding me with this right now?" She was beyond pissed off and speeding toward furious.

I waved a hand. "I'll get them to edit it out. Stop me when I'm lying. If we hadn't been interrupted, I would have had you yesterday."

"Had me? Like some sort of ownership? Please. *If* I slept with you it would've just been to scratch an itch, nothing more. Besides, you don't know what I would have done. I might have said no."

I gave her a confident look. "When have you ever turned me down?"

"Are you trying to be an asshole about this? Because you're doing a great job of it."

"I'm just—Carissa, I didn't like him kissing you." I didn't like the thought of her with anyone but me. It had always been me. I'd been her first and, before things went off the rails, I was going to be her last. I couldn't stand the thought of anyone else having that intimate knowledge of her.

"I'm no longer required to worry about what you like and what you don't."

"I don't want to argue."

"Then don't."

"Was something going on between you and that guy?"

"His name is Jordan."

"Carissa."

"What, Malachi? It was a dare. You're the one who was determined to win this thing. We're winning. We'll lose the weight, you'll finish getting in shape, you'll be back in the NFL, and you'll be gone. You should be happy. You have exactly what you wanted. And by the way, in case you forgot:

you lost the fricking right to worry about who I kiss years ago."

Marcy and Bliss walked in the room. "Are you ready to answer some questions?"

"I think we've answered enough," Carissa said with enough heat that Bliss didn't challenge her. She took a step back as Carissa swept past her.

Ren walked in the door Carissa had just stormed out of and slammed shut behind her. "Trouble in paradise?"

"Ha!" I laughed humorlessly. "This may be many things, but paradise is not one of them."

"You won today," Bliss reiterated with the camera rolling.

"Did I?" Where I was sitting, it definitely felt like I had lost something. Something important and irreplaceable.

"Well, you won the challenge. Is the competition what you expected it to be?"

"No. Not at all." I stood up and pushed past the crew. "Y'all have a good night." I strode down the hallway and upstairs to the suite of rooms Carissa and I were sharing. Walking through the tiny suite of two bedrooms, cubicle-sized living area, and a bathroom, I realized she was not there. For a moment I had the chilling thought that she was with Jordan. That she'd already chosen to be with him and shut me out. That thought terrified me. The idea that someone else could take her away before I even got the chance to figure out if I wanted her back and could win her back. Then I looked out the window and saw her sitting outside in the courtyard beside the fountain. I wanted to go to her, I wanted to talk, I wanted to hold her. More than anything else, I wanted to turn back the clock and have us be us again. Was this just because I was spending time with her again after avoiding her for so long? Was this just because a part of me thought she and I were meant to be together? Was it just an itch that needed to be scratched so that we could move on? Was this just me being selfish? The truth? I had no idea what would happen if and when I decided to put back together what I'd broken with Carissa or if it could even be done. With a sigh, I went to my room and shut the door behind me. It had been a long damn day and there was a line of long damn days yet ahead.

10

You're very passionate about this

Carissa—Wednesday, June 10—11:28 a.m.

"Dear God, I hate working out," I puffed as I attempted to hold the side plank pose for another thirty seconds. In a show of pure sexism, the female contestants were sent to a yoga class while the guys went to run sports-related drills in the gym. I would much rather shoot baskets than contort myself into a jiggly pretzel.

"What was that, Carissa? Did you have a question?" Darcy asked.

"Nope. Not at all." I tried not to groan as I released the pose and rolled into downward facing dog.

"Oh, this is totally not natural to be doing with clothes on," Niecy said.

"Girl, don't even remind me," I muttered.

"Would you two shut up so we can get out of here?" Suzette bitched. Aggravated bitching was par for the course for Suzette. Where Niecy and I grumbled with as much good nature as we could muster, Suzette indulged in recurring bitch sessions where clearly the world had conspired to make her miserable. If not the world, me. She was convinced that I spent copious amounts of time thinking up ways to make her life miserable. I didn't have to; she did fine all on her own. We were used to it by now. Constant bitch and moan from that one.

My only source of entertainment today was watching Suzette struggle even harder than I was to contort her fleshy extremities into these positions.

We huffed and strained through another forty minutes of yoga torture before collapsing onto the mats.

"Hydrate, ladies!" Paul called out from the front of the room.

I reached for the water bottle and drank deeply. Okay, so maybe I was pretending it was flavored vodka. A girl could dream.

"Ladies, we're going to have you meet with the therapist now. Suzette isn't feeling well, so she'll do her session later. Niecy and Carissa, you can meet Dr. Julie in the common room." Suzette fled the room without a look back.

"Dr. Julie?" I asked sardonically. "Are they serious with this?"

"It's very Hollywood," Niecy agreed. "Is it me or does it seem that our dear Suzette is always under the weather when there's an all-girl activity to do?"

"Under the weather?" we both repeated with air quotes.

"Is that what we're calling it? And no, it's not you."

"I mean, damn—she truly cannot stand you."

"The feeling is mutual. We competed for everything back in the day and I came out on top more often than not." Truly I felt Suzette should be over it by now, but it seemed like wounded negativity was all she had to get her through these days.

"I wonder why she even agreed to do the show if she hates being around you that much?"

"Probably the same reason we're stuck on this thing: more dollars than sense."

"Amen," Niecy said as we climbed awkwardly off the floor and gathered our things to head for the common room.

"Not that I'm not giddy to have you, but besides our brief catch-up convo, you never gave me the details on why you decided to do this show. What got you here?" I asked out of curiosity.

"You know I went through that breakup with Finn. . . ."

"I refer to him as Freakin' Finn, but yes." Niecy had been dating Finn Wilson for close to five years. Finn was a guy who had to be dragged into grown-up-ness kicking and screaming. Easy to look at, hard to live with. He always had some reason why the relationship could not be taken to the next level. Every step forward in their relationship had been the result of Niecy prodding and pushing and pleading. Personally, I didn't think it was supposed to be that hard. Eventually, she agreed with me and broke it off. Then again, what did I know? I sat around with Malachi's ring on my finger for about the same length of time without getting a Mrs. in front of my name. I was in no position to judge.

"Anyway, I ran into him back in April and he said some things that got me thinking."

"What kinds of things?" We arrived in the common room.

A whisper-thin blonde with a severely short haircut stood to greet us. She was dressed all in black and her lips were coated in a blood red lipstick. We both paused. It was a little much for a middle-of-the-day look in sleepy Belle Haven, Louisiana.

"Hi, Carissa. Hi, Deniece." She extended a hand to both of us. "I'm Dr. Julie. I'm here to talk through the psychological side of your weight gain."

Niecy and I exchanged glances and shook her hand. This would be yet another ride on the fun train. It seemed to never end around here.

"When you walked in, you were talking about Deniece's ex-boyfriend. Do you want to continue that conversation?"

Were they bugging the hallways, the water bottles, the T-shirts we wore? We looked at each other with resignation. We could talk about it with her in a controlled environment or we could try to talk privately and have things we said taken out of context.

We sat down on the sofa in front of Dr. Julie.

"So anyway . . ." Niecy drawled with an exaggerated eye roll. "Finn said that one of the reasons he wouldn't commit to me was because I was 'over-confident' about my appearance." She used the air quotes on overconfident.

I was appalled. "What was he trying to say?"

"He was trying to say that my ass was big and he wanted a skinny bitch."

"Oh, Niecy, come on. You've been the same size for as long I've known you and you've always looked fabulous. You were the same size when you met him, so all of a sudden he didn't like what he was hugged up on for months on end? That boy damn near begged to get with you."

She waggled her shoulders. "Who knows? Anyway, it occurred to me that I'm not getting any younger."

"True dat," I agreed.

"And would it kill me to, one: lose some weight; two: spend the summer with you; and three: get out of Finn's reach for a few months?"

"Good points all." I nodded.

"And so here I am in the middle of hot-ass Louisiana, sweating out my curls on nationwide TV."

"But we're having so much fun, though?" I giggled.

"Oodles." She winked at me.

Dr. Julie interjected, "Deniece, have you always been full figured?"

"Nice wording." She flashed a grin at the doctor to let her know it was okay. "Pretty much my entire life, but I've always been disgustingly healthy so it wasn't a problem."

"But now that you've been rejected by a man, you consider your weight to be a problem?" Dr. Julie queried.

We both frowned because that wasn't even close to what Niecy had said. "I think it's more a case of 'if I'm going to do this, why not now' more than anything else," Niecy answered diplomatically.

Dr. Julie turned to me. "Why do you think you've had such a drastic weight gain, Carissa?"

I expelled a breath. "You know, one thing you guys on this show could work on is a little tact and sensitivity. Most people who are overweight know that they are overweight. Those of us who used to be teensy and aren't anymore? It's especially painful. It's like fat is the last thing that people feel okay being rude and insensitive about."

"I wasn't trying to be insensitive."

"You referred to my weight gain as drastic. Which, of course, it is. But surely I don't need you to emphasize it," I explained with as much Southern hospitality as I could muster.

She nodded in acknowledgment. "Point taken. No one has ever told us this before."

"I can't imagine why not. Fat people do not want to be told we are fat. Even if we're just slightly overweight, we'd prefer not to be slapped around with it. Let us deal with our body issues as we see fit. No pun intended."

She sat back in surprise. "No offense, but you do not come across as sensitive about your weight."

"Okay, like what you did there: By saying I wasn't sensitive about my weight, you imply that my weight is a problem. As if I'm not living a full life, in spite of not being a perfect size 6. Happy comes in all sizes. The things that have gone wrong in my life aren't directly related to my weight. The opposite, in fact," I informed Dr. Julie.

"What do you mean?"

"Self-esteem and self-confidence are often issues of plus-sized folks. You just stumbled across me and Niecy, who don't really have problems in that area. We get that cute comes in all sizes, colors, and creeds."

"Okay." She took some notes on her iPad.

"Anyway, let me answer your question. My case is fairly classic. There were things missing in my life that I replaced with food. Unfortunately, the more things I lost, the more food I replaced them with, which coincided with me becoming less and less active. So more food, less movement, and here we are."

"Can you identify the things that you were missing so that it doesn't happen again?"

"I was missing me," I answered directly. "I placed the needs of others before mine and somewhere inside I knew it. Then I lost one of the people whom I had considered integral to my continued happiness. Over the past few years, I kind of found myself again, but I decided the weight wasn't that big of a thing."

"Do you think you will keep it off after this?" Dr. Julie asked.

"I guess that depends."

"On what?"

"On how much I lose and whether I'm healthy and what's important to me along the way. I'm not losing weight for a man or for some bright shiny life that only skinny people achieve. I'm losing weight because it's time and I'd be more comfortable in my own skin."

Dr. Julie scribbled furiously. "You two have a very

healthy outlook. I'm optimistic that you are prepared to handle the psychological ramifications of rapid weight loss."

Niecy blinked. "What might those be?"

"Well, a lot of times, you get more attention, you start obsessing over your looks, things like that. Your appearance becomes more important; other areas less so."

Niecy guffawed. "Did you miss the part where we talked about our cute? We've always spent more time worrying about how we look than we should. We're vain, at any size. Welcome to the South. Yeah, I don't think you really need to worry too much about us down the road."

"Carissa, would you like to talk specifically about Malachi and his impact on your mental well-being?" Dr. Julie asked out of the blue.

"No. I absolutely would not." I had to draw the line in the sand.

"But you do know that he impacted and probably continues to impact how you feel about yourself?"

"Malachi Knight impacts a lot of things, but what he can no longer do is change the way I feel about me. No, that's not an option. If I learned nothing else from our split, I learned I needed to be okay with me, no matter what. And that's not going to change whether I'm wearing an 8 or an 18." Niecy high-fived me.

"You're very passionate about this," Dr. Julie observed.

"About me?" I smiled. "Why, yes. Yes, I am. As a matter of fact, I love me some me."

"Girl, you're a hot mess," Niecy said with an amused shake of her head.

"If I don't love me some me, who will?" I raised my arms to ask.

Dr. Julie scribbled some more and then looked up. "I think we're at a good stopping point. I'll check back in with you from time to time. Feel free to give me a call if you have anything you want to talk about."

"Thank you, Dr. Julie," we intoned at the same time.

She gestured to the door. "You can head on over to lunch."

"Yummy. Carrot sticks and naked chicken," I murmured to Niecy.

"You know it." We locked arms and walked in slow resignation.

11

Are you sure you know what you're doing?

Malachi—Friday, June 12—6:12 a.m.

"What are you really asking me?" I responded to one of Meshach's questions with a question of my own as I finished my last round of reps on the butterfly press. Shifting to the Nautilus machine for leg curls, I adjusted the weight and slid onto the bench. Double-checking that my knee brace, which I needed less and less, was secure, I depressed the weight with both legs and then brought it back up slowly. After the third rep, I glanced up at him.

"I just want to make sure your head is on straight," Meshach cautioned as he settled onto a bench across from me.

Raising a brow, I had to needle him a little. "Are you going to work out or just sit in your pretty blue suit and lecture me?"

Meshach had a thriving law practice based in New Orleans, at least a ninety-minute drive from here. Yet here he was at six in the morning dressed in his Armani suit, taking time out to talk to me. Shach wasn't the kind to talk just to hear himself talk. If he had something important enough to track me down to say, I was going to listen.

"I'm heading into New Orleans after I talk to you. No workout needed. In case you forgot, I'm the natural athlete in the family."

"You're the natural bullshitter, that's for damn sure." I exhaled after the tenth rep. Some people actually liked strength training. I wasn't one of those people. I did what I had to do and went on to the next thing.

"Mal . . ." he started tentatively. Meshach was rarely tentative.

"Shach, you know you don't have to sugarcoat shit with me. We've never been that way. Just say it."

"Let's start with the career. Do you want back in the NFL just to prove you can do it or because it's what you really want?"

"You know it's what I've always wanted."

"Yes, but let's be real. Football came easy. You never thought about doing anything else. You've invested here and there, you've got some lines on other fields. If football isn't your passion anymore, don't do it."

I looked at him in confusion. "I still love it. I was miserable when I couldn't play. Even more because I had cut myself off from the sport."

"You were miserable without football or without Carissa?"

"Football. I learned to live without Carissa."

"Because football and Carissa are mutually exclusive."

"I know that."

"Do you? Cuz it kinda seems like you want to get everything back jus' the way it was. You can't do that."

"I know that, Shach," I repeated. "Just make your point."

He took a deep breath and unloaded. "I don't want you to get tangled up with Carissa again if you're going to leave her behind when you head back to the NFL."

"Tangled up?" I was looking for clarification.

"You know what I'm saying here."

"I don't know that I'm getting back to the NFL. No one knows that yet."

"C'mon, now. You damn well do know and it's not like you to play coy."

I tilted my head and acknowledged his statement before moving to the next machine.

He began again. "Listen, Mal, you weren't here when she came back. She was . . ."

I paused in the middle of a lift and met his gaze. "What? She was what?"

He clasped his hands together and looked down. "She was broken, Mal. Carissa had always been a live wire, full of energy and sass. All that fire, all that spark—gone. She was just a shadow of her former self for a while. And you know you had to be heavily responsible for that."

I let go of the bar I was pulling on and exhaled. I'd forgotten that as much as Carissa had been a part of my life, she was a part of my family's life as well. When she hurt, they hurt. The fact that

I was responsible for that weighed heavily on me. "You know, it really kills me to hear that. I never meant to do that to her."

"I know you didn't. But it took her a long time to come back. To find herself again. I wouldn't want—"

I got up and moved to the free weights, interrupting him as I moved past. "I know. I do know. I may be a little slow, but I'm not an idiot. I admit I didn't realize what I was doing to her before. You know she always just . . . I don't know."

"She always just did whatever you wanted. No questions asked," Meshach explained.

"Well, yeah. It didn't occur to me that she didn't want exactly what I wanted."

He huffed out a breath in frustration. "You're still not getting it, Mal!"

"What?" I was confused. What was I missing?

"She did want what you wanted for you, just not at the expense of what she wanted for the both of you and for her. She put you first. Every time. Your wants, your needs, your ambitions."

Okay. I had to set down the weights on that. It was like a lightning bolt struck me. I had never thought about it like that. Not at all. I was so focused on what I was doing and how to take the next step. I had been thinking about our relationship from my point of view. And then I thought about it from her point of view. But not until this moment had I considered our point of view—together, as a unit. Maybe I'd been too young when we met and got used to things a certain way. Maybe it took me a while to mature. Maybe being apart and alone and hurt and disillusioned made me see now what I didn't then. It was now clear that my inability to move us forward as equal partners had been a major part of the problem all along.

I sat down next to Meshach and stared unseeingly at the ground. "I don't think I want to do without her. But I'm not sure how to get us there," I admitted.

"When you figure it out for sure and you know how to make it work? That's when you make your move. Otherwise you're being the same self-obsessed asshole she ran away from."

My head snapped up and I glared at my brother. "Whoa! What's with the name-calling, bro?"

"You earned it, bro."

"When?"

"Right around the time when you started believing your own press," he said wryly.

"Jesus, was I that bad?"

He snorted. "Worse."

"Why didn't someone say something?"

"Carissa did. For all of us. Many times. You quit listening to any damn body."

I gave him a small shove. "You should have kicked my ass. Wouldn't be the first time."

He leveled a solemn look at me. "Remember I tried?"

"Oh yeah." Vaguely, I remembered Meshach, Burke, and Pierre coming to see me in Houston shortly after Carissa bolted, but before I injured my knee. I was in an asshole phase at that time, I could admit it in retrospect. Shach had tried to tell me about myself, but I wasn't hearing it. "I believe you referred to my attitude as 'stank'?" I'd called him something worse in retaliation and he drew his arm back to throw a punch. Pierre stepped in between us and reminded Meshach that assault against a brother was still considered assault and did we really want to go there? I sighed as the scene came back to me. It wasn't pretty. "My bad?" I put my fist up.

Meshach bumped me and nodded. "Definitely your bad. That's why I'm sitting here like a bayou-assed Dr. Phil all up in your business. If your head isn't fully pulled out of your hind parts, if you are not ready to be all in? Please for the love of God, leave Carissa Wayne alone."

"Duly noted," I agreed.

"All right, then." He looked around the gym I was using on Havenwood's campus. "What's with this candy-assed workout? When are you getting back on that field and testing that knee for real?"

"All in good time, Meshach. Everything will be as it should, all in good time."

"Oh, okay, Oprah. Are we still talking about your knee or are you dropping knowledge on the state of the universe?"

"You got jokes. I'm just saying I'm hearing everything you said this morning. I'm going to put everything back to rights if I can." Of course, I had no idea how to do that or if my idea of back to rights aligned with everyone else's.

Meshach called my bluff. "Are you sure you know what you're doing?"

I shrugged and replied honestly. "Hell no."

"Well, all right, then. Good luck."

"I sure need every bit of it."

"Later, bro."

"Shach?" I called out before he crossed the threshold.

He spun back to look at me. "Yep?"

"Thanks."

"Thanks for actually listening."

"Don't wrinkle your suit driving to work."

"Don't let your head get too big to fit in the helmet." He slammed the door behind him.

12

Challenge from hell

Carissa—Wednesday, June 22—3:34 p.m.

"I'm sorry." I squinted in the direction of Darcy and the other trainers. "You want us to do what now?"

Jim tried to look sympathetic but didn't really pull it off. "Form new teams for this event. We're shaking things up today. We're going to do girls versus guys. So you, Niecy, and Suzette will compete against Mal, Jordy, and XJ."

"Why?" Niecy was even less pleased than I was.

"We thought it would be fun," Jim answered.

"What exactly are we doing?" Malachi asked with enough impatience that I knew he was close to the end of his rope.

These were long hot days of physical torture and sensual deprivation. We were tart, testy, and tired. And we hadn't hit the halfway point of this competition yet.

"It's kind of like a treasure hunt!" Jim announced with way more enthusiasm than any of us felt.

"For real, though?" XJ asked with a scowl.

"I'm afraid so. Are we ready to get started?"

Niecy waved a hand in a "bring it on" motion. "Let's do it and be done already."

"Ladies, if you could line up to my left and fellas to my right."

I resisted the epic eye roll and stepped into place. Instead of standing on the other side of me where there was plenty of space, Suzette jammed in between me and Jim. I sighed and slid over a step. Jim handed Suzette the first envelope. She opened it, read it, and started walking away. Jim called her back.

"Suzette, this is a team event. Your score will depend on your entire team finishing ahead of the men's team. In addition, there will be a bonus or penalty for teamwork, leadership, skill, and speed."

"What he's saying is," I snapped, "do you mind scooting back over here and sharing with the rest of us?"

She looked not the slightest bit chagrined as she handed over the note card.

Niecy read, "Head to the center of town, find the historical landmark commemorating the town's founding father. Somewhere nearby is your next clue."

I frowned. "There are three landmarks with Josiah Somers."

Malachi groaned. "Why do you know that?"

"Some of us paid attention on the field trips?" I teased.

"Do the guys have the same clue and we're wasting time listening to Mal and Carissa flirt?" Jordan asked.

"If you think that's flirting, you're a little rusty," Mal zinged.

Jim put his hands up. "Contestants, please. The clues are the same. You have to solve them perfectly and get through them quickly to maximize your point totals."

"Any other rules?"

"We've taken all your keys so you can't drive from one place to the next. Oh, and the losing team is on kitchen cleanup for the rest of the week. Is everyone clear?"

"Clear," we all intoned.

"Ready, set . . . go!"

I would like to say that we took off running, but really . . . we girls did not. We'd been biking all day. Which gave me an idea. As the guys headed down the road on foot at a fast pace, I stepped over toward the gym and motioned for the girls to follow me.

"Carissa, what are you doing?!" Suzette shrieked. "The guys are getting ahead of us! I am not scrubbing dishes for a week because you always play by your own rules."

"Just this one time, Suzette; can you just trust me?" I reached into the equipment shed and started pulling out the bicycles.

"Ah yeah." Niecy grinned and hopped on.

I held a bike out to Suzette. "Unless you'd rather walk it?"

"Okay, this wasn't a bad idea," Suzette conceded grudgingly.

Quickly, we caught up to the guys. "See you in

town, fellas." I grinned and pedaled faster, ignoring the screaming in my thigh muscles.

"Hey!" Jordy called out as we whizzed by. "Is that against the rules?"

"He said we couldn't drive our cars." Niecy waved and followed behind me. Suzette was behind us and managed a giggle or two. A camera crew pulled alongside us and started filming.

Once we were on the main street back into town, I started complaining. "My thighs hate me."

"You? Girl, everything from the neck down is in rebellion."

"God, you two like to hear yourselves talk," Suzette complained.

I exchanged a glance with Niecy and held on to my thoughts about kettles and pots. We rode the rest of the distance in silence. When we pulled up to the main square, I said, "Niecy, you take the one on the left, Suzette the middle, and I'll take the right."

"Why can't you take the one in the middle? It's bigger and in the middle of some bushes," Suzette argued.

"Mary, Margaret, and Joseph. Fine! I'll take the middle statue." I swear to God if I'd said the sky was blue, she would say it was pink just because. We rested the bikes against a bench and started scouring the statues for clues. Five minutes in and I still hadn't found anything. With a sigh, I pushed between the scratchy bushes and started searching the hind parts of the horse Josiah Somers was seated on.

"Doesn't it just figure that you would be staring at a horse's ass?" Suzette cackled.

"I find I spend a lot of time around horses' asses these days," I shot back before turning my attention back to the statue. Was that? Yes! There under the back hoof was a long thin envelope. I pulled it out and waved it. "Got it!"

We met back by the benches and opened the envelope. Puzzle pieces fell out. "They are killing me," Niecy said as we settled down on the sidewalk to put it together. Every time I set a piece down, Suzette picked it up and moved it.

"This right here is going to lose us teamwork points. Let's do the outside first and work our way in, okay?"

"Why do we have to do it your way?"

"Do you want to clean up after XJ for the next seven days?"

She subsided and slid the right corner piece into place. A few minutes later we stared in confusion at the picture we'd put together.

"It's a picture of a box sitting on top of something?" Niecy wondered.

"It's a boat deck." I tilted my head.

"Yeah, but which one?" Suzette lamented. "This is the kind of town where every other body has a pirogue or shrimping boat tied up out back."

"But this is a nice deck, and here in the reflection, what is that?" I looked closer and made out the letters R-H-O. "I know where this is." I saw the guys straggling toward us and lowered my voice. "I'll tell you on the way there." We quickly took apart the puzzle, slid the pieces back in the envelope, returned it to its hiding place, and hopped on the bikes.

"Where ya'll headed?" Mal called out.

I rolled my eyes. "Wouldn't you like to know?"

"I surely would."

"Figure it out." When we'd pedaled out of earshot, I announced, "It's the Bissets' boat by the marina."

Niecy shook her head. "How did you figure it out?"

"The lettering on the reflection is the beginning of Taylor's shop. Rhone's Fine Arts, Gifts, and Framing." Though I was hot and cranky, I was glad Taylor's store would get some exposure.

When we pedaled up to the marina, one of the crew was kind enough to hand us some bottled water. I was tempted to dump it over my head but knew from past experience that this tank top and capri pant combo stuck to you like glue when wet. I settled for drinking almost half of the bottle as I retrieved the box from the deck of the boat. I handed it to Suzette and she opened it.

"Go fly a kite."

"Beg pardon?" I asked, frowning at her.

"That's what it says." She showed us the writing on the unfolded box.

Niecy closed her eyes. "Please tell me that Taylor sells kites."

"She does sell hand-painted kites." We turned toward the store next to the marina when a huge pickup truck pulled up beside us. Mal, XJ, and Jordy climbed out of the back. My eyes narrowed as the windows rolled town and two young women peeked out.

Mal smiled at them. "Thanks, ladies. I appreciate your kindness on a hot summer afternoon."

I rolled my eyes as they giggled. "Anything for you, Blue Streak. We just love you. Good luck with the competition! Call us when you have a night off or something." The more forward of the two handed him a business card out the window. He accepted it with another smile.

"Again, much obliged, ladies. Have fun in New Orleans."

They spun off and all eyes turned to Mal. He shrugged. Then, making sure I noticed, he ripped up the business card and discarded it in the trash can. "They were headed through town and were kind enough to offer a ride."

"Um-hmm." Of course they did. That was the kind of stuff that happened to Malachi all the damn time. I wasn't sure why it still irritated me so. I had no claim on him and no say-so about whom he decided to spend time with.

XJ laughed. "That kind of thing never happens to me." He looked over Suzette's shoulder. "So kites, huh?"

Niecy and I gave Suzette a look. After all her bitching, she couldn't even hide the clue? Without a word, I walked into Taylor's store and pushed the door open. "Hey, Tay. We're here for the kites."

Taylor stepped out from behind the counter dressed in her nicer jeans and a funky tunic top. "I've got them right here for you." Strategically, she had our kites at the back of the store so that the cameras followed us past all of her merchandise on the way there. Along the back wall, she had a variety of kites hanging—some with scenes of the Louisiana countryside, others with inspirational messages, and a few with abstract designs. There were box kites and traditional diamond shapes, along with complicated swirls and others.

"Which one is ours?" I asked.

She smiled slowly. "Well, here's the tricky part. You have a choice of three designs to choose from, and you have to put it together. Take it to Belieux Fairgrounds and fly it for five minutes without crashing. And you do have to walk or run to the park from here. No riding of any kind." She pointed to a table with six kite-assembly kits stacked. "Choose wisely."

"I think we should get the box kite with the picture," Suzette announced.

I bit my tongue. The old-school diamond with lettering looked like it would be easier overall, but I didn't want to get into it.

"I vote diamond with Belle Haven written across it," Niecy said.

"No," Suzette said. "I have kids, I know kites, and we're doing this one."

I reached out, grabbed the one she wanted, and turned for the door. "Fine. Later, Tay." Stepping outside, I finished my water and started stretching. "The fairgrounds are two blocks over. Y'all ready to jog?"

Suzette opened her mouth to argue and Niecy cut her off. "Girlfriend, you got your way on the kite. Take the win and let's get through the rest of the day, shall we?"

To my surprise, Suzette backed down and took off at a slow trot. Thank God we didn't have far to go. As I suspected, Mal and the guys came out and quickly passed us by. I noticed Mal had the simple diamond kite box in his hand. Right then, I knew I would be spending the rest of the week wiping out the microwave in the common kitchen.

We got to the park, and though we wanted to collapse on the ground, we took out the kite pieces and the instructions and got started. Four long sticks, four short sticks, string, connectors, and the fabric. Suzette looked at the instructions, looked at the materials, and announced, "This isn't right."

"Yes, it is, you're just doing it wrong."

"I am not!"

"Let me see the instructions."

At this point, I was so weary and frustrated that I wanted to lie down on the grass and weep like a child. I was PMSing, I wanted chocolate, and I wanted a bubble bath. Instead, I was handed some Powerade, a protein bar, and a cool cloth to mop my brow. I sat cross-legged and watched Niecy and Suzette battle. This was the challenge from hell.

Niecy snatched the instructions out of Suzette's hands. "These four make the box. We cross the small ones at the top and the bottom for support, wrap the fabric, and we're done."

"I don't agree," Suzette said. "I think you wrap the fabric around the short and use the long to extend the kite."

Niecy almost snarled. "How does that make a box, Suzette? What laws of geometry make that work? Please share." She looked at me. "Cari, I know you're trying to play nice with Princess today, but ain't nobody got time for that. I need you to get on board and kick this kite's ass. C'mon, now."

With a sigh, I sat up. "Niecy's right, you're wrong. Connect the support sticks so we can attach the others." Suzette didn't move. "Please?"

Giving a dramatic huff, she started snapping the pieces together. We hadn't even built the frame when the guys shouted. "We're done!" Sure enough, we looked up to see Mal running up and down the field with the blue and green Belle Haven kite high in the sky.

Suzette snapped two of the sticks in half and threw them. "Dammit! If you had let me do it my way, we'd be done by now."

"If you'd picked the kite Carissa wanted, we'd be done by now," Niecy hissed.

Ren came over to us. "If you can't finish, it's a forfeit."

I walked over to the remains of the poor defenseless kite sticks and picked them up. "Maybe we can tie some string around them and bind them back together, just enough to get it up in the sky?"

Mal came over and looked. "Maybe, but then you need to use less fabric so the kite won't be too heavy."

"Good idea." I nodded and started trying to fit the pieces back together.

Suzette yanked the sticks away and broke them again. "I'd rather lose than have you save the damn day."

Everyone's mouth fell open and we stared at her in disbelief.

"And there it is." Niecy shook her head and fell back onto the grass. "The entire reason we'll be scrubbing pots and taking out trash: Suzette would rather sink the boat than have Carissa be the captain. Jesus."

The production truck pulled up and Jim climbed out. "So it's settled?"

"I'm afraid so." I used his words from earlier.

"No one completed the hunt?" he asked.

XJ put his hands on his hips. "Man, listen. We hot, we mad, we funky. The girls forfeited. Can we be out?"

Jim flashed his smile. "Perhaps the ladies would accept a blind challenge to make up for the loss?"

"Perhaps I'd rather slit my wrist and swim with sharks," Suzette said.

"So that's a no." Jim smothered a laugh.

"A no," Niecy agreed.

"That's it for today, then. Good job, guys. Ladies, we'll see each of you separately in the confessional."

Ren waited a few moments and then called out, "That's a wrap for this location."

We nodded and headed for the van to take us back to campus. Mal sidled up beside me. "I may be in possession of a Snickers bar. What will you give me for it?"

I may or may not have whimpered. "Fun size? Regular? Whatcha working with?"

"You know I only deal in king size." He smirked.

My mouth watered. Not for his innuendo but for that chocolate wrapped around nougat; that caramelly, peanutty goodness. "What do you want for it?"

His eyes darkened. "I can think of so many ways to answer that, girlie."

I shook my head. "I look beat from tip to toe and must smell like all of the bayou and you're thinking nasty thoughts?"

"Around you? Always."

"Boy, I'm not about to do you for a Snickers bar."

"What will you do me for?"

"Are you that desperate to be done?"

"Like I said: With you? Always."

"How about I let you take the first shower tonight and we call it even?" I offered.

He considered for a minute. "Care to join me?"

"Boy, give up." I chuckled.

"Not likely. But I'm easy—I'll take the first shower and you can have the Snickers. Will you save a piece?" He climbed onto the bus and we settled into the back row.

I slid him a sideways glance. "Will you save me some hot water?"

"Deal."

"I don't know, Mal. I might've got the better end of the deal on this one."

"Which one of us is on kitchen duty for a week?"

My face fell. "Oh yeah. And I ache all over. I could use a hot shower."

"I could give you a little massage later, work out some of the kinks?"

I smacked him on the shoulder, though the

offer was hella tempting. "I'll just enjoy the Snickers and worry about my own kinks, thank you."

He whispered in my ear. "Sounds nasty."

"Everything sounds nasty to you."

"You used to love that about me."

"Hmph." Yep. That was my witty comeback. I was spared having to say anything more intelligent as we pulled up in front of the dorm.

13

Now I'm not ready

Malachi—Monday, June 27—9:14 p.m.

I had to admit that the *Losing to Win* folks did not miss a beat. No pun intended. They decided to make tonight's challenge a Zumba dance-off. The three teams would be challenged to first watch, then mimic dance steps inspired from the popular dance workout craze, Zumba. Each combination would be more complicated than the last. The couple that showed the most accuracy and style and learned the most steps won the challenge.

In a savvy twist, the production team had opened up the event to the whole town and surrounding communities. The ballroom on the ground floor of City Hall hosted Town Hall meetings, the Christmas pageant, and the Veterans Day dance. This year, it was hosting the Belieux County Brazilian Dance-off sponsored by *Losing to Win.*

A few hundred people had ventured out on

this steamy Monday night, dressed in their versions of club gear, and getting their samba, cumbia, and salsa on. Sad to say I witnessed my parents doing some sort of dance that could have stayed forbidden for my well-being.

"Boy, you don't know nuttin' 'bout dat!" my dad cackled, and swiveled his hips in a way I won't soon burn from my memory.

"I'm so sorry I saw that." Carissa's voice floated over my shoulder and I turned around.

"Ni-ice!" I hissed as my eyes took in her flirty purple wrap dress with a ruffle that stopped above the knees and ridiculously sexy high-heeled sandals. "You are looking right, Carissa Wayne."

She checked me out in my black dress shirt tucked into black pants. "I'm just trying to keep up appearances, Bayou."

"Well, you're doing a hell of a job there, Teach."

Meshach walked past. "Did you see our parents out on the floor?"

"Man, I can't *un*-see it."

Carissa snickered. "Reverend Young had an inappropriate grip on my mother's hips two songs ago. I had to walk away."

Jordy, Suzette, Niecy, and XJ had come over. "When does this thing start for us?" Niecy asked.

"In about fifteen minutes," Bliss called out as she headed toward the stage.

"Well, that's enough time for me to steal a dance," Meshach announced and pulled Niecy out on the floor with a haste I found interesting.

I reached for Carissa, but Jordan was already

drawing her along with his hand around her waist. I narrowed my eyes as he looked over his shoulder and caught me watching. It was going to be like that, huh? Okay. Game on.

"Suzette, do you want to take a quick spin?" XJ asked.

"Not really." She flipped her hair over her shoulder and walked off.

"Dude," I said to XJ.

"Right? Suzette is some maintenance and a brother is tired. I called her husband every day this week to come spend some time with her. Got me hemmed up in that tiny-assed suite night after night with old girl. Sheesh."

"She wasn't always this bitter. I mean, she was shallow, she just wasn't mad at the world."

"Well, she's sure as shit mad now. You get the feeling she's out of her element and would be happier someplace else. She can be bearable when Carissa's not around."

"Yeah, they've always been oil and water and Suzette wanted to be a big fish in a big pond. Belle Haven is a small pond without space for . . ." I stopped talking as Jordy pulled Carissa in close and slid his hand down her waist to her hip.

"Uh, Mal, I don't need to stand here and make sure you don't rip somebody's head off, do I?" XJ said in a half-nervous, half-serious tone.

I patted him on the shoulder and kept one eye on Carissa and Jordy dancing. "Xavier, I'm a receiver. Don't you know we don't like contact?"

"Ha! I've seen you almost full-body slam a cornerback that got in your way. You don't fool me."

I smiled at him. "No worries, I won't be delivering any hits tonight." I watched as Jordy dipped Carissa over his arm and spent way too long admiring her cleavage as he pulled her back up.

"How did you ever let that go, man?" XJ asked in an awed voice as Carissa danced some sort of fancy kick-step ending in a spin with her arms over her head.

God, she looked amazing. The slow burn of desire and possession started spreading in my gut as I shook my head slowly. "It's a long, sad story."

"I mean, but . . ." He paused as if not sure how much to say. "You gotta get that back, right?"

I really did.

"Yeah, he does." Renard and Ruby had been standing behind me watching me watch Jordy and Carissa as well.

"Only if he knows what he wants this time." Ruby sucked her teeth. "Ain't nobody got time to be put through your changes, Malachi Henry."

"Yes, ma'am," I answered.

"Why didn't you come get her?" Renard asked. "Before this?"

"First I was mad. Then I was proud. Then I was hurt. Then I'd waited too long."

"And now, Malachi? What do you want with my sister now?" Ruby asked with a hand on her hip.

"I'm trying to figure that out exactly. But I know I want her."

"You always have. And then what?" Ruby probed.

"Ruby, let the man have some breathing room. I'm sure he wouldn't start anything if he couldn't do right by Carissa this time. Now, would you?" Renard pinned me with a glare.

"No, I wouldn't do that. Not this time," I swore.

Ruby said, "Hmm. Good luck convincing her of that."

I nodded.

"Ladies and gentlemen, if we could have the *Losing to Win* contestants come to the stage?"

"We're up," XJ said with a sigh, looking around for Suzette.

I headed for Carissa and held out my hand. "You ready to do this?"

She slid her hand into mine. "I'm ready to win this."

We grinned at each other. No need to be modest; we had an unfair advantage. We'd been dancing together for years. I was a natural athlete and Carissa could always cut a step. Our only real competition was Jordy and Niecy. And while they might hold their own, they were no match for us in this challenge.

We climbed onto the stage. Jim came out from wherever he'd been hiding and waved at the crowd. "Hello, Belieux County, Louisiana!"

The audience applauded politely.

"Y'all ready to see these folks get their groove on?"

Carissa whispered, "Should we tell him to never say 'y'all' or 'get their groove on' again? Like ever? He's not Southern and he's not hip. Bless his heart, though."

I cleared my throat to hide the laughter bubbling up. "After the points are tallied, you can tell him whatever you'd like."

"Good point."

Jim went through the instructions and rules

and then introduced the dance instructors who
would be leading and judging us. Within moments,
we were learning a cumbia hip swivel followed with
some Bollywood arm movements and ending with
a reggaeton "stop and drop it like it's hot" move.
We walked through it once.

I shot Carissa a smile. "You got this?"

She raised a brow. "You want the extra style
points?"

"Bring it."

Not even twenty minutes later, I was regretting
challenging her. Her last move resulted in her ass
brushing my pelvis as she dropped down and came
back up. Lord have mercy, I thanked the roomi-
ness of these pants. I could not stand in front of all
these folks sporting wood; at least the pleats cam-
ouflaged my condition somewhat.

When the instructor said we were going to slow
it down a bit, I actually broke out in a sweat.

"Let's put a little tango in here, shall we?" the
instructor enthused and it was all I could do not to
groan. They demonstrated twice, once slowly and
once to tempo. As we stepped together in the first
set of the next routine, Carissa looked up at me
through her lashes. The mischievous sparkle let me
know she knew what she was doing all along.
"You're killing me right now, you know that, right?"

"I had an idea," she said with a total body
shimmy against me.

"You've turned into a tease."

"Me?" she asked with false innocence.

"You know I want you and you're playing me.
Is it payback?"

"Mal, come on. This is just a little seductive suspense. It's not like I, say . . . promised to marry you, strung you along for years, and forced you out of my life with nothing but a Benz for a parting gift. Now, is it?"

I stopped dead still for a second as her words hit their mark. "Ouch."

"See?" she said with a dazzling smile as she danced in a circle around me. "Now that's payback."

I glanced around and started moving again, my mind no longer in the dance or in the foreplay. "I thought we were getting past it?"

"I'm working on it."

Improvising on the steps we'd just seen, I wrapped my arm around her waist and dragged her close. "Well, I want another shot." I whipped her away from me in a spin and pulled her back in close.

Our breath was labored from more than the efforts of the footwork. "Another shot at what? Me?" She turned away and turned back quickly before we pranced sideways together with hands clasped.

I put my hands on her shoulders as she slid down my leg and gritted my teeth as her hands got a little familiar on the way back up. "Oh yeah."

"What are we talking here? Sex?"

"To start. I think I'm finally ready for you," I whispered as we pressed our cheeks together for the last phase of the dance.

"Well, that's something," she said breathlessly as the dance finished.

"What?"

"Now *I'm* not ready."

"I'm right here when you are."

"Really," she drawled. "You, Malachi Knight, are going to wait for me?"

"It's my turn, don't you think?"

Her eyes went wide and she had nothing to say.

"Carissa and Mal, come over here and tell us where you learned to dance like that!" Jim crowed.

We both blinked as we realized where we were and what we were supposed to be doing. I put my hand in the small of her back and gestured. "After you."

She flicked an uncertain glance my way before affixing her "television" smile and walking toward Jim.

I had my work cut out for me here. But I was definitely up to the challenge.

14

I needed to eat, I needed to sleep, and I needed to think

Carissa—Friday, July 1—9:02 p.m.

"Carissa, you've lost a little over eighteen pounds in three weeks, and while that's very impressive, it's also too fast. Since your initial weigh-in, you are down twenty-six and a half pounds. You're averaging a loss of four and a half pounds a week and your body is going to rebel. We'd like you to lose between two to three pounds a week."

I had been coached to quit rolling my eyes so much on camera, so I flashed a carefree grin and asked, "Does this mean I'll be having a fried crawfish po' boy for dinner tomorrow night?"

Hannah, the nutritionist, shook her head and laughed at me. "I don't think you'll be seeing fried anything for quite some time."

Of course not. I resisted the urge to heave a sigh and listened while Darcy, super perky trainer extraordinaire, rambled on about pacing my weight loss and concentrating on replacing fat with muscle. Loose skin and jiggly flab were the enemy. I nodded at the appropriate intervals and then thankfully stepped off the scale.

Mal stepped on; he'd lost seventeen pounds in three weeks and got a different lecture about muscle fatigue and hitting the wall. The guest judge this week was in sports rehab, so he and Mal talked about how much stress he could put on his rehabbed knee.

Niecy and Jordy lost ten pounds each over the last few weeks. Suzette and XJ had been up and down but combined for a total weight loss of seven pounds. Apparently, they had been caught on film tipping over to Ruby's to have a decidedly NOT low-fat, not low-carb, not sugar-free dinner plus dessert.

In the end, Mal and I were ahead not only in weight lost but in competition wins as well. When we were paired together we won extra points for sportsmanship and partnership. There had been no more silly-assed challenges requiring us to bare our personal business. We had put whatever issues or conflicts we had to the side for the sake of trying to maintain some dignity throughout this competition. One time with the blind challenge was more than enough. We had no desire to see what kind of crazy scenarios they would put us in if given the chance. All I had to do was get through the last of this weigh-in and then we were off for the Fourth of July weekend.

By off, this meant we were allowed to live in our own homes without microphones or cameras dogging our every step. We were expected to work out and stick to sensible diets, but we had four whole days to interact with people not affiliated with this damn show. Four days where I could walk around in a bathrobe and not fear that my ass was jiggling on primetime television.

Plus . . . let me just be really real for a second. I needed a break from Mal's brooding intensity. And Jordan's hungry gazes. Yes, that kiss he'd laid on me at the "truth or dare" challenge threw me for a loop. I did not know he had that in him. At all. He kissed me like the answers to the puzzles of the universe could be found in my mouth and he wanted to take the time to discover each and every one of them.

That thirty-second kiss instantly moved him out of the friend zone and into the "What have we here?" category. He'd taken a few opportunities to talk with me since then, and so far, I liked what I was hearing from him. To be fair, I couldn't take too many steps toward Jordy until I dealt with whatever was still left between me and Malachi.

Clearly we still had the chemistry, but was that it? I was not going to reinvest in the Malachi Knight brand if he was going to turn back into that guy. So far, he had been open and communicative. We worked well together, we laughed, we talked— it was almost like it had been, before the adulation and the game turned him into more of a personality and less of a boyfriend. He was warm, engaging, and more like the guy I originally fell in love with decades ago.

Given the tug-of-war between whatever I felt for Malachi and the curiosity about what I could feel for Jordy, I was exhausted. Add in Suzette's constant malevolence, the cameras, the production schedule, and the two point two bites of food per day? I was ready for this break.

"Carissa, did you hear what Hannah said?" Jim asked from the podium.

"Honestly? No. I'm daydreaming about sleeping in my own bed without a 4:45 a.m. wake-up call."

Hannah piped up, "I was reminding everybody to stay on their dietary plans over the holiday."

"Who do we need to beg for permission for a piece of barbecue?" Niecy asked.

Paul, her trainer, laughed. "You can have one piece if you add an extra ten or fifteen minutes to your workout, wash it down with water, and skip the potato salad."

XJ sighed deeply. "Barbecue without potato salad? That's downright un-American!"

Jim chortled loudly. "It may be un-American, but it's the *Losing to Win* way. Good luck over the weekend and remember, we'll be checking in on you. See you next time!"

We stood still with fake smiles on our faces until Bliss called out, "And we're clear. Thanks, everybody! Carissa, can I talk to you for a second?"

I wanted to stomp my foot and say no, but then I remembered that I'm supposed to be a grown-up woman. "Sure, Bliss."

Bliss, Marcy, and Ren circled around me and led me over to a cluster of rooms they had set up as production offices. Once inside one of the meeting rooms, they closed the door and sat down to face me.

I raised a brow. "What can I do for y'all?"

Bliss gave me her most engaging "I want to be serious with you" look. I didn't trust it. "Carissa, we've conducted the focus group, where we show a few episodes of the show to a market research team, some focus groups, and our network execs."

Hoping it sucked and was about to be canceled, I answered with cautious optimism. "And?"

Marcy bounced in her seat. "They love you. People absolutely love you!"

I blinked twice. "What? Why?" I hadn't exactly been warm and fuzzy.

"You've got that certain something that people can relate to. You're pretty, you're real, and you are a bit of a drama magnet. Whatever the combination, you're a hit. We're a hit. They are predicting the biggest ratings ever this season."

"Oh. Well. Good for you," I responded lamely.

"Good for all of us," Ren added. "Of course, the tension between you and Malachi is testing uber high."

"Really," I said drolly. "Who knew my discomfort could be others' entertainment? I'm here to help."

Completely ignoring my sarcasm, Marcy continued. "Yes. After the first few episodes, the people in the focus group started taking bets on whether you'd end up with Mal or Jordy. Isn't that awesome?"

My brows drew into a frown. Perfect strangers betting on which guy I'd end up with and I hadn't made a move in either direction? Wasn't that even more damn intrusive than before? "Awesome, when does the first episode air?"

"Sunday night. This means that we're going to spend more time focusing on you. You were always the centerpiece of the show, but now you're the crown jewel!" Marcy added.

"Does the crown jewel get a little more privacy and respect?" I asked hopefully.

"Um . . . 'fraid not. Pretty much the same as it is now," Bliss answered with a twist of her lips.

"Does the crown jewel get an extra check?" I wondered out loud.

"Well . . . actually. That's one of the things we wanted to talk to you about. We're hoping to do some additional footage of you with members of your family, friends, and townspeople. That sort of thing."

"Uh-huh." It felt like they were building me up for something so I waited for the other shoe to drop.

"And we are going to want to feature you in some promos. Commercials, ads, things like that. You will get extra money for that."

"Uh-huh." Still waiting.

"And we'd like to offer you your own reality show after this one wraps."

"I beg your pardon?" No. As a matter of fact: Oh hell no.

"Yes, sort of like 'what's next in the life of Carissa Wayne.' Of course, we'd be thrilled if you ended up with Malachi and that would be extra viewership, but you're fun enough that you'd make a great show all on your own."

I snorted with laughter. "Doing what? Believe me, when I'm not battling old high school neme-ses or sparring with ex-fiancés, my life is not that fascinating. I teach teenagers. I mentor teenagers. I hang around with my friends and family. I sit at home and watch documentaries on the History Channel. I am not sexy. Truly."

Bliss shook her head. "We disagree. But take some time to think about it. Think of the exposure for you and the community. You don't have to decide right now."

"All right, then. Thank you. No offense, but I hope not to see you for the next few days."

"Understood. Have a great long weekend."

I fled that production office like the hounds of hell were on my heels. The last damn thing I needed was more exposure. I wanted to lose another twenty or thirty pounds and then slink back into semi-obscurity. I still couldn't understand what it was about me basically bitching and moaning my way through this process that was engaging. But somehow, I had managed to snag the attention of the network. Apparently my pain was everybody else's damn entertainment.

I was tempted to pull a *Gladiator* during the next confessional and hurl a knife at the audience while screaming, "Are you not entertained? Are you not entertained?" Let's see how that plays with the focus group. Shall we?

Giggling to myself, I grabbed my purse, keys, and laptop bag and practically skipped to my car. XJ, Suzette, Niecy, Jordy, and Mal had cleared out the minute the panel was over, so I didn't have to say any good-byes to anyone.

Settling in my one concession to vanity, the

Benz, I headed home with a smile. I considered the car to be my "thanks for playing" parting gift. I loved this car. It drove like a dream and never gave me a moment's drama. Unlike its rightful owner.

Speak of the devil. As I pulled into my driveway, I noticed several parked cars, Mal's included. So much for getting some alone time to dance around in my bathrobe sans jiggle worries.

I waltzed in the front door. My mom, Ruby, and Renard were sitting in the long living room on my sectional with Mal, Meshach, and Niecy. Lounging nearby were Pierre and Mal's parents, Henry and Val.

"Hi, everybody," I called out. "Am I having a party and didn't realize it?" Through the doorway, I saw Sugar, Middle Mike, Tay, and Mac in the kitchen. Something smelled amazing and not the least bit fat free.

"We just wanted a quick get-together to check on you and Mal," Eloise said.

"So you thought you'd come over and cook things I'm not allowed to eat?" I joked.

Valentine laughed as she got up to give me a hug. "We wouldn't do that to you, baby. Ruby has been working on approved recipes with Hannah and we think we've come up with one or two that you'll like. You look wonderful by the way, dear." She patted me on the arm.

I glanced down. The dreaded yoga pant tank top outfit wasn't as tight as before, but I still had a long way to go.

"She always looks good," Meshach said with a smile in his brother's direction. "Isn't that right, Mal?"

Mal's eyes tracked up and down my body. "I wouldn't kick her out of bed. Then again, I never did."

I gasped. "Malachi Henry! There are parental units in the room!" So embarrassing.

Henry guffawed. "Baby girl, how do you think we became parental units?"

Ruby threw up her hands. "We've entered the oversharing zone."

"Most definitely," I agreed and strode into the kitchen. Taylor and Mac were fighting over a large pot of something that bubbled on the stove. As I watched, Tay grabbed the spoon from Mac, he grabbed it back, and when their hands touched, they both froze before pretending like nothing happened. I held back a sigh. Could the two of them fall naked on top of each other already? Sugar was pulling some wheat rolls out of the oven and Middle Mike was stirring up his infamous party punch. No one knew exactly what was in that stuff, but it had five different types of liquor and "mystery" juices. I never attempted more than two small glasses of the stuff at a time.

Mal came in behind me and settled his hands on my shoulders. "What part of this meal are we allowed to eat?"

Taylor grinned. "This is guilt-free étouffée with brown rice and roasted veggies. If you limit yourself to half a whole-grain roll with the butter spread, you're clear. Everything here has been inspected and blessed by your Bod Squad."

Mac piped up. "By the way, the bod is starting to look right, Cari."

"How many men in this town are checking out

your bod?" Mal asked in an exasperated tone of voice.

I wasn't going there with him. "I have no clue, but no doubt after this first episode airs on Sunday, the number will be going up," I replied cheekily. "Are we not to speak of the Mal Knight groupies that have started to show up on set?"

Mal shrugged. "I pretend not to notice."

Pierre walked in. "Speaking of groupies . . . Cari, are you going to tell everybody about the offer you got today?"

I forgot Pierre was my agent too and had obviously already received word of the network's offer. Before this damn show, I hadn't needed or wanted an agent.

Sugar stopped in the process of setting the long table. "Girl, you holding out. What's up?"

I waited for everyone to file into the kitchen before I spoke. "Well, apparently, Malachi and I are a hit." Pierre sent me a look. "Okay, apparently *I'm* a hit," I amended. "And the chemistry between me and Mal is an audience draw. They want me to do promotion shoots. Film extra scenes around town with me and all of you fine people."

"And?" Pierre prompted.

I sighed. "And they offered me a reality show of my own after *Losing to Win* wraps."

Niecy flung back her head and laughed. "How much do you hate the idea?"

"More than life itself. I'll do the extra scenes and the promos, but my life as a 'reality show chick'?" I punctuated with air quotes. "That ends with this show."

Mal grinned. "Are you sure? You're really good

at it. I've seen some of the dailies. The camera loves you and you have a comic timing that works."

I shot him a look. "I'm positive, Malachi. You're the one headed for the bright lights. I just live in the shadows, remember?" Oops. That slid out before I could self-edit.

The whole room fell silent in the wake of the verbal jab. Mal put his hands up and backed away, turning to place napkins on the table. Dammit, now I felt bad. Clearly there were a few things I was still sensitive about from our past, but now was neither the time nor the place to zing him with it. Glancing at his crestfallen face gave me a moment's shame. Now I'd hurt his feelings.

There was too much going on, too much happening, and I felt like I was being pushed and pulled in a bunch of different directions. Hell, I was just tired. I needed to eat, I needed to sleep, and I needed to think. No need to skewer Mal over things he had already apologized for. "I'm sorry, Mal—everybody. I'm just over all of this. I'm ready for my life to get back to normal."

Mom brushed my hair back from my face. "Baby, who's to say what normal is now? All the businesses benefitting from this show . . . By the time they finish, there will be a new normal around here. Maybe for you too. Even if you don't do the next show, don't close yourself off to whatever the future has in store for you."

She slid her arms around me and I snuggled into her hold. "Thanks, Mommy, you're right."

Mike raised the pitcher of mystery punch up high. "Well, I always say it ain't a party until someone starts telling the truth. Now it's a party! Let's get it started, cuz." He poured some red liquid into a glass and handed it to me. I took it and walked it over to Mal.

I held it out to him. "Apology . . ."

". . . accepted." It was how we used to apologize to each other before there were really serious things to be sorry about.

Someone passed me a glass and we all raised them up. Meshach spoke first. "To friends and fam. Always."

"Always," we echoed.

15

I reckon I know just enough to be dangerous

Malachi—Saturday, July 2—8:05 a.m.

It was already ninety-four degrees in the shade on my old high school football field. It was early, I shouldn't have had more than one glass of Middle Mike's mystery punch last night, and my boys were of no help to me. Pierre, Burke, and Meshach stood on the sidelines, sipping iced coffee beverages while watching me running backward to the twenty-yard line, up to midfield, sideways toward the bench, and then back to the thirty.

"The knee looks good," Burke said.

"Yep," Meshach agreed.

"Not bad at all," Pierre cosigned.

"Any one of you bums care to step onto the field and toss me a few balls or are you just going to watch me sweat for the next thirty minutes?"

"You mean for the next hour, doncha, son?" a

familiar voice called out from the opposite end zone. Looking up I saw my dad coming across the field with my high school coach.

"Coach Robinette!" I jogged over and embraced the tall, broad-shouldered, graying man with a booming voice and personality to match. "What brings you out here?"

Earl Raymond Robinette, Earl Ray to his friends, had been coaching high school football in Belle Haven for over twenty-five years. He was like a second father to me. The day after I got hurt, he'd shown up at my door in Houston and said, "Let's talk about what comes next for you." He was the first person to tell me that I should attempt a comeback. I hadn't been ready to hear it then, but I was damn glad he'd made the suggestion and happy as hell to see him here today.

"Now boy, we can't have you out here half-assing your comeback. The pride of Belle Haven is at stake. I heard you've been trying to train on your own and that just won't do."

"I don't want to put anyone out." Actually I did. I really did need and want the help.

"C'mon now. We go too far back for all of that." He turned to the side and blew a whistle. Five guys came running out onto the field. "Now these are some of my fellas. Dixon here is at LSU now, Riley is at Auburn, Joe is still in high school even though he's as big as a barn, and I believe you know these two fellas." The last two guys were NFL players: Lee played one year with the Stars before finishing his career in Seattle, and Corey and I had played against each other in more games than I could count. He was an All-Pro cornerback in San Diego. We slapped each other on the back and I high-fived the other guys.

"I appreciate this, fellas—I really do. I've got this one last shot and you know—"

"—it's all or nothing," Lee finished, nodding his head. "Man, if I had a shot to go back and play, even if one more game?"

One of the young guys said, "Hey, I just wanna get there."

From around the side of the field came some of the production staff from *Losing to Win*, along with my mom and some other folks from town. Someone brought out a few coolers and it looked like a portable grill was being set up. You had to love Belle Haven. Everything was an excuse for a community get-together.

"This is awesome," the high school kid who was built like the side of a barn said. "Think they'll grill some ribs?"

"I'm not allowed ribs," I mumbled grouchily.

"Man, that's harsh!" Corey said. "One rib ain't gonna kill ya."

"You're telling me?" Even before I finished speaking, I noticed Darcy, the personal trainer from hell, bounding out of the locker area heading toward us.

Coach Robinette blew his whistle. "You ladies can form a knitting circle later. Let's get some work done. Meshach Knight?"

"Yes, sir?" my brother answered from the sidelines.

"You suit up and get your ass out here on this field. You still know how to throw a decent spiral, doncha?" Meshach had played quarterback for two years of college before he decided he was happier in a law library. I couldn't hide my amusement as he resignedly set down his fancy mocha-choco-latte-whatever and headed to the locker room. "Burke Bisset, you get over here and set these cones out, two by two. I know you remember the drill. When you finish that, go on ahead and grab a stopwatch."

Burke had also played high school football under Coach Robinette. He shook his head and stepped forward with swiftness. "Yes, sir."

"And who is Fancy Pants?" Coach asked, pointing at Pierre, who did look might fancy in some severely pressed linen pants.

"That's my agent and business manager, Pierre Picard." I introduced him with a smirk.

"Picard, you too fancy to record some stats?"

With a deep sigh of the beleaguered, Pierre trotted out onto the field and took one of the clipboards from Coach Robinette.

Coach looked him up and down. "Do you know football, son, or are you only good with facts and figures?"

Pierre shot me a look clearly indicating he was not appreciating the verbal shellacking. He answered politely. "I reckon I know just enough to be dangerous. Are you going to start with warm-up and flexibility or go straight to agility and speed drills?"

Coach gave him an approving nod. "You'll do, Mr. Fancy."

Meshach walked onto the field in some training gear. He knelt down and retied his shoelace. Then he paused to check out the assortment of Gatorade in one of the coolers.

Coach looked at my dad. "I know you didn't raise any lollygaggers, Henry."

"Step to, Meshach—daylight's burning!" Henry hollered.

If looks could kill, the look Meshach sent me would have struck me down immediately. If I could have gotten away with falling down on the field to roll around laughing, I surely would have.

The whistle blew twice to signal the start of practice. "Line up along the forty-yard line, men. We're going to start with flexibility and then go straight into dip and slip, followed by quick foot fire cones. I don't wanna hear any moaning and groaning. First one to slow us down earns wind sprints for the lot of you. Let's go!"

Two hours, multiple drills, and three sets of wind sprints later, I dragged my tired body toward the showers. Even though I was dog tired, for the first time I actually felt like I was going to make it back.

"Mal," Earl Ray called out to me. I almost wept at the interruption, I was so eager to get under that hot spray of water.

"Yeah, Coach?"

"You look good out there. Another four to six weeks and you'll be back at peak level. Your speed is almost there. Plus you're smarter now. You've started playing with your head instead of putting your body on the line for every play. Your hands are good."

"Aw, thanks, Coach." Hearing his validation pumped me up. I was really doing this.

"Don't thank me yet. Your footwork is sloppy and your timing is off and you still take it personally when someone hits you. You ran a slant when it should have been an out, you ran post instead of skinny post. We've got work to do yet. I'll be out here with you every Saturday until you're ready to go."

"I feel like I should pay you and the guys something for your time," I offered.

"Boy, please—can you not tell when people are having the time of their lives? This here television show kicked in for the supplies. And with the money this little show is bringing in, we're happy to help out." He slapped me on the back. "You just get back out there and make us proud, that'll be payment enough."

"Yes, sir. I'll do my best."

"You do that." He nodded and walked away.

I turned back toward the showers.

"Malachi Henry!" my dad's voice called out. Was I never going to get that shower?

"What's up, Dad?"

"I didn't see your girl out here, cheering you on. What's that about?"

I knew who he was talking about, but I wasn't going there with him right now. "I don't have a girl, Dad."

"You sure as hell do and you better do something to lock that woman down before someone swoops in and snatches her from right underneath your nose. I hear things, you know. There's another fox in the henhouse and he's angling for your chick. You might want to step up your game." He wagged his finger at me.

Having my father preach to me about foxes and hens while telling me to step up my game was for sure going down as one of my least favorite moments in a summer filled with moments I didn't care to repeat. Anyway, I was not chasing Carissa Wayne. I had made it clear I wanted her; the next move was hers. "If she wants me, she knows where I am."

He barked out a laugh. "Ha! That hard-to-get shit only works if you don't give a damn. And you, Mal? You definitely give a damn. Life is short. Football or no football, that's a good woman. You're not gonna find another like her and you know it."

I sighed. "I'm tired, Dad. I'm going to get a shower, pretend I don't smell those hot links cooking on the grill, and go sit somewhere without a camera in my face for a few hours."

"All right, son. I hear ya talking." He patted me on the shoulder. "Just think about it, will ya?"

When I wasn't thinking about getting back to the NFL, I was thinking about getting back with Carissa. Those two thoughts occupied all my spare time. "You can bet on it."

16

This is a small town and an even smaller show

Carissa—Saturday, July 2—6:37 p.m.

"**S**uzette, what is your general problem?" I voiced my irritation as discreetly as I could. I was standing in the lobby of Sugar's bed-and-breakfast, The Idlewild. The Idlewild was a former plantation that had been converted into a twenty-two-room inn. Burke and Mac Bisset had done a great job on the restoration and the old house shone through like the Southern treasure it was. Rich dark woods combined with light airy walls; it had the feel of stepping into a stately home that just happened to have all the modern conveniences.

The Idlewild hosted the contestants who did not live in town, when they weren't trapped on campus—with the exception of Mal, who chose to rent a place from Burke. A lot of the crew was staying at the Idlewild as well. A few of Mal's friends from his NFL days had checked in to help him train for a few weeks, so the place was busier than I'd ever seen it. This afternoon, I had popped over to drop off my updated paperwork and ran into Suzette on my way out.

I supposed an explosion between the two of us was just a long time overdue and inevitable. She didn't like me, I didn't like her. We'd never clicked. Not from the first time we'd laid eyes on each other in middle school. I thought she was mean, shallow, and petty. She thought I was standoffish, snobby, and siddity. To my credit, I had tried several times to extend the olive branch and let the animosity go. Unfortunately, every time I tried to bury the hatchet, she attempted to bury it in my back. After a particularly nasty hair-pulling incident on the playground, I gave up.

To say that our mutual disdain was long lived and abiding was an understatement. Today, only one of us was trying to be classy about it. The minute she saw me, she launched into a litany of insults. The least hurtful involved her calling me fat for the fiftieth time this summer; the most offensive was her accusing me of sleeping with all the male members of the cast so I would be the most popular contestant on the show.

I was sick of it. My timing may have been poor, but I was calling her out once and for all.

"You are my general problem," she hissed, not bothering to lower the volume of her screechy voice.

"You've always thought you were better than anyone else around here," she continued. "You walk around with your nose in the air like your shit doesn't stink, when in reality you're just a washed-up prom queen with no man, no kids, and no real accomplishments. You act like you're so far above it all when you are no better than a trashy bitch. Your mama is blue collar and your daddy is a known womanizer who'll lay down with anyone who smiles at him twice and buys him a beer. I guess you take after him. You've slept your way into anything you've ever gotten. I don't think Queen Slut is a career aspiration for young girls. How they allow you to teach kids is beyond me!"

"Now wait just a damn minute," I lashed out, angry to the point where I had no more damns left to give. The fact that I could hear feet scurrying and knew that signaled rolling cameras were some-where close by should have stilled my tongue, but it didn't. The words tripped from my mouth with force and ferocity. "Maybe I'll let you call me what-ever you can dream up as acid drips from your lips. Maybe you can talk about my father. But best be-lieve you will not besmirch the good name of my mama. I'm not about to stand here and let the chick who gave blowjobs to the principal just to get a seat on the student council call me all sorts of tramps and sluts. No, ma'am. I am not going to let a chick who ballooned up from a size 3 to a tight size 30 call ME fat again. Not today."

She sniffled and let two fake tears run down her cheeks. "I have four kids!"

"Well, bless their hearts. Girl, please! What you have is a ready-made excuse for everything you've ever jacked up, and that list is plentiful. I don't think that I'm better than everybody else, but I'm a damn sight better than you."

"You always wanted what I have!" she accused in a shrill tone.

I shrieked with laughter. "What exactly would that be? I have never wanted anything you had. Not. One. Damn. Thing. I started the rumor saying I thought Jerome Allendale was hot so that you'd go after him and quit jock-riding Mal for half a second."

"You did not. You totally wanted Jerome and you hate that I have him."

"Yes, all those years I was cozied up to Mal's fine self, I found myself longing for Jerome. You think? And really, Suzette—if I had wanted Jerome, don't you think I would've found a way to have him? I mean, let's take it there. I'm just saying."

"You bitch!" She swung her hand back and I put a finger up.

"Uh-uh. If you hit me, it better be the hit of your life, because not only will I snatch out what's left of your listless hair, I will knock you the hell out up in here. Then I will proceed to have you arrested for assault, I will sue you for damages, and I will take every last dime of Jerome's money that you have not already spent." I looked her squarely in the eye. "Whatcha gonna do, Boo-Boo?"

She wavered for a minute as if considering her options. I shifted my purse to my left arm in case I needed to actually swing on this woman. I was done taking the high road. Her eyes narrowed when she noticed I wasn't backing down. "This isn't over!" she screamed and backed away.

"Uh-huh." I sucked my teeth and nodded. "Just as I thought. All talk and hot air. Let's just be real.

We don't like each other. We never have. At this point, we never will. This is a small town and an even smaller show. But why don't we agree to stay the hell out of each other's way and leave it at that?"

She stepped around me with her head held high and muttered "Bitch" as she walked past.

I took two quick steps backward and blocked her path. "That's your last freebie. You call me anything else besides my name and we can go there if we have to, okay, Suzette?"

"Nobody is scared of you, Carissa Wayne!" She flung her hair with extra drama and stormed out the door.

Sugar came running over clutching a broom in her hand. "I don't know, cuz. I'm a little scared of you."

"Girl, what were you about to do? Sweep her up outta here?"

"I had your back!"

"Yeah, if some lint balls flew out her mouth, you were right there for me."

We dissolved into laughter. Noticing all eyes were still trained on me, I twirled in a circle in the lobby before taking a bow. "Show's over, folks. Nothing to see here!" I received scattered applause.

"This is why they love you on that show. You're a damn drama magnet," my Aunt Elaine said as she came around from the registration desk. She took the broom out of Sugar's hand and walked back toward the kitchen muttering to herself about these kids today.

"You know what you need?" Sugar asked me. We strolled toward the door.

"A gallon of rum and a paid vacation to Jamaica?"

"I was going to say a hot bath and a hot man to relieve you of your stress."

"I can make that bath thing happen," I admitted with a smile.

"You could make the man thing happen. With a phone call."

"I'd be lying if I said I hadn't thought about it."

"What's holding you back?" Sugar looked at me curiously.

"Didn't you just call me a drama magnet? Add a man into the equation and it's like drama squared." And all evidence to the contrary, I really did not like drama.

"But the man could be worth it, right?"

"Worth it in the interim, yes. In the long run? Not so sure about that one."

"Two of Mal's friends checked in, did you hear?" Sugar asked.

"Yeah, I heard. Which two?"

"Corey something and Lee McAdoo."

I nodded. "I know both of them."

She leaned forward. "Give me the 411. What's the scoop?"

"You do know no one says 411 anymore, right?"

"Girl, dish already!"

"Corey is a wolf in sheep's clothing. Comes across all sensitive but is a heartbreaker. The Western United States is scattered with the ashes of his former flames."

"Oh, a churn-and-burn type?"

"Most definitely," I affirmed.

"What about Lee?"

"Oh, he's both a looker and a sweetheart, if I recall. He and his wife split up after he retired. He rejoined the league and I don't know if he's got someone right now or not." I noticed the twinkle in her eyes. "If you're interested, that's not a bad direction to go. Is he still fine?"

"Like you wouldn't believe," she said in a dreamy voice.

"Oh, I'd believe. You should go for it," I encouraged her. She could do a lot worse. Lee was one of the good guys.

"You know what?" Sugar said while a huge grin spread across her face. "I believe I will. See how much good this show is bringing to Belle Haven?"

"Bringing you a man is good?"

"Always, but business is good, things are good all the way around, Ris. Thanks to you."

I held myself back from rolling my eyes. "That's me: the savior of Belle Haven." I pushed open the door and looked up and down the street to make sure Suzette was nowhere to be found. I dug out my keys and unlocked the car.

"All right, Ris. Try not to fight nobody on the way home."

"No guarantees!" I called out and backed away.

17

This is who we are, this is what we do

Malachi—Sunday, July 3—10:02 p.m.

"Next week on *Losing to Win...*" the announcer's voice blared from the television on the far wall of Carissa's living room. I was lounging on the chaise section of Carissa's couch dressed in cargo shorts, T-shirt, and flip-flops. Even though I was sore from yesterday's workout, I was enjoying the time off. Tomorrow was the Fourth of July and the day after that, we had to be back on set. The immediate cast, some family, and friends were gathered here to watch the premiere.

It was far more entertaining than I had expected. Everyone had personalities that worked well on camera and kept the pace of the show engaging. Watching our lives unfold in sequences was surreal. The cameras managed to pick up a lot of interactions that we weren't aware of. Suzette spent a lot of time on the phone to her husband complaining about everyone and everything, particularly Carissa. Suzette clearly hadn't expected some of her words to be aired. Soon after the first scene revealed her spewing dirt about her cast mates, she got up and slipped out of the house.

XJ apparently spent a lot of time finding new and innovative ways to sneak off to restaurants around town. The problem was, the cameras caught him every time. Many townspeople had been interviewed and shared their stories or tidbits about us on camera. Carissa was considered a bit of a town hero for coming back to Belle Haven and contributing. People were very polarized about me. They either thought I was a great guy or a total asshole. One thing they all agreed on was that they wanted to see me do right by the town and by Carissa, whatever that meant.

The first episode had wrapped with me and Carissa standing in our mud-soaked clothes accepting the blind challenge. So I knew exactly what the teaser for the next episode would be. Carissa was seated across the room wearing one of those maxidress things in a shade of orange that looked great on her. As if feeling my gaze on her, she turned her head to look at me. We shared a look of resigned what-the-hell-ness and looked back toward the TV.

I watched as the onscreen Carissa stood up and stepped into Jordan's arms. I hated seeing it again now as much as I had the first time. I kept watching as the onscreen me stood up with clenched fists and stepped forward. Everyone watching held their breath as they cut away for another teaser.

With the exception of those of us who had been there, the room broke into conversation as soon as the commercial went off.

Sugar's voice rang out. "Whoa, cuz—love triangle?"

"Shut it, Sugar. No triangle. I'm an island."

Ruby laughed. "Didn't someone say no man—or woman—is an island?"

More laughter diffused the last of the tension as people started getting up to leave. I leaned back and stayed put. Jordan looked over at me from his position near the door. I crossed my arms across my chest and rested one ankle across my knee. I speared him with a "whatcha gonna do, player?" look and he gave me an "oh, it's about to be on" head nod.

He walked over to Carissa and leaned down to whisper in her ear. She sent him a sweet smile that caused my stomach to clench, but then she shook her head no. She beckoned him closer and whispered something in his ear. I narrowed my eyes. He nodded, trailed his hand down her arm, and walked out. I had been noticing that Jordan Little always found a way to put his hands on Carissa Wayne. As he passed the doorway, he sent me a quick look I interpreted as "Yeah, I'm leaving, but I'll be back."

Maybe he would, but not tonight. I stood up, stretched, and chatted Renard, Mac, and XJ along to the front door. I made small talk with Ruby and Sugar as they sashayed out. Picking up a few empty paper plates and plastic cups, I wandered toward the kitchen, where I stopped short in amazed disbelief.

Mashed up against the pantry were Niecy and my brother, Meshach. Breathing all heavy, kissing like their lives depended on it—when had this started? My brother's hands were not in a PG-13 position. "Damn, girl," he whispered into her neck as she arched her hips closer to him. Okay, I'd seen more than enough.

"Am I interrupting?" I asked, knowing full well that I was as I tossed the trash into a container on the side of the counter.

They sprang apart guiltily and gasped for air. Meshach pointed at me. "Bro, your timing!"

I sat down on the barstool. "My bad. How about y'all take that somewhere more private?"

Niecy shook her head. "Woo, you Knight brothers. Let me escape before I get into trouble."

Meshach grumbled. "I was *trying* to get into some trouble."

"You were getting into something," I laughed as Niecy backed out of the room, running into Carissa on her way out.

"What's up?" Carissa asked, looking at Niecy's hasty retreat toward the closest exit from the house.

"I'll call you in the morning!" Niecy said, practically sprinting out the front door.

Cari looked from me to Meshach and back again. "What did you do?"

I held my hands up. "For once it wasn't me! This one"—I directed my thumb toward Meshach—"had his paws all over your line sister. Lips too."

"Is that right?" Carissa grinned widely, sliding

onto the barstool next to mine and resting her chin on her hands. "Do tell."

Meshach shrugged. "I like her. I'm going to get to know her better."

I snorted. "That was you initiating a conversation just now?"

He grabbed his keys off the counter and came around the bar to give Cari a kiss on the cheek. "I'm out. Lookie here, bro, don't be projecting your sexual frustrations in my direction. See y'all tomorrow."

He strolled out the front door, completely missing the finger I flashed at him. As the door closed behind him, Cari swiveled toward me on the barstool with an animated expression.

"Mal?" Her voice was silky.

I looked over at her to see a wicked grin on her face. "Rissa?"

"Are you sexually frustrated?" she said in a teasing, singsongy voice.

A slow smile crept across my face. That sounded like an invitation to me. If she wanted to play, I was more than ready. Standing up swiftly, I yanked her out of the chair and started backing her toward the staircase. "Not for long, babe. Not for much longer at all."

She opened her mouth to either agree or protest and I took the opportunity to cover those pretty lips with my own. Testing delicately, I gave her a second to push me away. She didn't. I wrapped both arms around her and pulled her in tight. With a sexy moan, Carissa slid her arms around my neck and gave as good as she got.

This kiss was possessive, aggressive, and filled

with a thousand words we needed to convey. Slick, hot, enticing, and addictive, our tongues spoke to each other in languages never forgotten. Carissa smelled of vanilla and gardenias; she tasted like sweet wine and heaven. I pressed her against the wall next to the staircase and ran my hands along her back, her arms, her thighs, everywhere I could reach quickly. Our hands flew across each other's bodies, reacquainting ourselves with new curves, new angles, new textures, but the same feelings remained. Heat, passion, and eagerness for more were always in the forefront when I got next to Carissa.

I was too impatient to say and do all the things I needed to do right now. If I wanted to do this the right way, I would say sweet things and ease into each phase with light, teasing touches and soothing caresses. But everything inside of me was screaming, "Now! Now! Now!" I just wanted her to be mine in every way possible. With the last ounce of willpower inside of me, I pulled back slightly. "Do you want me to stop?"

"I don't know," she whispered with her hands on my chest. I couldn't tell if she was pulling me closer or pushing me away. Her lips were swollen, her lids were heavy, her breathing as erratic as mine. The two of us together like this felt like an inevitability.

The thought that she didn't feel the same frantic need that was racing through my veins drove me crazy. I put my hands on her hips and tilted her pelvis in alignment with mine, dragging her close. I was hard as iron, pressed against her velvet softness. I wanted her to feel the urgency of my want, the desperation of my need. "You don't know?" I whispered into her neck as I licked a path from her bare shoulder to just behind her ear, where she was particularly sensitive. She shuddered in my arms and I nipped the spot lightly with my teeth.

She groaned. "I don't know."

Sliding a leg between hers to open her up, I grasped her wrists in my hands and pulled them over her head. I shifted my hips forward and then back, applying pressure against her heat and then backing off. Waves of heat echoed back and forth between us, cocooning us in hot steamy air. I kissed her lips with the same staccato rhythm. Then I paused. Her hips chased mine, her lips pouted for more. Her mind may not have known what she wanted, but the rest of her was completely on board. I waited for her lashes to rise and our eyes to meet before I spoke. "Maybe you need reminding."

"Reminding?" Her eyes went cloudy with confusion and desire.

I turned her so she was facing front against the wall. I surged against her and kept her arms above her head. "Leave them there." I commanded before reaching for the tie on the halter top of her dress. I released it, then flicked open the bra underneath. Both of us groaned as her breasts fell into my hands. I'd definitely missed these. They were ample and overflowed my hands as I squeezed and molded them. I rolled the hardened nipples between my thumb and forefinger. She held her breath and released it in a choppy moan. The sound of that moan raked across my nerves, arousing me further. I'd missed that sound.

"Later on tonight, when I'm not hustlin' to get

inside you, I'm going to play with these with my tongue and my lips and my fingers over and over again until I watch you come apart. You were always so sensitive here. I could take you over with just two damp fingertips. Remember how I used to do that?"

She flung her head back and let out a low keening sound but didn't speak. She ground her hips into my hardness, enticing me to hurry. I gritted my teeth against the temptation.

No way was I letting her get away with that. I dropped my hands to her hips and held them still. "Answer me. Do you remember?"

"Yes. I remember." Her voice barely registered above a whisper.

"I thought you did. I can't forget. Do you how many times I've been in bed at night thinking about how we were together? I would touch myself wishing it was you. Thinking about all the ways we burned together. How you used to melt into me, match me, challenge me, satisfy me?" I raised the hem of the dress and pulled down the pastel panties she was wearing. "Do you know?"

"No." She shook her head frantically.

I slid a finger through her moist heat and she gasped. "It's happened more times than I can think about. You are so wet, Cari. Is it mine? Is it all for me?"

"Oh, Mal," she implored me.

"Tell me, is it me that makes you steamy and dripping, hungry? Is all this hot honey for me, Carissa?" My fingers explored her, reaching the tight quivering nubbin of sensation. I caressed it in slow circles, reveling in the unevenness of her breath. How she quaked when I stroked just so and purred when I rubbed right there, there, and twice more with two fingers and a squeeze there. I slid one long finger inside her warmth and her walls clamped around my finger.

"Mal, please!"

Nothing in the world like having the woman you want begging for more. Nothing. "What do you want? What can I give you, baby? Talk to me."

She whipped around with her eyes flashing and reached for the fastening on my shorts. In record time she had them open and down on the floor. I pulled off my shirt and she pushed her dress the rest of the way off. She reached into my boxers and freed the straining, desperate part of me that leaped at her touch. "You know what I want. Stop. Playing. Games. With. Me." She punctuated each word with a squeeze and a downward stroke of my hardness. I had to lock my knees to fight the swell of sensation.

I pushed her away and turned her back toward the wall. We had to do this my way. Reaching down, I grabbed my wallet out of my pocket and extracted a condom. I rolled it on and looked up at her. Tempting as it was to stop and slowly taste my way back up, I had more urgent needs to deal with.

I pressed myself full length along her back before adjusting her position. I tilted her so she was leaning against the wall balanced on her hands, her hips aligned to mine, her ass out and raised to receive me, her legs slightly spread. "God, you look so sexy right now. You remember that time when we'd just bought the house and I came up behind you on the stairs. Do you remember?"

"I remember." She whimpered, straining closer to me.

"Do you remember how I bent you over, pressed against you, and you wiggled your ass against me? How I wrapped my hand around your waist?" I wrapped my arm around her to hold her steady. "And then I slid inside of you just like this?" I slid inside of her warmth in a single stroke, inflaming the both of us. "Do you remember, Cari?"

"Oh my God. Yes. I remember everything." She clenched her internal muscles around me and I growled low in my throat.

I drove into her with long, deep strokes, driven by a tidal wave of emotion and pleasure and things I wasn't ready to define. I struggled to stay in control. A part of me just wanted to stop and bask in the fact that I was wrapped around Carissa Melody Wayne and she was wrapped around me. That in this moment she was mine and mine alone. That in this moment, we were happy and together and there was no future and no past, just this one perfect sensation of oneness. Me, encased in her heat, savoring every liquid slide of my length. So many more thoughts and feelings bombarded me than I could control. "Just remember how this feels, Carissa. This." I plunged. "And this." I retreated. "And this." I dove in again. "This is us. This is who we are. This is what we do. This is how we make each other feel. No one else. Just you and me. Are you listening?"

"Yes."

"Tell me." I slowed to short, shallow strokes teasing every ridge and nerve ending inside of her. It was addictive, the heat of her, the smell of us, the feel of this. How had I ever let this go?

"God, you make me crazy when you get like this," she breathed, raising up on her tiptoes as I hit a sensitive spot inside of her.

"Like what, baby?"

"All alpha male."

I grinned. "You love it when I make you feel. When I make you sweat. When I make you come."

She peered over her shoulder at me and rasped in a sultry voice full of promise and tension and sex, "Remind me."

Two little words and I went wild. I couldn't get deep enough, fast enough. I wanted everything she had to give. I slammed into her with everything I had and snaked my other arm up to tweak her rock-hard nipples. Every time I brushed her nipples, she clenched tighter around me. It was heaven, it was hell, I couldn't get enough. Stroke, tweak, clench, stroke, tweak, clench . . . it was too much for both of us. She screamed and her molten walls fluttered around me, triggering my release that erupted from the depths of my soul. I shouted her name as the sensations flooded through me and I had to brace my knees to keep both of us from falling backward. Long moments passed while aftershocks sparked from her to me and back again, before our breathing settled and our brains re-engaged. With extreme reluctance, I pulled out of her and went to dispose of the condom in the hall bathroom.

When I walked back toward her, she was lounging back on the staircase, resting on her elbows. "Had a point you were trying to make, Mr. Knight?"

I loved it when she was like this with me. This was one of the things I adored about her. She was a lady for the entire world to see, but then with me, in our private time when she let down her guard, she was open, uninhibited, daring even, and a little brash. My equal in every way. I stood in front of her, uncertain of what would come next, and shrugged. "We tend to do our best communicating with elevated heart rates."

"Hmph," she snorted while eating me up with her eyes. She was staring at me with consideration and something else I couldn't clearly define. But it was stirring me up; I felt myself starting to rise to the occasion.

I raised a brow. "What?"

She stood up and started ascending the staircase. "I guess this part was inevitable."

"The naked part?"

"The naked, got-to-have-you-give-it-to-me-right-now part, yes."

"With you and me, it's always just below the surface." I stood at the bottom of the stairs wondering if I was about to get kicked out on my ass.

She paused and looked down. "And now that you've unleashed the monster . . ."

"Yes?"

"I want more. Suit up, baller; you've got some work to do."

I snatched my wallet off the ground where I'd dropped it, praying I had more than one condom still left in there. It promised to be a long, produc-

tive night. "Yes, ma'am. Reporting for duty, ma'am,"
I joked and jogged up the steps. When I entered
her bedroom, she was lying in the middle of the
four-poster bed on her back.

"But Malachi?"

Uh-oh. Here it came. The catch.

"Yep?"

"This is just about the sex right now. Okay? I'm
just looking for a little kitty maintenance, not trying to resurrect our dead romance. Understood?"

Ouch. That hurt. A lot. Our romance was dead?
I didn't think so. But I also did not want to be
kicked off of kitty maintenance duty. Especially
knowing someone else was waiting in the wings to
pick up anything I left behind. If that's the way she
wanted to play it, so be it. God knew some of Carissa was better than none at all. "I don't necessarily cosign, but since I'm not sure what I'm bringing
to the table for the long term, I understand." I
crawled across the comforter and gently bit the tip
of her right breast while twirling the tip of the left
in my hand.

"God, you're good at that." She leaned back
and closed her eyes.

I pinched lightly to get her attention. "But one
thing, Cari?"

"Um-hmm?"

I rolled so she was lying on top of me, her
breasts level with my mouth. She arched her back
as I sucked passionately, and when she least expected it, I smacked a hand across her butt cheek.

Her eyes flew open. "What the hell? Have you
gotten kinky? Kinkier, I should say?"

I chuckled. "Just making sure you're paying attention when I tell you this." I smacked her again lightly and watched her squirm not entirely in displeasure. Hmm. Kitty liked a little slap and tickle. Something to play with later.

"I'm listening, Mal. What is it?"

"I don't share."

She frowned down at me. "I don't cheat."

"I'm just saying. I know Jordy is feeling you and I don't know what is between you two, but while we're like this, for however long we're like this? He gets none. Nothing, nada, nary a taste, never a whiff. Understand?"

Carissa rolled her eyes. "I'm not an idiot. And I do know you, Malachi. I know what you will and won't put up with. We're on the same page here. And same goes for you. Until we both agree to walk away—"

"—or to stay," I interjected.

"Not likely, but fine. Until we both agree on what's next, we're a party of two."

I kneaded her ass and spread her legs before sliding myself along her already moist slit. "Good, 'cause we've got a lot of catching up to do, here."

She wrapped her arms around me and lightly bit my shoulder. "Well, time's a-wasting. Let's get to it. Slow this time and then fast again."

"As you wish." I was always good at being coached.

18

She has a point

Carissa—Tuesday, July 12—10:57 a.m.

"I'd like to thank you for joining us today, Mrs. Wayne," Dr. Julie greeted my mother as we walked into the room. How damn clichéd was it for a therapist to ask you to bring your mother in for a session? Just how screwed up did she think I was?

"Baby, let's just go and see what the woman has to say," my mom had lectured me this morning on our way in. "Nine times out of ten, these things aren't as bad as you make them out to be. You know you've always had a flair for the dramatic."

I let that go. Everyone knew Ruby was the drama queen in our family. All I wanted to do was make it through the day without airing any more dirty laundry on film. Simultaneously, we settled into the two deep club chairs in front of Dr. Julie, crossed our legs, and folded our hands in our laps.

Dr. Julie smiled reassuringly at us, nodded to the cameras to start rolling, and then dropped a bombshell.

"I'm wondering, Eloise—can I call you Eloise?" she addressed my mother.

My mother inclined her head regally in assent.

"Eloise, do you think it's possible that the repetitive abandonment by her father caused Carissa to be insecure in her relationship with Malachi?"

Both of our mouths dropped open. "I beg your pardon?" my mother asked.

"What I'm wondering . . . what I've been thinking is that due to the unreliability of her father, do you think Carissa was ill equipped to handle a man like Malachi, who was in the spotlight, frequently absent, and not forthcoming with his intentions?"

Well, hell. I sat back in my chair with a huff. Ain't this some shiggity? Not once did I consider that Blue's shiftless existence played a role in the outcome of my relationship with Mal.

My mom reached over and grasped my hand. "I think Carissa, more than anybody, has amazing depths of coping capacity. I also think that her father did us no favors with his actions and I'm sure I'm partially to blame for allowing it to go on for so long."

"Oh, Mom—"

"Hush now, let me talk. One thing you need to understand is that Blue is a big talker. And when he talks, you find yourself believing him. Mostly because you want to but also because he's an excellent bullshit artist. For years, Blue would call and tell Carissa and Ruby that he was coming back and that when he came back, we were going to be a real family. And every time he came, he disappointed us all and left. Now, I fully expected to be disappointed by Blue, and Ruby is just the sort of person who never takes anything that seriously. But Carissa wants to believe in people. She needs to believe in their inherent goodness. Especially in the people she loves. So time after time she believed that Blue was going to do right by us and he never did. The worst time—"

I winced, knowing where she was going with the story. "Mama, you do not have to tell all of this."

"Baby, she needs to understand." She patted my hand and continued. "One time, when Carissa was about ten or eleven, Blue came and took her away with him for the weekend. Ruby was at camp and didn't go. Blue promised to take Carissa with him to Dallas for the big Texas State Fair. He was performing with that band, I can't recall the name. Won some Grammys that year, three albums? Anyway . . . off he went with Carissa in tow, thinking that she'd won the jackpot weekend with her father." Her voice thickened and she threaded her fingers through mine. I squeezed as she took a deep breath to steady her emotions.

"Anyway, they got there and Blue patted Carissa on the head and then promptly turned her over to one of the groupies and told her he'd be back after the show. She watched him play and that was the last she saw of him for that day and most of the next. The groupie finally called me the next day to come get Carissa because she didn't know where Blue had gone. I don't even want to think of where my child spent the night and in whose company. I got to Dallas that night. I will never forget seeing my baby girl sitting on a curb outside of a 7-Eleven clutching a suitcase and a Cherry Slurpee. When we tracked Blue down, he was climbing on a tour bus to go to the next gig. He'd completely forgotten about his daughter's existence. He actually looked surprised to see us standing there. He got off the bus, gave both of us a kiss on the cheek, and said he'd see us before long. Carissa waited until he was almost back on the bus before calling out to him. 'Daddy?' Her little voice halted him in his tracks. 'Don't bother coming back.' He just smiled, told her she didn't mean it, and climbed back on the bus. We didn't see him for about five years after that. By then, none of us cared anymore."

The room was silent while everyone digested that pitiful tale from my childhood.

With a deep sigh, Eloise finished making her point. "All of this to say I think you have it skewed. I don't think Carissa was incapable of dealing with Malachi. I think she was unwilling to put herself in a situation that might mirror mine at all."

"Now, Mom, this has nothing to do with you."

"Oh, yes it does. All you saw was me allowing a man to yo-yo back and forth into our lives and you were determined to be nothing like me."

"No, Mom. I *am* like you, in so many ways. Creative, stubborn, smart, outspoken but polite to a fault. But I don't have your patience and forgiveness. I damn sure did not want a relationship where I couldn't count on the other person in it. I saw what waiting on Blue to do right did to you. I just couldn't wait on Mal, Mama. I just didn't trust him to ever do the right thing."

"And what was the right thing?" Dr. Julie asked.

I realized she was still in the room and the cameras were still rolling. "The right thing would've been marrying me and not making me wonder what he was doing and who he was doing it with."

"And then what would've happened?" she probed.

I blinked in confusion. "What do you mean?"

"What happens after the man of your dreams marries you and does right by you?"

"I'm guessing that 'they lived happily ever after' is not what you're looking for here."

She smiled. "I think you need to figure out what happily ever after would look like before you expect a man to give it to you."

"She has a point," Eloise murmured.

I shifted on the chair. I knew she had a point.

"If you are going to move forward in your quest for overall wellness, you have to come to grips with your feelings for Malachi and what you would want either from him or whoever you decide you want to build a life with."

"Mal and I are somewhat okay with the past. We're trying to be friends again." Yes, that was a massive understatement for how much time we'd spent naked in each other's company over the past few weeks, but I didn't see where that was relevant right now.

"Friends?" My mom snorted. "Is that what you call it?"

"Mother."

"I'm not in your business. I'm just saying, I'm not blind."

Dr. Julie's eyes flicked from my mom to me and back again and she looked like she couldn't decide what she wanted to ask next. "Regardless of the current status of your . . . affiliation with Mal, you owe it to yourself to do a little bit more work on Carissa."

"Before or after I run the stairs in the stadium for the fifth time?" I joked.

"Maybe at the same time; I'm told you're a multitasker," the doctor joked right back.

Eloise cackled as I rolled my eyes.

"I think that's enough for today. Thank you both for taking the time to talk with me today."

"Like we had a choice," I muttered under my breath and stood.

"Carissa Melody, be nice," my mother said.

Holding back the deep sigh I ached to give, I extended my hand. "Thank you, Dr. Julie, for all your insights."

As we headed down the hallway, my mom released a breath. "That wasn't as bad as I thought it was going to be."

"Were you expecting a rectal exam? 'Cause that was plenty painful."

She crowed and laughed. "You *are* like me with your dramatic self. Let's go get some of the cucumber mint water; I've grown kind of fond of it."

"And there is where we differ. I miss sweet tea."

"You'll live." She patted me on the back. "We will all live."

I shrugged, knowing she was referring to more than beverages. "It's what we do. We're Waynes."

19

You're different

"Just follow us and we'll get you out of here," I screamed over the wind to Jordy and Niecy in the flatbottom swamp boat behind ours. This challenge is what the hell happened when folks who didn't know a damn thing about the swamp tried to do something fun in the swamp. It was supposed to be a ride up a pretty fork in the bayou to an obstacle course and then a race back down the swamp in the boats.

The day started off poorly. I had some business to attend to and then my drills ran late. I had to race over to catch up with everybody. Then we had to give out a few lessons on how to pilot a swamp boat. And then came the weather. No one checked the forecast before sending people out on a body of water? Suzette got violently sick less than a mile out, so she and XJ had turned back. How sad was it that people were actually wishing for seasickness to get out of this challenge?

After arriving at the site, the skies unloaded and there was no way we'd be doing anything on that soggy ground. Standing in a windy tent on swampland waiting for the rain to stop was another on a long list of things from this summer I had no desire to repeat.

The next issue kicked up when the motor went out on Jordy and Niecy's flatboat. We tied it to the back of ours and were trying to get back to the dock before the sun went down. If the bayou was a bad idea in the daytime, it was worse at night.

Carissa was standing beside me; we had two of the crew seated behind us. The rest of the crew took the powerboats and were probably somewhere discussing what a bad idea this turned out to be. As if reading my thoughts, Carissa spoke up. "Someone did not do their research. Whoever dreamed up this challenge needs a severe beat down."

"At the very least," I agreed, maneuvering the craft closer to the shoreline.

"You're different," she said, watching me steer.

"What?" We had to scream at each other to be heard.

She cupped her hands around her mouth and yelled into my ear. "I said you've changed!"

I glanced over at her briefly. "Hold that thought a second." I pulled the boat up and motioned for her and the crew to hop off. They looked overwhelmingly relieved to be back on solid, dry land. I navigated forward so Niecy and Jordy could exit their disabled craft as well. Cutting the engine, I grabbed the rope, jumped to the dock, and secured both vessels. "That will have to do."

"That was some quick thinking and fancy navigating. Good looking out, Captain." Niecy smiled at me and I gave her a half-assed salute.

"We're going to ride back with the crew. Carissa, you coming?" Jordan asked.

She shook her head. "You two go on ahead. We'll catch up."

The four of us looked at each other for a moment before Niecy linked her arm through Jordan's and turned toward the van. "Later, you two."

By mutual accord, Carissa and I climbed into my car and rode to my rental house in silence. Weird as it sounds, I enjoyed these moments of silent comfort with Carissa as much as I did our more energetic activities. There was something about being able to just chill with someone who really knew you that made all the stresses of the day ebb away.

Probably because of the earlier storm and drama, for once there was no one following us with cameras and we pulled into the garage without incident. We walked through the living room and I paused. "Bath or dinner?"

"Bath, please."

Those Bisset boys could build the hell out of a bathroom. This one featured a deep and long soaking tub set into a glass-tiled platform wide enough to sit on. I sat on the edge of the tub testing the temperature of the water. Tossing in a few muscle-relaxing salts, I turned toward her.

"I'm not like your father."

"I know that!" she protested.

Where's that coming from?

"I hope so. I would hate for you to think the men in your life just use you for their convenience. I'm not like that."

She sent me a soft smile. "Believe me, I know that."

"Earlier you said that I've changed. What did you mean?"

"I mean, you've changed. We've basically blown a whole day in really uncomfortable conditions and you've been a trooper, a leader even. There was a time when you would've let everyone know how important your time was and how we were all wasting it and how someone was going to have to make it up to you."

I winced. "I wasn't that bad."

"Mal, you made our last housekeeper cry because she vacuumed on your day off."

"I was tired." A football player usually had only one true day off during the season. Those hours were precious.

"It was two in the afternoon," she returned wryly, toeing off her socks and shoes before setting them to the side.

"Oh. Well, I could've been more sensitive about a lot of things, I guess." I kicked my shoes off and watched as she retrieved them and placed them by the bathroom door.

"That's what I'm saying. I think you've matured." She pulled her shirt off over her head and set it on the counter before wriggling out of her pants.

I tugged my shirt over my head and dropped

it on the floor. Interpreting her look, I reached down to pick it up and set it on the counter. Carissa liked things in their place. "When you say matured, that sounds like aging. Maybe I've mellowed."

"Fine. Mellowed." She smirked and put her hand on my shoulder. "It's nice to see."

"Did you think I'd stay the same selfish asshole I always was?" I pulled the drawstring on my shorts and pushed them down with my boxers. I pitched them toward the hamper.

"Who called you that?"

"Just because you didn't use those exact words doesn't mean I didn't take your point, Ms. Wayne. I was selfish, I was thoughtless, I was shallow, I was arrogant, I was greedy, I was shortsighted . . ." I stopped talking when her underwear came off and she slid into the water.

"Keep going, you're on a roll." She smiled and scooted forward to make room for me.

"Feel free to cut me off and correct me." I slid in behind her and pulled her up against me. We both leaned back with a sigh.

"I'm too mellow right now. I can see where you've made some improvements. I didn't love you because you were perfect. People always thought I hero-worshipped you, but that wasn't it."

"What was it?" I handed her a washcloth and a bar of soap.

She started sudsing the cloth. "I saw through all of the other stuff and I liked what I saw. Plus you're easy on the eyes."

"Ma'am."

"And you adored me. God, I loved being adored like that."

I was glad she couldn't see the stunned expression on my face. "You think I quit adoring you?"

"You quit showing me how much you did."

"I took you for granted. But I'm better now."

"Are you?" She ran the washcloth along my arm before picking up my hand and toying with my fingers. She rested her palm against mine. Her small hand with pink-tipped nails sat in contrast to my larger one that had a scar across the back and nails that needed trimming.

"I'm starting to get to you, Carissa. You say you see the real me? You tell me. I'm not that guy, right? I'm not still the guy who let you down. You're not still the girl who let me hurt you and then walked away without trying to fix it."

She caught her bottom lip between her teeth and frowned. "This isn't us. We don't talk like this."

"No, this *wasn't* us. We *didn't* talk like this. But we're here now."

"I don't know what you want from me. Besides the obvious."

"Sure you do, you just don't want to talk about it because you're scared."

She turned to look at me. "Oh yeah? What am I scared of?"

"You're scared you want the exact same thing. You're scared I'm going to hurt you. You're scared of history repeating itself. And you're scared of what comes next."

She kept her eyes cast downward and maneuvered us until she was straddling my lap. Out of habit, my arms went around her as the water sloshed around us. "You know what I'm scared of right this very minute?"

"What might that be?"

"I'm scared the water will turn cold before I've had my way with you."

I recognized her stall tactic for what it was. But neither of us were going anywhere for weeks yet; I still had time. "Well, that won't happen," I reassured her.

"And why's that?" she murmured, draping her arms over my shoulders.

"Built-in heater. The water stays hot as long as it's full." I licked along the side of her throat before biting down lightly on the pulse beating strongly at the base.

"Remind me to thank the Bissets."

"I will and I'll also pick this conversation back up where you abandoned it."

She tilted her head back and met my eyes. "You've definitely changed."

"For the better, I hope."

"Time will tell."

"Indeed." I covered her lips with mine and soon all conversation became unnecessary.

20

Dessert items were far more innocent conversation

Carissa—Thursday, July 21—4:31 p.m.

"Wha—?" Niecy grabbed my hand and pulled me down the hallway at a near sprint.

"Come with me."

"Okay, but slow down; you know that peppy, sadistic Darcy kicked my ass on those squats today and my entire body is screaming." What I wouldn't give for a spa day and mountain of chocolate right now. Oooo, yes: spa, chocolate, shrimp scampi, and champagne! Champagne sipped off of Malachi's abs, which were coming back to definition in fine form. Mine were still missing in action. I snapped back to the moment at hand as Niecy yanked me into a janitor's closet just down the hall from the confessional.

"I need to talk to you before you go in there," Niecy whispered urgently.

"Well, all right, then." I snatched my hand back before she tore my whole arm from the socket. "Why are you whispering?"

"I wouldn't put it past these people to have bugged the mops and brooms up and through here. Ever since they caught Suzette 'reuniting' with her husband in the indoor sauna? I've been extra paranoid."

The *Losing to Win* staff were doing the utmost to catch us in ratings-worthy compromising positions. It was a daily chess match between the crew and the contestants. Suzette's husband had come down to visit for the holiday, and instead of staying behind closed doors, they decided to "celebrate" all over Belle Haven. The cameras were rolling the minute they set foot on Havenwood's campus. Why she thought it was a good idea to get naked with her husband in the sauna we used every day was beyond me. The cameras captured that hot mess of a hookup using that eerie green night-vision lighting. Not flattering. I almost felt sorry for Suzette. Right until she had the nerve to go on camera with some story about me trying to steal her man for the last fifteen years. Like really? Jerome Allendale hadn't aged any better than Suzette, and even back in his cute days, he had the personality of a wet walrus stranded on dry land.

But back to Niecy. "Um, is that why you have Meshach climbing up the emergency staircase like Spiderman damn near every night?"

She gasped. "You know about that?"

Six people living within thirty feet of each other had very few secrets. "He climbs into Malachi's room, which is attached to mine, girl."

"Oh," she said, chagrined.

"What did you need to talk to me about?"

"Well, along this same subject . . . so you're doing Malachi again, right?"

Like I said: few secrets. "Jesus, Mary, and Joseph—can you put it another way?"

"Sorry, Prom Queen. Are you engaged in sexual congress for the purpose of mutual orgasm with Malachi once again?" she singsonged in a teasing voice.

I elbowed her in the side. "Fine, smartass. Yes, I'm doing Malachi. Why?"

"How are you doing it?"

Blinking twice, I had to clarify. "I beg your pardon; do you want an instructional video? Power-Point slides? An illustrated manual? Kama Sutra checklist? What are you asking me?"

She smacked my arm. "No, silly. I mean, the producers suspect, but as far as I can tell, they don't have you guys on film or microphone yet. So where and how are you getting it on so that it's not 'film at eleven?' "

"Oh, you mean how logistically." She'd worried me there for a minute.

"Yes, fool."

I snickered. "Okay, because I was like—damn, girl, I know it's been a while for you, but it really is like riding a bike. Once you hop back on, it comes to you."

"Oh. My. Damn. Can you just answer the question so we never have to talk about this again?"

"You brought it up," I reminded her. "Bathrooms, dressing rooms, and locker rooms are no mic/no camera zones. It was in the fine print of the contract. The only thing is, stay clear of the door and play some music or run some water because they've been known to stand outside the door with the mic."

She slapped her hands on her hips. "Seriously?"

"Girl, seriously."

"This is some bullshit."

"I told you. Also, if you can sneak off campus, Sugar's bed-and-breakfast is all clear if you're not down in the lobby. Our houses aren't wired, but there's no way someone wouldn't notice both of us going into one of those homes, so . . . we've had to get creative."

"Or you could just stop until filming is over," she suggested.

A look of pure horror crossed my face. "Girl, what? I'm starving. I'm wearing spandex on camera. I'm sweaty 80 percent of the day and my hair is a frizzy hot mess. They filmed me having high tea with my mother yesterday, for Christ's sake! You think I'm giving up the only guilty pleasure this long-assed summer affords me?"

"That good, huh?" She slid me a look.

"Oh, you know I don't kiss and tell."

"Carissa, throw me a bone here."

"You know how Julie Andrews stands and twirls on the mountaintop singing about the hills being alive with the sound of music."

"Yes."

"Better than that. My entire body is alive with multiple orgasms."

"Whew!" She fanned herself. "I suspected he had some moves."

"He's got moves on top of moves. On top of

some more moves after that. It might run in the family, girl. You might wanna get on that Knight train."

A blush crept up her cheeks. "It couldn't be worse timing, but he is such a nice guy. You've known him forever; what can you tell me?"

"Let me say this. If I had any choice in the matter, I would've fallen for Meshach instead of Mal. If Mal is the bad boy who done good, then Meshach is the good guy who always wants to do better. He's just that rare combination of Southern gentleman, good looks, sweet personality, and something else I can't define."

"Hotness?" Niecy supplied.

I laughed. "Okay. Anyway, there's not a mean bone is his body, but he is apparently a shark in the courtroom."

"I might have to send Jordy to Sugar's for the night and sneak Meshach in. Jordy could use a night out anyway; I think you broke the boy's heart."

I sighed. "I'm actually pretty torn about that. I mean, don't get me wrong; I'm having a hell of a time with Mal. But he's already proven that he's not a forever kind of guy, you know? Jordan has me intrigued. He really shook me up with that kiss. He's got some skills, girl. He surprised the hell out of me. The thing is, he's the kind of guy who sticks, through thick and thin. Mal—well, he didn't stick so well, now did he?"

Niecy shook her head at me. "You truly believe you're with Mal just for the sex?"

"I'm not *with* Mal. I'm having sex with Mal. Period."

"But you could see yourself with Jordy long term."

"I think I could. I definitely owe myself the opportunity to find out."

"You should tell him that."

"Who?"

"Jordy."

"I should tell Man B to please wait for me to finish sexing down Man A because I think maybe somehow we can have something real?"

She covered her mouth with her hand and snickered. "Find a better way to say it."

"Ri-ight. I'll get right on that. When are you giving Meshach the cookies?"

"Girl, cookies?"

"What, we're too grown to say cookies? Cupcakes? When are you serving Mr. Knight your special cupcakes?"

She expelled a deep breath. "As soon as I can find a plate to serve them up on."

A knock came at the door and we both jumped. Yes, we had forgotten we were hiding out in the janitor's closet.

"Um. Yes?" I asked tentatively.

"Are you two talking about dessert?" Marcy's voice came through the door.

Niecy and I exchanged glances and nodded. Dessert items were far more innocent conversation. Sure, let them think we were talking about sugary treats.

"We miss cupcakes. Well, one of us does," Niecy answered with a giggle.

"Aren't you supposed to be in the confessional, Carissa?"

With a muffled sigh, I reached for the door and yanked it open. I looked back at Niecy. "I'm heading to the confessional, then I'm shooting promos. No time like the present, girlie. You hear what I'm saying?" This was my clever way of telling Niecy that most of the production staff would be with me for a while if she needed to sneak out to see a certain Knight brother.

"Bless you and good luck in there!" She grinned at me.

I had become a pro at the confessional. I gave cutesy answers that didn't reveal too much but made great sound bites. I bitched semi-good-naturedly about the workouts and the strict diet. I made sure to mention local businesses and talk up the town and then I wrapped it up. The show was using me, I was using them. I should have suspected that they would up the stakes of the game the minute I thought I had it conquered. But I didn't suspect because I'm just not that damn devious. So I was not prepared when I walked into the confessional and found Jordy already seated there. He looked up and a brilliant smile crossed his handsome features. "Hey, girl."

I smiled back. "Hey yourself, good looking." I couldn't help flirting a little. He was looking good. Though he hadn't shed a lot of pounds, he had flattened a lot of that belly and replaced fat with muscle. His face had started to chisel out around his jaw. If Mal was starting to look like a combination of a muscular Idris/Denzel, Jordan was starting to look like a Boris Kodjoe/Shemar Moore combination. I slid onto the sofa next to him. I glanced at the cameras before meeting Jordan's eyes. "To what do I owe the pleasure?"

"The pleasure's entirely mine." Jordan put his arm around me for a quick squeeze before we settled in to await whatever the production team had up their sleeve this time.

"We thought we'd shake things up a bit, mix up contestants in the confessional," Marcy announced from behind the lights. "You ready to get started?"

"Sure." I shrugged, anticipating some hot mess.

"Jordan, you and Carissa shared a kind of heated moment a few weeks back. Where does your relationship stand today?"

You would think I would be used to it by now, but I wasn't. I just never got comfortable with people being all up in my business and thinking it was okay. These folks were just gangsta. There was nothing sacred here. You couldn't show them the slightest bit of weakness or scandal because they would exploit the hell out of it for all the world (or the reality TV–watching public) to see. After seeing how they took comments out of context and spliced scenes together to make them look like something they weren't, we had all learned to be extra cautious.

Jordan reached over and squeezed my hand. "Carissa and I have been friends for years and we continue to be."

"But don't you want more?"

"I think the important thing is that Carissa and I know where we stand with each other and we're okay with it."

"Are you okay with it, Jordy?" she pressed.

"I'm not a child. If I want something, when I want something, I'll ask for it," Jordan answered with some steel in his voice.

"Carissa, how does Mal react to the closeness you have with Jordan?"

I was tempted to say "none of your damn business" or "how Mal reacts is not my concern," but I knew that would only add fuel to the fire. So I smirked and said, "You really have to ask Mal how he feels about things. I wouldn't dare speak for him."

Sensing that was as far as they could take it, Marcy switched gears and started asking us about the competition and how we were feeling. We gave our customary wow-this-is-hard-but-sure-gonna-be-worth-it-in-the-end answers and they cut us loose.

Jordan and I escaped into the hallway and walked silently to the elevator. "Can we talk a minute?" he asked as the doors slid open. He gestured for me to enter ahead of him. Stepping inside, he leaned next to me against the side wall and pushed the button for the first floor.

"Not here." I shook my head and gestured toward the camera.

He tilted his head down near my ear and spoke quietly. "Should I not stand so close?"

I didn't want to play games with him, but I didn't want to discourage him either. I liked Jordan and was genuinely interested in him. But the timing was terrible. I'd just started something back up with Mal. Yes, it was super-incredible sex, but I'd be lying to myself if I said that's all it was. Not with our history. When it ended this time, and I was sure it would end, I wasn't going to be broken with nowhere to land. If that made me selfish, so be it, but I was going to play it straight all the way around and let the chips fall where they may. I looked up at him through my lashes. "Who's pushing you away?"

"Rissa, am I in danger of getting my ass kicked here?"

"For talking to me?"

His voice went low and sultry. "You know I want to do more than talk to you, Carissa."

I flicked a glance at the cameras and inched a little closer. "I know. The interest is mutual. I'm not averse to the idea of exploring our affiliation further. But the timing . . ."

"I'm always one step behind that damn Malachi, aren't I?"

I reached out to stroke his arm. "It's not about him."

"C'mon, now," he chided.

"Okay, not *all* about him. Will you do something for me if I ask?"

"Just about anything."

"Give me a little time."

The elevator reached the lobby and the doors opened, but neither of us stepped off. He turned toward me, bracketing his arms on either side of me. "I'm sorry, are you asking me to wait on the sidelines while you sweat Malachi out of your system, and be okay with that?"

I winced. "It sounds bad when you put it like that."

"I'll tell you what. Your boy's tryout is in August, right?"

Apparently everyone knew of Malachi's aspirations. I nodded. "Yes."

"You've got until the day after his tryout and then I'm coming for you. I'll only ask once. If you say no, I finish the show, head back to Georgia, and I'll send you a holiday card on Facebook once a year. But if you say yes, you have to be all in. No more me or him, no more waiting, all in. Agreed?"

I nodded. "Agreed." We stepped out of the elevator, through the lobby, and out into the courtyard. People were milling around waiting to film some promos, so we paused far enough away that no one could hear the conversation.

"This would be easier if you just tell me now that you're not interested."

When had my life become this complicated? Here I was twenty feet away from the guy I was sleeping with and flirting with a different guy. No wonder the audience was feeling me. My life was turning into a soap opera. "I could tell you that, but it would be a lie. I *am* interested and you know what else?"

He let out a breath. "What else?"

"I'm so totally worth it." I grinned at him.

"Good thing because we're starting to attract attention and the Bayou Blue Streak is about two seconds from sacking me in the end zone."

I snickered. "He plays offense, Jordy. He doesn't tackle people."

"Does he know that?"

Over his shoulder, I saw Mal stalking toward us with quite the look on his face. I sighed. "I'll save you."

I stepped away from Jordan and headed straight

to Mal. "Don't start something and I'll make it worth your while later."

He glowered at Jordan over my shoulder. Jordan strolled down the sidewalk with a grin on his face. "He's pushing his luck," Mal said.

"He's pushing your buttons."

"As long as he's not pushing *your* buttons."

Not yet, I thought. "Mal, stop grimacing. I'm sure they are filming the hell out of this."

His chocolate eyes cut to mine and he raised a brow. "You're going to make it worth my while? How?"

These men were wearing me out. Was it only two months ago that I was man free, drama free, and camera-in-my-face free? Then again, in the past sixty days I'd become thinner, less in debt, better "maintained," and more my true self than I had been in years. I stood up on my tiptoes to whisper into his ear. "Let's play let's remember."

He looked around as if considering the quickest how and where to get us naked. "Here? Now?"

"We'll keep our clothes on. You remember that trip to the Pro Bowl when we got lost driving back from the shrimp shack on the North Shore?"

"Um-hmm."

"That thing we did on the abandoned beach as the sun went down?"

His nostrils flared and he shifted toward me. "I remember."

"If we get through these promos without any drama, I'll do that thing again. Tonight."

He sucked in a breath. "What?! For real, though?"

"For real, though."

He stepped away and clapped his hands together. "People, can we do this? I'm ready for my closeup."

Jerry raised the camera onto his shoulder. "Someone's in a hurry all of a sudden. You got a date tonight, Bayou?"

"You wish you knew." Malachi grinned and stepped to his mark to start filming.

I saw Jordan smiling and chatting with XJ by the production staff. He slid me a private look before turning away. But not so private that Malachi missed it. He frowned slightly and then gave a small shrug as if deciding it wasn't worth his time to make an issue of it right now.

I exhaled a ragged breath. One way or another, things were heating up around here. I just had to survive the summer and then everything could go back to normal. Whatever that was going to look like. For the first time in forever, I had no idea what the next few months of my life were going to look like. Even weirder: I was almost okay with it.

"Carissa, you ready? You're going to be on camera one." Ren pointed and held up some cue cards.

"Ready!" I called out and turned toward the camera with a smile.

21

Care to tell us what better thing you have to do?

Malachi—Friday, July 30—6:18 p.m.

The days fell into a blurry routine. We were up between 5:30 and 6:30 every weekday morning. I usually got up forty-five minutes earlier to lift. Then we met to eat as a group in the common area. Sometimes we cooked; often it was easier to just create smoothies. Most of the time, they provided pre-prepped meal options for us.

From there we spent a half hour acting like we were a group of people who hung out regularly discussing weight loss. These on-camera conversations frequently devolved into revelations about who was getting on whose nerves and what if anything could be done about it. We talked about the things we missed from our "real lives" and how much longer until we could get back to them. Then we trained for at least two hours. We had a short break for personal time (which was not at all personal and always filmed). We ate lunch or what they were serving that passed for lunch. Then we had meetings either with the production staff, the trainers, the nutritionists, the special guests that were brought in, or I met with Pierre and other members of my business team.

To date, Carissa had lost over forty-five pounds. I was close to that same total. Niecy and Jordy were down about thirty pounds each. As expected, XJ and Suzette lagged behind, but even they had lost a little over twenty pounds each.

Then came the competitive workout activity. It was almost always some crazy obstacle course or rock wall or three-mile hike through the swamp. Yesterday was at least a swimming challenge that got us out of the heat of the damn day. Grudgingly, I had to hand it to them: they kept coming up with new and camera-friendly ways to make us sweat . . . literally and figuratively.

The competitive workout challenge was followed by the on-camera wrap–up. Then came the showers in the tiny bathrooms, where the hot water always ran out no matter how quick you tried to be. There was an option for whoever came in last to opt in for the blind challenge. The blind challenges always involved some tomfoolery where they tried to pit us against each other on some sort of personal level. If we were blessed, no one felt like taking the challenge and we were free to go to dinner. Not that dinner was anything to write in to the Food Channel about. After dinner came the day-in-review confessionals. On a good day, we were free to retire for the day at around ten p.m. On a bad day: midnight or later.

It made for short tempers and long-suffering tests of patience. We needed a break, badly.

For today, we had one more competitive activity to complete before we wrapped for a long weekend. I needed that long weekend like a starving man needed steak. I was tired. No, scratch that: I was exhausted. Mentally and physically spent. I needed at least a twenty-four-hour stretch without a camera following me, without a workout to finish, without a playbook to study. In the past few weeks, some sports reporters had started showing up in Belle Haven and on set. While on the one hand it was gratifying to know they were still interested, on the other hand I felt like the pressure was coming at me from all sides. All eyes were on me. Normally, I enjoyed the spotlight. I worked best under pressure when everyone was counting on me. But right now I wanted to grab my girl, turn off the phones, and forget about the world for a minute.

There were only so many ways we could get freaky in the tiny bathroom in the dormitory. Neither of us was eighteen anymore. Quickies while trying not to slip and fall on that cold white tile? I was way the hell over it. I wanted a bed. A king-size bed with a pillow-top mattress with bedsprings that didn't creak with the slightest movement. I wanted a room larger than a cubicle, with climate control that worked not just when it felt like it. Call me spoiled, but damn, I missed sheets that actually had a thread count. I missed my steam shower big enough for two with the never-ending hot water supply.

"Malachi, are you listening?" Jim Swindle asked in a condescending tone.

I was too tired to lie. "No, Jim. I am not. I was daydreaming about a steam shower. What'd I miss?" I grinned with a shrug.

"I said that you and Carissa are exempt from this activity because you have won three in a row. So unless you want to participate, you both are free to go."

I turned toward Carissa and raised a brow. She put a hand on her hip and squinted at Jim. She wondered aloud, "What's the catch?"

Jim shrugged with one of those used-car salesman grins we'd come to mistrust. "No catch, though if you decide to stay and you win the competitive activity, you're exempt from the next three competitive activities."

I'd learned to ask for the fine print. "And if we should happen to lose?"

"You'd have to take the blind challenge to maintain your current standing."

"What's today's super-fun activity?" Carissa asked.

Jim pointed at the track. "Five-mile run. First team with the best combined time to finish—whether it's run, walk, or crawl—wins."

One look at Carissa's face and I already knew. She was not a runner. She would dance, do stairs, bicycle, swim, walk, lift, and stretch, but she was not about running. I was a good runner, but I liked sprints, not long distance. Jordan had become a pretty good runner and Niecy would probably speed walk to a decent finish. XJ and Suzette would give their normal half-assed effort. Yes, I liked to win, but enough was enough for now. It was not worth it to chance having to face some crazy-assed "what can we dream up to get in your business" challenge when we could just walk away now. Plus, I had plans for the weekend, none of which involved shin splints. Not too much more discussion was needed. "We're out. Y'all have fun."

"You act like you have something better to do?" Jim called out in a teasing voice.

"I most definitely do." I grabbed Carissa's hand without thinking and started to walk toward the parking lot. I'd completely forgotten that we weren't showing any overt affection on camera. She paused a second, looked down at our clasped hands, and met my eyes. It was too late now. The cameras were rolling. With a roll of her eyes and a shrug, Carissa laughed and we kept right on walking, picking up the pace to a light jog.

"Care to tell us what better thing you have to do?" Ren asked as he, Jerry, and the microphone guy who were my constant shadows ran along beside us.

The hell with it. As my grandfather used to say, in for a penny, in for a pound. With the grin that won me the cover of ESPN magazine twice, I looked straight at Carissa. "What better thing do I have to do?" Carissa shrieked as I scooped her up and threw her over my shoulder. "Her. She's the better thing I have to do!" I ran the last few feet and unlocked the car door.

"Mal, where are y'all headed?" Ignoring the reporters hustling our direction, I dropped her in the passenger seat and sprinted around to the other side.

"Does this mean you're back together?" another reporter called out as I hopped in the driver's seat and shut the door.

I flashed the grin, hit the horn twice, and backed out of the space. "Wait! Do you have time for a quick interview?" Someone called out another request. I held up the peace sign and pushed harder on the accelerator.

"You are CRAZY!" Carissa announced as we barreled out of the parking lot.

"I may just be, but you've got a bag packed in the trunk, your purse is under the seat, and we are out of Belle Haven for the weekend," I announced proudly. I couldn't wait to see her reaction to my surprise.

"What? Where are we going?" she asked excitedly.

The fact that she didn't argue and didn't get mad that I hadn't asked her first, told me just how far we had come. I reached out and squeezed her thigh. "How do you feel about the Big Easy for a few days?"

"Yes! I love New Orleans. But of course, you know this." She pumped her arms over her head. "No cameras, no hard-ass twin bed . . ."

"No Meshach tipping in and out in the middle of the night," I tacked on.

"No Suzette, no Bliss, no Marcy." She sat back with a contented sigh.

"A real bed," I added. "With room service."

"Room service," she echoed reverently.

"Room damn service, baby!"

"I'm going to cheat on my diet," she whispered giddily.

"I'm not going to tell," I reassured her. As much weight as she'd lost, she could afford to take a few days off. Personally, I liked her with a little extra cushion and most of that was gone. I was no fool: I kept those thoughts to myself. We were going to have a pleasant, drama-free weekend for the first time in years and I planned to enjoy every minute of it. If she was happy, I was happy.

"No Mom, no Ruby, no Sugar!" she crowed triumphantly.

"No Ren, no Jerry, no Jordy . . . ma'am." I shot her a look.

She shook her head. "I don't care what you say. Nothing can spoil this. I'm so happy to be outta here for a minute!"

We flew down Main Street and took the left toward the interstate. Waiting for the light to turn, she opened up the sunroof and stood up on the seat. "Carissa, what are you doing?" I asked in alarm.

"Woo-hoo!" she yelled with a wave before sitting back down and looking at me. "I started to scream ' 'Bye, bitches!' and flash a peace sign, but then I noticed a camera crew out in front of Ruby's. You know they would open the show with that shot. Damn hot mess–loving cameras." She fastened her seat belt with a sigh.

I smirked at her. "Ya good?"

"Oh yeah. Very good and getting better by the minute."

"All right, then, we're outta here." With a quick turn onto the service road, I accelerated onto the highway. We'd be on Canal Street in less than two hours.

She bounced on the seat. "I can NOT wait. Oh, and Mal?"

"Yeah, babe?"

"In case I don't tell you later, I had a great weekend." She leaned forward and brushed a soft lingering kiss on my cheek.

It was just a short, sweet kiss on the cheek, but my heart leaped in my chest. Aw, dammit, I'd fallen back in love with her. Not sure if I'd ever fallen out. Seeing Carissa Wayne happy made my entire life fall into place. My father, my mother, Pierre, and everyone else who'd offered an unsolicited opinion were right. Getting back in the NFL or not, whatever came next, it would only mean something to me if I had her with me. I was in it now. With a deep sigh, I smiled at her. "If you're happy, I'm happy."

"Really?" She considered my words seriously.

"Indeed, it's your weekend. Whatever you want, you get."

"Spa services?"

"Done."

"Dancing at Tipitina's?" she queried.

"All night if you want," I promised.

"Hmm, who are you and what have you done with Malachi Henry?"

"Oh, come on, I've pampered you before." I shot her a quick look in my defense.

She leaned against the door and crossed her arms. "It's been more than a minute, player."

"Let's just say I'm making up for lost time."

"Is that what you're doing? Making up for lost time?"

I didn't want her to turn skittish on me. It was better not to let her know that I was more than making up for lost time, I was setting up a foundation for our future. I wanted the whole package. Her and me forever. Till death did us part, the whole nine. But she was nowhere near ready to hear it. Instead, I kept it light. "I'm having a nice weekend with my best friend. Can I do that? Is that okay?"

She tilted her head to the side and studied me as though she was trying to figure out what I was up to. After a long silence, she nodded. "Okay, let's have ourselves our weekend."

I turned on the satellite radio. Smooth R&B poured out. Her station, not mine. I tended to listen to more hip-hip classics. She started singing along, a little off-key but very enthusiastically. Something she only did when she was happy. My girl was happy. We were on our way.

22

In your world, does "not bad" mean "drop-dead gorgeous"?

Carissa—Saturday, July 31—10:34 a.m.

"Oh my God, oh my God, oh my God!" I moaned in ecstasy. "That is perfect. You have the most magical hands!" The masseur dug into the knots in my shoulders and worked out the tension that had settled there for God knew how long. Whatever magical thing he had done with hot stones and essential oils had to be illegal. His thumbs ran down my spine ensuring the last of the tension was released there.

"Okay, Miss Wayne, you're all done." He draped the towel back over me and I slid bonelessly off the edge of the table. Yes, I was done. Or redone, in this case. I felt like a brand-new woman. Last night, despite all of our big plans, Mal and I had pulled into the portico of the Ritz Carlton in New Orleans and given in to exhaustion. We'd showered, changed clothes, had room service delivered, and were asleep before ten p.m. Very sexy.

This morning, after a sold nine hours of the best sleep I could remember in a long time, he got up early to go work out and I headed down to the spa. For the past ninety minutes, I had been buffed, scrubbed, polished, and buttered up one side and down the other. One last trip to the salon for a mani/pedi and to have my hair revived and I was ready to take on the world. Amazing what a little maintenance could do for a woman.

I dashed up to the room to change clothes and grab my purse before heading out to shop Magazine Street. I sent a text to Mal to let him know where I was. He said to text him back when I started trying on things and he'd come over to help. Ha! I just bet he would.

I was trying very hard not to read a lot into whatever was going on between me and Mal. At some point, we'd moved beyond the "sex only" to this interesting limbo we were in now. I wasn't complaining. It was quite a nice place to be. Here all was good, all was fun, even if I was pretty damn sure it was temporary. I wasn't going to think past the moment. For once I wasn't looking back or worrying about what came next. The here and now was awesome. With a smile, I texted him back with the name of the store I was stopping in first.

Stepping into the trendy boutique, I circled the floor twice and then picked out two dresses and headed back to the dressing room. Zipping into the first one, I was surprised to find the dress was way too big for me. The saleswoman knocked on the door. "How are we doing in there?"

Why do salespeople say "we," as if trying on clothes was a group effort? With a smile, I swung open the door and stepped out. "I suspect I no longer know what size I wear," I confessed while grasping the extra fabric billowing around me.

She took one look at me and laughed. "That dress is a sixteen; you're at least two sizes smaller. Have you not tried on clothes in a while? Lost weight recently?"

"Something like that," I muttered.

She took a closer look at my face. "Hey, you're that girl from *Losing to Win*, aren't you?"

"Um, no—I just look like her," I denied. I was not in the mood to be "that girl from *Losing to Win*" right now.

"Cari, you back there?" Mal's voice boomed out from the front of the store. I peeked over the door of the dressing room. There he was, all six foot four inches of chocolately gorgeousness. Just by entering the room, he owned it. He was in black jeans and a silk-blend T-shirt in light blue. He had that whole "I look good and I know it" vibe working for him. I suddenly regretted falling asleep so early last night. The things that boy and I could do to each other. Whew!

"Hey, Mr. Knight. You're looking sexy today." I infused my voice with enough suggestiveness that he could guess my thoughts.

His answering grin lit up his whole face. "Hey yourself."

The saleslady looked at him and back at me and raised a brow. We'd pretty much given ourselves away. Ah well, at least no cameras were following us. I shrugged. "Busted. I am that girl. He is that guy. We're playing hooky."

"Well, I love the show. You two are so much fun to watch. Are you back together?" she asked excitedly.

He and I exchanged glances. "No comment," I responded in a deliberately neutral tone.

"That's fair enough. By the way, you both look great. Carissa, let me get you a size 10." She almost skipped back out front, she was so thrilled. "Your friend is in the first room on the left," she told Mal, giving him an appreciative once-over.

He strolled back. "Look at you, all pretty, relaxed, and half dressed." He inched closer.

I snickered and put a hand up. "Do not start anything up in here, Blue Streak. We've got a perfectly lovely bed and an air-conditioned room waiting for whatever shenanigans you can dream up."

"Whatever I can dream up? 'Cuz you know, woman, I have an awesome creative streak."

"Don't you, though? And I say amen to that," I agreed as the saleswoman came back with at least ten dresses over her arm.

She held out a cute short dress in teal green with an embellished neckline that plunged before the material fell away to stop a few inches above the knee. Simple but elegant with a little bling. I looked at it suspiciously. "It looks small."

"It's an eight, I think it'll fit."

The last dress I'd bought was a size 16 or an 18. I had lost a lot of weight, but half my size? I doubted it.

"Try it on, Ris," Mal said.

I shrugged and took it into the dressing room. I pulled it over my head and it fell into place, no problem. Wow. I twirled back to look in the mirror. Now I needed a better bra, but overall? I looked damn good.

"We're going to need some help. What was your name?" Mal asked the sales clerk.

"I'm Heather." She smiled extra wide and batted her heavily mascaraed baby blues.

Of course she was. Perky blondes who stared at Mal with the worship eyes were always Heather or Mandy or some such.

"Heather, she's going to need some underthings, some shoes, and some accessories. Can you help us out?"

"We don't have everything she needs here, but we partner with the lingerie shop across the street. I can go get some stuff. Size 36C?"

"38D," Mal and I said at the same time. I rolled my eyes at him.

Heather handed me the other dresses. "You might like these too. I'll also get you some jeans and a few other things that might work." She took off almost running. Heather might look like a lightweight, but she was no dummy. She smelled the potential for a huge sale.

"Why am I buying all this stuff?" I asked him. My plan had been to get a pair of jeans and a party dress and call it a day.

"Why not?" he reasoned with a lift and drop of one shoulder. "I know you're sick of the workout gear and yoga separates. You might as well get a few things while we're here. Not that you'll have it on for long."

I shook my head at him while secretly looking forward to it. "Behave."

"I haven't stepped in there with you, have I?" He flashed me an innocent look. "I think I'm displaying massive amounts of behavioral goodness."

"You're the epic soul of restraint," I cosigned while trying on a red strapless dress. Tentatively, I stepped out in front of the three-way mirror. "Not bad."

"Sure. In your world, does 'not bad' mean 'drop-dead gorgeous'?" He rose up from the dainty sofa where he had been sitting and started toward me. The heated look in his eyes told me exactly what he had in mind. If I let him (and I was seriously considering it), he would have this dress off me and his hands all over me in two minutes flat. Before he could follow through, the store door flew open and Heather hurried in with two women trailing her. One had her hands full of lacy things and the other was juggling six shoeboxes.

"Size 7 shoe?" Heather asked.

"Yes." I smiled as she slid the top off of a box and handed me a silver sandal with crystal embellished straps and a chain-link ankle wrap. The heel was high and narrow. I raised a brow at the overtly sexy, purely decorative shoe and wondered where the hell I was wearing those in Belle Haven. Not exactly appropriate for parent-teacher conferences at Havenwood. I slid them on and fastened the back zipper before taking a few tentative steps. Not too bad, actually. Rare that a stiletto was both decorative and comfortable. I performed a slow pirouette and put my hands on my hips. "Thoughts?"

"Many, many thoughts." His voice was a growl.

"But I doubt you want me to share them here and now."

"Mal," I breathed, trying to keep things PG-13. "Should I get it or not?"

"She'll take the whole outfit," Mal said in a low voice and glanced at the lingerie still clutched in the other salesperson's hands. "And all of that. Any teddies in that stack?"

Okay, he was losing it. "Mal, seriously—why do I need teddies?"

"So I can see you in them. And then see you out of them," he declared as if I was asking a very foolish question. With a grin tossed over his shoulder at me, he pulled out a credit card and headed to the register. I made a motion to stop him and he shot a look that clearly said "don't even try it."

I wondered if now was a good time to discuss what was going on between us. He was buying me stuff. Stuff I could buy on my own. And he clearly planned on being around to see me wear these things. By my, his tryout was in a few weeks. If he was picked up by the Stars, he was headed back to Houston and I was in Belle Haven trying to broaden the minds of teenagers. History showed that we struggled to keep it all together while in the same city; what was the long distance going to help? With a shake of my head, I dismissed the more serious thoughts.

"He said you have to try a few of these jeans as well," Heather announced, handing me a stack of various denim options. I reached out to take them from her and she handed me some tops as well. "He likes these too."

I could pretend to be indignant, but truth be

told, Malachi knew my taste as well as I did and there wasn't a single thing he picked out that I didn't like. Some of it was a bit more clingy or low-cut than I would normally wear, but overall, not bad choices. Deciding that tomorrow was soon enough to think about the bigger picture, I closed the dressing room door and got started.

Almost two hours later, I was sick of trying on clothes. I was done. After determining that this sale would more than make up whatever quota they had for the day, the ladies had locked the front door and spent the time handing me items of clothing and chatting with Malachi. Baller Charming had talked them into knocking 30 percent off the entire thing with a wink and picture for each of their Facebook pages.

That sort of thing used to drive me crazy. Now, I just laughed it off and stepped into one of the new bra and panty sets Mal had spent a considerable fortune on. It was a peacock blue creation of lace and satin with little pink bows on the straps of the bra and the high-cut thighs of the panties. It was beautiful lingerie. I wanted to feel guilty; actually, I didn't. I didn't feel guilty at all. Three-hundred-dollar lingerie was not in my budget, no matter how much the show was paying me to suffer on camera week after week. He seemed happy buying belts and shoes and whatever else they dreamed up, so I decided to let him be that. But a girl could at least say a proper thank-you.

"Mal, could you come back here for a minute?" I said in a breathy voice.

"Excuse me, ladies. Can you have all of this sent over to our room at the Ritz Carlton? Thanks so much." He jogged back and peered over the door of the dressing room. I loved how his jaw went slack in appreciation before he hitched one brow upward in surprise. "You're looking a little underdressed to go to lunch, babe."

I opened the door and pulled him inside. "You're looking a little overdressed for what I have in mind." I shoved him backward and he landed on the little bench. I pointed at him. "Don't. Move." I cracked the door open an inch. "We're going to need a few minutes to make some final decisions on these last few items. You all should take Mal's credit card and go indulge in a latte . . . or two, with biscotti," I suggested.

They giggled. "We'll be back in twenty. You guys rock!"

"We do, you're awesome. Buh-bye, now!" I called out as they left the store and locked it behind them. I swung back toward Mal, who sat with his jaw hanging open again. I put a bit more sway in my hips as I neared him, watching his eyes track my every movement. It had been a long time since I'd felt this way. Sexy, confident, in control, hot. Everything was exactly as it should be in this moment and I intended to enjoy the hell out of it. I leaned down and bit his lower lip. "Close your mouth, Mal Henry, or put it to better use." I straddled his lap and put my arms around his neck.

"Seriously, it's like that?" His voice rumbled out as he shifted my hips closer.

"Seriously, it's exactly like that." I plunged my fingers into his dense wavy hair and settled my lips against his. We always kissed well. We started with lips and then added tongues, exploring and dueling. We caught fire instantly, his arms tightening around me like steel bands. I writhed against him, trying to get as close as I could. I could admit it: I loved it. I loved being in his arms, I adored the way he held me, the way our hearts started to beat to the exact same cadence when we were close like this. I loved that I didn't have to play coy or pretend to be anything other than what I was. I loved that all I had to do was nip his ear and whisper, "I neither require nor desire any foreplay." He knew exactly what I wanted.

His hands flew to his jeans, undoing the buttons and unzipping in record time. He'd barely shoved his boxers down when I shifted my panties to the side and settled atop him. I licked my lips and uttered a greedy groan as I took him inside me with one swift downward stroke.

"Damn, girl!" He caught my hips to still my motions and I batted his hands away.

"I can't wait." I used my thighs to lift up once more before rotating my hips and sliding down every steel hard inch once more.

He hissed. "Good Lord, woman! Condom?"

I paused midstroke and met his eyes. "I'm set for birth control unless you've got other worries?"

He shook his head rapidly. "Naw, I'm clean. I'd never endanger you like that. God, you feel good. So damn hot."

I rotated on the down stroke once more and tightened my inner muscles around him. I used my fingernails to scratch lightly across his back. I felt a shiver run all the way through him and he shuddered over and over again, straining his hips toward me. He met me stroke for stroke, groaning in the back of his throat as I changed tempo. I'd reduced this big strong man to a quivering ball of nerves. I loved that I could do that to him. A slow smile crossed my face. "You good, Mal?"

"You're killing me." His head fell back against the wall.

"Well, hold on, baby; let me put you out of your misery. We're gonna do this quick and dirty." I shifted slightly to get better leverage and then began riding him at breakneck speed. "God, I love the way you fill me up."

"Yes!" he hissed threw his teeth and held on for dear life.

For the next electric moments, all you could hear was the sound of flesh kissing flesh, meeting and separating in heated, liquid claps of sensation. The air was perfumed with our passion, sweat beaded on both our brows, breaths turned into ragged gasps as we strained toward completion.

"Carissa, I'm gonna . . ." he ground out through gritted teeth, arching his hips to delve deeper.

"I'm right there with you. Right there." I slammed down on him one final time and convulsed into an ocean of pleasure. He tensed and let go inside of me, my wave feeding his wave and back again as we clung to each other to ride out the storm. Aftershocks sizzled through me as I leaned against him.

"What got into *you?*" he panted.

"You did. Quite magnificently." I smirked and patted his shoulder. "Thanks, I needed that."

"I think you took advantage of me," he teased, pulling me tight for a hug.

"I was trying to thank you for buying me these

lovely things." I patted his cheek as our heart rates slowed to within normal range.

"A thank-you? Woman, that was a full frontal attack."

I howled with laughter. "Poor little lamb, do you feel violated? Want me to kiss it and make it better?"

"Definitely. Later. I'll hold you to that."

"You do that."

"And you are most certainly welcome. If I knew how hot buying you a few dresses would get you, I'd own boutiques across the country."

"Ha! All of that is not necessary." Lifting off of him, I had to deal with the messy practicalities of post-sex hygiene. "Hand me my purse, I have some wet wipes and bottled water in there."

"Why do you carry wet wipes?" He looked confounded as he handed my bag to me.

"Girl Scout motto: Always be prepared."

"That's Boy Scouts, and you were neither."

I cleaned up as best I could and handed a fresh wipe to him. "We're always sweating on that damn show; I got tired of seeing film of myself glistening from head to toe."

"At least you're pretty when you sweat; they have more shots of me looking shiny as hell."

"You look hot when you sweat and you know it. They never fail to catch you standing around shirtless." I eyed him up and down in admiration. He looked amazing. He was chiseled and fit, back in playing shape, from what I could tell.

"I worked hard to be able to stand around shirtless again."

"Yeah, ya did. Look here, stud: tip on out there

and grab me a pair of drawers from the counter-top. These are done." I slipped a slinky maxidress over my head and stepped into peep-toe wedge espadrilles before shimmying out of the sodden underpants.

"Oh yeah?" He grabbed them from me and sniffed. "Daddy likes." He tucked the blue boy-shorts into his back pocket.

"You are so nasty."

"You like me like that."

"True. Go get me some drawers so we can be outta here. I'm starving!"

"You worked up an appetite . . . seductress."

"You like me like that," I teased right back.

"I love you like that," he said and walked away before I could respond.

Whoa. He loved me loved me? Or loved me when I was naked and riding him like a cowgirl? Or did I even want to open that can of worms right now? He handed me a pair of panties with pink and blue hearts on them and I stepped into them.

"I want seafood," I announced, pulling my purse onto my shoulder, playing the avoidance card.

"Whatever the lady wishes." He nodded and smoothed my hair back into place, letting me get away with it.

We were standing by the register innocently when the sales staff returned from their extended coffee break.

"Everything work out?" Heather asked, only needing to hit the TOTAL button on the register to finish us up. The register spit out what seemed like miles of receipt. She tore it off and handed it to

Mal. I tried to glance at it and he tilted it away from me.

"It certainly did." Malachi nodded, tucking his credit card back into his wallet and signing the receipt. "We appreciate your help today." He took my hand and led me toward the door.

"Thanks so much!" I echoed.

"Good luck on the show!"

"We'll need it!" I called back as we headed out. I glanced back at the store and then up at him.

"Did you forget something?" he asked.

"Just one thing," I said, reaching up and kissing him on the lips. "Thanks for a great day."

"Aw, babe, we're just getting started," he promised.

23

Last thing I ever would have put on my bucket list

Malachi—Saturday, July 31—11:02 p.m.

"**B**lue Streak! Looking good! Got your best girl with you, huh?" some random reveler at the Blue Nile called out as Carissa and I took to the dance floor. We'd just come from an amazing dinner at Dooky Chase's restaurant in Tremé. I was making good on my promise to take her dancing.

"Yessir, you know it!" I replied and spun Cari in a quick circle before pulling her close. She looked sexy as hell. She was rocking a hot pink halter dress that showed off all her hard work. Her skin glowed and her curly hair was glossy and fell around her pretty face. Even more than looking smoking hot, she looked rested, happy, and carefree. I hadn't seen her look like this in years. The fact that I had a part in her happiness made me feel ten feet tall and unstoppable.

The live band was excellent. The lead singer was crooning about moonlight on the bayou. I swayed Carissa around the floor, loving every minute of this closeness. I closed my eyes and ran my hand across her smooth back.

"This is nice," she murmured, tucking in closer to me.

"Mmm. Definitely," I agreed. The music changed to an up-tempo zydeco and I took a step back. "Ready to show me what you're working with?"

She twirled once with her arms upraised and pointed at me. "Try and keep up, Knight." She did some complicated footwork that was doubly impressive considering those sexy-ass stilts she was wearing and added some sort of shoulder shimmy.

"Oh, we really dancing? All right, then." I leaned in to match my steps to hers. We were rocking when a bright flash went off right next to us.

"Mal! Carissa! Smile!" a photographer called out. Then another and another. Suddenly we were blinded by flashes. What the hell?

"Are you two back together?"

"Mal, you ready for your tryout?"

"If Houston doesn't pick you up, will you come play in New Orleans?"

"Carissa, how's he treating you this go-round?" The flashes and questions kept coming one after the other.

"You have GOT to be kidding me!" Carissa hissed under her breath.

I linked our fingers and murmured in her ear, "Must be a slow news night. The sooner we give them a photo op, the sooner they'll leave us alone."

We posed for a few minutes. Carissa was handling it like a pro. This was an area we'd had problems with before in my playing days. Carissa used to say she'd signed on to be with a man, not a personality, and she hated the whole pseudocelebrity thing. If I could thank the show for anything besides placing me back in her path, it would be getting Carissa comfortable or at least able to bear to stand in the spotlight for a few minutes without being too irritated.

"We're just enjoying a weekend off. Thanks for all your good wishes," Carissa stated without really answering any of their questions. As we turned to sit in the VIP section, a young woman with way too many assets on display stepped into our path. "Carissa, you really think you can keep him this time?"

"I'm sorry, what's your name?" I asked, holding Carissa's hand tighter when she moved to pull away.

She thrust her chest out, tossed her hair back, and flashed her overly whitened teeth at me. "I'm Leslie."

"Well, Leslie, that's rude. Not just rude but also disrespectful. To her and to me. Don't be that chick." I stepped around her and led Carissa over to the booth in the farthest corner of the VIP area. I sat on the plush velvet bench and she sat across from me. I tugged her closer until my legs bracketed hers and I could read her expression. I gazed into Cari's face, trying to gauge what she was thinking and feeling. "You mad?"

She studied me a long moment before answering. "No. Surprised."

"Why?"

"You never stood up for me in front of the groupies before."

"Sure I did."

"No. You didn't. You laughed it off and told me it was all part of the package."

I winced because the minute she quoted me, I knew I had said it. "Have I apologized for being an arrogant ass before?"

"You have." A slow smile started spreading across her face.

I leaned in and nuzzled her ear. "Is there anything I can do to make it up to you?"

"This weekend was a good start." She raised her face to mine and a flashbulb went off again. "This is crazy. We're not that famous. Well, *I'm* not that famous. Your Blue Streak mojo is killing us here."

"I'm sorry to burst your bubble, babe, but you, Carissa Wayne, are now a reality-television star. The flashes are as much for you as for me."

She rolled her eyes. "Ugh. Last thing I ever would have put on my bucket list."

"What IS on your bucket list?" I was curious.

"You want to discuss that here? Now?" She looked incredulous.

"Well, we don't have to get deep. I just wondered what your 'before I'm eighty' checklist looked like."

She leaned her head closer to mine. "The regular things, I guess. Get married, have some kids, open the youth center, teach a few kids a few things along the way, travel to as many tropical locations as I can, be healthy and happy, surrounded by people who love me." She put her hands up in a shrug. "Regular, right?"

I nodded. "Funny, my bucket list is the same. Just add win the Super Bowl, hoist the trophy, and do a victory dance in the end zone."

'Well, you don't want much," she teased.

"I don't think so," I teased back. I wanted to ask her if she saw me as her partner for those bucket-list plans, but I wasn't sure of her answer and didn't want to spoil this easiness between us if the answer was no. Not right now. We were having an epic weekend. I aimed to keep it that way. Out of the corner of my eye, I saw some guy holding up his iPhone filming us. "Okay, you're right—this is a little crazy."

"Mal?"

"Yep?"

"Do something for me?"

"Name it."

"Get us outta here."

"I thought you wanted to dance?"

"We can dance in the room."

"We CAN dance in the room," I agreed readily.

"We can dance in the room naked," Carissa said silkily, running her hand up my thigh. I didn't need any more prompting.

I motioned to one of the staff members and handed him my valet stub. "Can you have that brought around . . . quickly?"

"Yes, Mr. Knight." He took off racing toward the door.

Cari giggled and mimicked him. "Yes, Mr. Knight."

I stood up and pulled her with me. "Um-hmm, that's all you need to say the rest of the evening. Yes, Mr. Knight. Okay, Mr. Knight. More, Mr. Knight."

Her eyes heated up and she linked her fingers through mine. "So we're outta here," Carissa announced to the few people still snapping pictures and invading our privacy.

"Already gone," I agreed and strode for the door.

24

Guess who's back

Carissa—Sunday, August 1—2:00 p.m.

"I don't wanna go back," I whined. Yes, flat-out whined. We were less than fifteen miles away from Belle Haven and I wanted to go back to that hotel room in New Orleans where I only sweated for the best of reasons and didn't have to worry about saying the exact wrong thing to the American viewing public. I could not have planned a better weekend had I tried. Even with the crazy paparazzi thing last night, it hadn't dulled our enthusiasm for the city and for each other. The weekend was great because Mal and I had been together—alone—and that was all we needed.

But that idyll was over. We were less than a half hour away from life in the fishbowl, twenty-four yoga poses in forty minutes, tiny bunk beds, Suzette with the dagger, and watching every word I said lest it be broadcast to the masses. Did I mention I was pretty much over it?

Plus, the closer we got to Belle Haven, the closer we got to Mal's tryout and that uncertain future I wasn't prepared to face. No. I didn't want to go back.

As he'd responded with infinite patience each and every time I bitched and moaned, Mal again patted my knee reassuringly and answered, "It's not worth getting yourself wound up about. If you're done, you're done."

"And then what happens?" I said grumpily.

"Then we have choices. We can go to your house, my rented spot, or our home in Houston."

Our home in Houston? Did he really still consider that to be our home? When I drove away from there all those years ago, I vowed never to go back. I was so not prepared to deal with that right now.

He took his eyes off the highway for a second to flick a glance my direction. "I can hear the gears turning. What are you thinking?"

"The next move is one you're thinking we make together?" I danced around the issue.

"All of my next moves have you attached to them, Carissa. I don't know what you're thinking and you clearly don't want to get into this now, but know that at least. Whatever comes next, I want you there."

For how long? Until what? As what? And what happens to me when football takes over again? All questions I wanted to ask but didn't want to hear the answer to. Not yet. "Okay."

"Okay what?"

"Okay, I hear you."

"And?" he pressed.

"It's food for thought."

"You are so chicken."

"Not chicken." *Denial, we'll need a table for one*, I thought to myself.

"What would you call it?"

"Gun shy," I reasoned.

"You know, Carissa, you said you forgave me, but you act like you don't," he accused in a hurt voice.

And just like that we were talking about it. "I do forgive you. But don't think I've forgotten. You put me through some shit, Mal. Wait, let me rephrase that. It wasn't all you. I allowed myself to get lost in what you wanted and what you needed to the point where I didn't get to exist and I'm not doing that again."

"I'm not going to be that guy again. We aren't those people anymore. I wouldn't ask you to give up anything for me," he stated with a conviction I both envied and questioned.

The unspoken question, "What *are* you asking me?" hung there between us. In my mind, I weighed whether or not we should just go ahead and have it out now. What were we doing, where were we going, what came next? But it didn't make sense to have this conversation before his tryout in two weeks. I sighed deeply and reached over for his hand. "Can we talk about all of this after the tryout?"

"No matter what happens, I know what I want. The results of the tryout are not going to change what I'm thinking, but okay."

"Okay," I agreed.

"So what's it gonna be? We finish the show? We

break for freedom? We hide out in Hawaii? Whatcha wanna do, Cari? Back on campus, your place?"

Before I could answer, my cell phone rang. I dug it out of my purse and looked at the display. It was Ruby. "Hey, what's up?"

"You better get over here." She sounded stressed.

"Where is here?"

"Your house."

"You're at my house?" I echoed, confused. Mal glanced over with concern stamped on his features.

"Yeah, me and Mom. And Aunt Elaine. And a bunch of cameras."

That couldn't be good. "What's going on?"

"Guess who's back?"

I shook my head; I couldn't imagine whose arrival would stir up this much drama. "Who?"

"Stacy Wayne."

My father. Of course. The spotlight on Belle Haven was shining too brightly for him not to want a piece of it. Which would be okay if he didn't leave devastation and destruction in his wake whenever he breezed through. Like a vicious hurricane. Dammit. "I'm on my way." I flung the cell phone toward my purse and pressed my hands over my eyes. I did NOT need this right now.

"What's wrong, babe?" Mal asked.

"Blue."

The one-word answer had him tightening his lips and stepping on the gas. "We'll be there in five."

"Hey, Princess! Look at you looking better than new money!" Stacy "Blue" Wayne called out from the front porch of my house as I jumped out of Mal's truck with my purse on my arm. One undeniable fact about Stacy: he was attractive and he was charming . . . on the surface. Stacy was a pretty man the exact color of roasted cocoa beans with thick kinky hair; a reed-thin, tall rangy body; and scoundrel's smile. If you didn't know him very well, he was a hell of a guy to hang out with. He earned the nickname "Blue" not from the color of his skin or his love of the music genre but because his mother had stated (on many occasions), "This boy right here was born to give me the blues." The main problem with Stacy Wayne was that he was a spoiled little kid in a grown man's body who never took responsibility. The one thing you could count on Blue to do was let you down. Sooner or later, he always did.

My mother and Aunt Elaine stood off to the side looking as if they'd already gone forty rounds in the ring with the devil himself. Ruby and Renard stood in front of my door clearly blocking entrance. Cameras were set up to the side of the driveway capturing every tense expression and moment.

I knew, I just KNEW that the minute it looked like this show was bringing some shine to Belle Haven, he would show up as if his presence was requested, hat in hand, trying to get a piece of whatever action there was to be had. And here he was—literally, with a straw fedora in his hand and slick grin on his face—walking toward me with his arms outstretched as if he'd been any kind of a father to me. I stiffened. I did not want to snub him in front of the cameras, but neither was I going to pretend like we were all some big happy family. I kept myself from taking a step back.

Before he could embrace me, Mal stepped in front of him and grabbed his hand and shook it. "Blue. What brings you back into Belle Haven? Last I heard you were lighting up the Vegas strip."

Blue looked annoyed at the interception. "Last I heard you had broken my baby girl's heart and were nowhere to be found."

Okay, that was enough fodder for the cameras. "I guess we all have some things to catch up on. Let's go inside," I prompted, skirting around my father and marching up onto the porch. I motioned to Renard. "Make sure they don't film us inside the house, will you?"

"I got you, sis." He nodded as we filed past him.

Herding everyone into the kitchen, I swiveled and put my hands on my hips. "What do you want, Dad?"

"Ah no, come on now. Can't a man want to see—"

"Cut it," I interrupted. "Nobody here is buying it and the cameras and microphones are all outside. What do you want?"

"Eloise, you just gonna let her talk to me like that?"

"She's a grown woman, Blue. She has been for a long time now. I guess you'd know that if you stuck around without wreaking havoc for more than a minute," my mom said tiredly as she dropped into a chair at the dining table.

Remembering my manners, I walked to the fridge. "Anybody want something to drink?" Just because we were dysfunctional as hell, didn't mean we couldn't follow basic Southern hospitality rules. I spent the next few minutes handing out water and tea. Blue asked for a beer. Ruby snatched it from my hand and slammed it down in front of him.

"Just tell us what it's going to cost us to get you outta here so we can write the check and you can be onto the next," Ruby snarled.

"Write the check?" I asked in confusion. "Who has been writing him checks?"

The entire room fell silent. I looked around with mounting dismay.

"Wait a damn minute; you all have been paying him to stay away?" I was appalled. Not that I wanted him to stick around, but I wanted him gone without any of our money lining his lazy-assed pockets. No one would meet my eyes. "Why?"

Eloise shrugged. "That's all he wants anyway, and he makes such a pain in the ass, baby. It's easier to just cut a little check and be done with it."

Ruby nodded.

I noticed Mal was mighty quiet. "Mal? Not you too?"

"You don't want to go stirring up old history," my father said too quickly for my liking.

"Malachi Henry Knight, did you give my father money?"

He shrugged. "It was less drama."

All of a sudden, the answer came to me. "Was he blackmailing you? With what?"

"Ris, he threatened to make up all sorts of bullshit. Go to the press with anything he could come up with to make trouble for us. He just wanted a little piece of the pie, said it was his due as your father. Like your mama said, it was easier to just give him the money. I could afford it, it's not that big of a deal."

"It's a huge damn deal, Mal."

"Baby, I took care of it."

"How much over the years?" I snapped and noticed my father shuffling uncomfortably. "How. MUCH?"

"Probably around fifty grand total," Malachi announced and everyone except Blue gasped.

Tears sprang to my eyes, not just because my father was basically a con artist, but because Mal had shouldered this alone. "Mal, you didn't have to do that. You could have told me!"

"I wanted to protect you from this. You didn't need Blue drama on top of everything else. Besides, it would've just made you unhappier than you already were," he said sadly as tears ran down my face.

I could not believe that my father had basically been holding this family hostage for years. I could not believe the lengths that Mal went to in order to protect me from him. All of that ended today. Right the hell now. I snatched the beer out of my father's hand. "You will never see another red cent from this family or anyone affiliated with us. You do your worst. You cannot touch us anymore. Do you hear me?"

"Carissa Melody, I don't want no trouble. But it ain't right for the fam to be doing so good and not share with your daddy. I mean, you're here because of me. You got this fine house and this rich man, but you came from me. I'm your father. . . ."

"In name only. I'm here in spite of you, not because of you." I pulled Malachi over to me and brushed a kiss across his lips. "Thank you." He brushed a tear off my face with his thumb. I stepped back, wiped the remaining tears from my face and opened my purse. Taking out my makeup kit with shaking hands, I reapplied lipstick and mascara before fluffing my hair. I brushed nonexistent wrinkles from the bodice and skirt of my spaghetti-strapped navy blue maxidress. "How do I look?" I turned to Ruby.

She hopped up to stand beside me. "Ready to do battle. What are we doing?"

I tilted my chin up and stormed out to the front porch. I motioned for the cameras to come closer. "As you may know, my father has come to Belle Haven for a visit. I can count on one hand the number of times I've seen this man over the course of the past ten years. Blue Wayne is a selfish man. He is a deadbeat dad who has two good things about him: He's a brilliant guitarist and he had the good sense to pick a hell of a woman to birth his two children. Well, two that I'm aware of and acknowledge. I just found out that he has been extorting money from people I care about so that he won't make trouble for me. I'm not going to allow that to happen anymore. If anyone in this town or on this show gives my father money, I'm done. You can feel free to shut down *Losing to Win*, sue me for breach of contract, and pack up your cameras and go. He is not a part of my life. Are we clear?"

Marcy, who had shown up at some point, nodded with her eyes wide as saucers. No doubt she was already figuring out how to edit the latest Carissa Wayne melodrama into next week's trailer.

I poked my head back in the house. "Blue? You can go now."

"We need to talk about this, little girl!"

"We actually don't . . . Dad," I snapped out as Renard and Malachi ushered him out the front door.

Marcy piped up quickly as we were shutting the door. "When will you and Mal be back on campus?"

"Half an hour," I replied. Mal cleared his throat. I looked over at him. He gave me a look hot enough to burn through metal. We were going to need a little adult alone time. "Um . . . two hours?" He nodded.

"Okay, we'll be waiting for you two in the confessional."

"I'll just bet you will," I murmured and slammed the door shut.

25

Boys' night out

Here's one thing I've learned on this show: The problem with reality television is that very often, reality is completely staged. Take tonight, for instance. At no point in time in my reality would I have invited Jordan or XJ out for drinks. Nothing against either of them, but we weren't that tight. I'd barely known XJ when he lived in Belle Haven all those years ago and I wouldn't have known Jordan at all were it not for this television show. Add in the fact that Jordan made no secret of the fact that he was just waiting in the wings for me to mess up with Carissa so he could step in? Yeah, not my first choice of drinking compadres.

The producers of *Losing to Win* thought it would be "fun" for us to do a Boys' Night Out and a Girls' Night In, so instead of spending the evening dazzling Carissa with what a sparkling and enlightened man I was, I was sitting on the back deck of the Idlewild nursing a beer. I didn't really want a beer and I didn't really want to hang out with the guys, but "reality" waits for no one, so here I was. I hadn't seen any cameras, but I assumed that some footage of this evening would turn up somewhere. With these folks, it always did.

Meshach, Burke, Mac, Lee, and Corey had come out so it wouldn't be obvious that I was out on what was basically a grown man playdate with guys I didn't really know. We'd been here since around eight o'clock shooting the breeze about a number of topics. Having exhausted sports, weather, and what was new in the reality weight-loss world, the conversation took a turn to the personal.

"So XJ, what's your story?" Corey asked. "How did your wife feel about you spending the summer doing a weight-loss show in Belle Haven, Louisiana?"

XJ barked out a laugh. "Truthfully, I think she was happy to get rid of me for the summer, pleased about the extra money coming in, and willing to do anything to get a few pounds off my ass. As far as she was concerned, this was all win, bruh."

"Has she been out to visit?" Mac asked.

"She came out over the Fourth of July and said she'd see me in September," XJ offered as an explanation. "What about you fellas? How is it I'm the only one with a ball and chain at this table? Well, not you, Mal; we know your story."

I snorted. "I doubt it, but yeah, I'll let you guys answer that one."

Corey said, "I'm married. Wifey gave me a get-out-of-jail pass for a few weeks so I could come play with Mal, but I'm headed home after the weekend. Lee?"

"Oh, I'm single," Lee supplied.

"Not that single," Burke piped up. "I've been seeing you hanging around the lovely Ms. Sugar."

Lee grinned. "She is something, isn't she?"

Mac slid him a look. "That she is, but she's also a hometown girl, so if you were planning on hitting and quitting, you may want to slide out on that same plane with Corey."

Lee put his hands up. "Hey, I'm not that guy. Understood. I'm supposed to be playing a preseason game tomorrow in Denver. I've asked Sugar to come along. And then we'll see where she wants to go from there. I'm willing to see where it goes if she's interested."

I had to tease. "Well, is it something in the water in Belle Haven? Meshach is all up in his feelings over Niecy, you and Sugar getting sweet . . . Anything you want to share with the group, Mac?"

Mac raised his brows, looking both surprised and ambushed. "Not unless you know something I don't?"

Burke elbowed his brother in the ribs. "Seriously, bro? How long are you and Taylor going to do this dance?"

"I don't even know what you're talking about, so you can move on to the next and ask Jordan about his love life," Mac snapped and picked up his beer for a long draw.

"Jordan doesn't have a love life . . . yet," Jordan said with a glance my direction.

I really was going to let it go. But then I just couldn't. "Well, I wouldn't expect that to change anytime soon if you're looking where I think you're looking," I shot out.

"Oh, I'm planning on doing more than looking," he said with a smirk.

I slapped my beer bottle down on the wooden tabletop and made to get up. Meshach grabbed my arm and held me in place. "Not this close to the tryout. Not worth it. You've got too much to lose. Especially not when she'll be in your bed tonight. All you gotta do is keep her there."

Shach had a point. All Jordan could do was talk about it and dream about it. Carissa would be calling out my name before the sun came up. Of that I was sure.

"Keeping her? Good luck with that," Jordan added. This guy was begging to catch a Belle Haven butt-kicking.

"Bruh," Mac snapped at Jordan. "Mal may be the only one who's not allowed to kick your ass, but he's not the only one who can, hear? Carissa and I go way back and I don't like hearing her talked about like a damn piece of ass."

"I don't think of her that way," Jordan said. "She's not a trophy, no matter how others have treated her. She's the best person I've ever met."

My jaw clenched with the fervent unquenched desire to punch Jordan Little squarely in his pretty-boy face. Part of me knew he was speaking his truth; the other part of me knew that he was baiting me to see how far he could push. There may have been a time where I thought of Carissa as an attractive trophy, but all of that changed in the years without her. I definitely didn't need him telling me Carissa's worth. So with a self-satisfied smirk of my own I raised my bottle. "There's none better, son. None. You can believe that." I sat back with the satisfaction of knowing that I had first-hand knowledge of just how awesome Carissa Melody Wayne was in a thousand different ways that Jordan never would. Not while I had any say in the matter.

Meshach sent me an amused glance before turning back to Mac. "Really, Mac, you're going to act like you and Taylor aren't doing the dance of denial around each other? And before you say you don't know what I'm talking about, let me speak plain. You want to bone her and she wants you to . . . repeatedly. What's the holdup already?"

Mac motioned for a refill. "Taylor and I know each other too well. Well enough to know that once we scratched the itch, it would never work."

"You lost me," XJ said. "If she's your best friend and you have hot sex, don't you get to have hot sex with your best friend?"

Burke put his hands up and clapped them together in a "that's what I've been saying" gesture. "Speak it plain!"

Mac shrugged. "Just wouldn't work."

"You know what that sounds like? Sounds like the words of a chicken to me," Corey said.

"Does sound borderline poultrylike," Burke agreed, making a clucking sound under his breath.

Mac took a quick sip of his drink. "This is a small town. We have a fairly tight circle of friends and acquaintances. *If* we do this and it doesn't work out, the fallout would be epic."

"Wait, wait, wait," Lee interjected. "Are you sitting there telling us that you're not huddling up with that fine sister because shit may go wrong down the road and that would be awkward? More awkward than watching the two of you pretending that you don't want to jump each other every time you come within staring distance? I ain't even been in town that long and I see this shit. Dude, rediscover some balls."

I cracked up. "And this is why we keep Lee around. Straight, no chaser; damn the niceties; serves it up cold."

"How did we get on me anyway?" Mac complained. "What about Meshach sneaking all over town to do unspeakable things to the lovely Niecy?"

A slow smile spread across Meshach's face. "Who says the acts are unspeakable? They're pretty damn shout-worthy if I do say so myself. Though I don't, because I'm a Southern gentleman. We don't kiss and tell."

Jordan spoke up. "Please don't; that's my roommate. She's like a sister to me."

"Well, your play sister and I are speaking all sorts of truth to power. We are enjoying the hell out of each other. There's something there. Not sure what yet. Time will tell," Meshach admitted.

"You've definitely spent more time in Belle Haven this summer than you have in a while and I don't even pretend it has that much to do with me," I noted.

"You're finding the scenery in Belle Haven to your liking as well," Burke said.

"Oh, I've always liked that particular scenery," I drawled.

"You have stayed away and the scenery has always been this lovely," Mac said, sending me a look.

"I guess I'm the kind of guy who doesn't know what he misses until it's gone."

"Sounds risky. What if things aren't the same when you come back around?" Jordy asked.

"It was a risk I was willing to take before. But not now. I'm not that guy. When I see what I want, I grab it and hold on."

The mood turned tense while everyone waited to see what move Jordan and I would take next. He sat back and I turned back to Burke. "But what about you, Burke Bisset? Surely there's some lovely diversions lined up outside your door lately?"

Burke just gave a secretive grin. "If you all weren't so wrapped up in your own melodramas, you would know I've been seeing somebody this summer as well."

My eyes narrowed in thought. I thought about the times I'd seen Burke over the course of the past few months and whom he had interacted with. Suddenly my eyes popped open. "You're dating Darcy? The perky-ass personal trainer from hell?"

"I refer to her as my current boo thang, but you guess correctly, sir."

Mac's mouth dropped open. "How did that get past me?"

"Again, your eyes are focused in one direction only," Burke teased.

"Lord, what are Mama and Daddy gonna say when they find out you're dating a white girl." Mac guffawed. The Bissets put both the old and the school in "old school" and thought only women with

Bayou roots tracing back a few generations were suitable for their sons.

"They'll remember I'm over thirty, it's past the year 2010, and it's none of their damn business. But more to the point, it's not serious. We're just having some laughs before she heads back to LA." Burke shrugged.

Corey rolled his eyes. "Yep, that's how it starts."

"Ain't that the truth," XJ said.

This conversation could take a turn to get all of us in trouble. I put my hands up. "Okay, enough. I'm going to pull out aprons and knitting needles in a second. Who saw the preseason game between Houston and Indianapolis?" With that, the conversation turned back to sports. I glanced at my watch. In about two hours, I was bailing and going to crash Girls' Night. Damn the producers. Life was too short to waste time. Sure, there was a time when I would've appreciated hanging out with the guys. Right now, my focus wasn't there. Maybe this is how I knew I was finally grown, when I'd rather stay home with my woman and watch TV than sit in a trendy bar with the fellas. And you know what? I was okay with it.

26

Girls' night in

Carissa—Saturday, August 8—11:20 p.m.

"Well, Suzette, just feel free to leave." I pointed to the door after she complained about God knew what for the sixth time that night.

"I won't stay where I'm not wanted. I believe I will head on back to my room for the night," she said in her best Scarlett O'Hara voice. When no one tried to stop her, she pouted, snatching up her purse and slamming out the door of the suite. We were lounging in the penthouse suite of the Idlewild for this Girls' Night In that Marcy and Bliss insisted we do.

It was a three-room suite that used to be the fourth-floor attic of the great house. Unlike the other floors, this one had a completely contemporary look and feel. Sugar and Eloise had gone for an updated "glam meets Southern comfort" style. Plush beige carpets and blingy lighting meshed with oversized couches in sage and pale blue to dominate the living area.

I rounded up Sugar, Ruby, and Taylor to join me and Niecy. We were all dressed in variations of the blue and green *Losing to Win* loungewear sets, because don't you know that in "real life," grown-ass women dress alike? Never mind that one of the girls was a complete pain in the ass; we were expected to hang out and pretend that at any minute we were going to braid each other's hair, have pillow fights, and lip-sync to Taylor Swift songs. The click of the lock indicated that Suzette had indeed abandoned the evening.

"Whew!" Sugar said. "That woman puts the itch in bitch and takes it all the way there and back!"

Niecy shrugged. "Some women are just not happy and that right there is the manifestation of years of unhappiness."

"God, I hate it when women act like victims unnecessarily. She's been that way for as long as I can remember. I tried to like her, I've tried to be nice, I've tried to ignore her. Now I've just decided not to care." Taylor sighed.

Ruby shifted on the wide, teal velvet chaise. "Let's not waste any more time on Suzette. I'm trying to find out what's going on with Sugar and Sexual Chocolate down there."

I sputtered into the iced green tea I was drinking. "Are you calling Lee McAdoo Sexual Chocolate?"

"Doesn't he look the part?" Ruby cackled.

"Don't you have a husband?" I reminded her.

"Girl, even if the store is closed, you can window shop." She grinned. "And I'll bet Lee would look good oiled up standing in a window."

"Oh Lord," Sugar moaned. "The last thing he needs is a bigger ego. He asked me to come to Denver to watch him play tomorrow."

"You going?" Taylor asked.

"Hell yes."

"And then what?" Niecy asked.

Sugar twirled her wine in her glass. "I don't know. I guess we'll talk about it after we get through the weekend."

Ruby huffed. "You and Carissa with these easy breezy 'who cares what the future holds' attitudes. I don't know how you do it."

"I care what the future holds," I explained. "I just don't see any good in fretting about it right now."

"How do both Jordy and Malachi feel about that?" Niecy wondered.

"I couldn't say. They can either love it or leave it alone. I'm doing me," I stated jauntily.

"Oh, all right then, Carissa X. Go militant, why don't you." Taylor chuckled.

"Well, Ms. Rhone, it's better than doing nothing at all." I arched a brow in her direction.

"I know where you're going with this and I don't want to talk about it," she said shortly.

"Of course you don't. That would be acknowledging that there's something to talk about. Okay, then." I turned my attention to Niecy. "What about you, ma'am? Looks like since we had the cupcake discussion, you are dispensing all flavors of sweet treats to Attorney Knight."

Niecy beamed with delight. "We're enjoying ourselves. A lot."

Sugar piped up. "And to quote you, 'and then what?' "

"He said he wants me to come back to New Orleans with him when the show is done."

I squealed. "Are you going?"

"I can't see any reason not to," she said with a coy smile.

"Damn right," I agreed with a nod of my head. I was about to ask for details when the suite door flew open.

"Where the women at?" Lee bellowed as he led a motley crew of fellas into the henhouse.

Mal, Mac, Burke, XJ, Jordan, Corey, and Lee entered with complete disregard to the producers' plans for the night. Apparently the separation of the sexes was not working for them. I was surprised at Mal. Back in the day, a night out with the guys would mean I wouldn't see or hear from him for hours. Lately, he didn't let more than a couple of hours pass without giving me a call or sending a text.

As if sensing my thoughts, Mal walked straight over to me, scooped me up, and sat down with me in his lap. He kissed me with a bit more ardor than we usually showed in public. I was breathing heavily by the time he pulled back. "Hey, babe," he said quietly.

I raised a brow at him and glanced sideways at Jordan. He crossed his arms in front of him, stared at the two of us, and said nothing. I turned my attention back to Mal. "Hey yourself," I replied. It was both ridiculous and unfortunate how glad I was to see him. This was getting deep. This was supposed to be lighthearted and fun only. But as I leaned my head against his shoulder and he stroked my hair, I had to acknowledge that it felt like more.

XJ threw his hands up. "I see where this is headed. All the love in the air and whatnot. I'm off to call the missus. Y'all keep it real."

Corey nodded. "I'm out too. I'll come around and say good-bye before I head out."

Lee walked over to Sugar and slid an arm around her waist. "Hiya, gorgeous."

"Hi yourself." She giggled up at him. They were actually kind of cute together. I hoped it worked out for her. Living in a small town, the guys to date and mate with were slim pickings. Sugar deserved to at the very least have a little fun for a while.

"Okay, I'm going to find my husband."

"See if Renard will do that baby-oil thing you were talking about," Sugar called out.

"What?" Mal said. "What have you ladies been discussing?"

"Don't even worry your pretty head about it, Malachi Knight," Ruby declared. "I am going to ask Renard right now. Shoot, like XJ said, here y'all go with this lovey-doveyness. Let me go find my husband." Ruby got up and followed Corey and XJ out of the suite. Without uttering a word, Jordan turned and departed as well.

Meshach sat down next to Niecy and tugged her close. "Baby oil?"

"I'll tell you later," she offered and rested her hand on his thigh.

That left Burke and Mac standing. Burke looked over at Taylor, who was perched on the edge of a lounge chair, and then back at his brother with a brow raised. "Just do it already," he muttered under his breath.

I looked with wide eyes as Mac took a deep breath and stalked toward Tay. "Stalked" was the only way I could describe it. He was prowling like a lion looking for a meal and she was the chosen morsel. Her eyes snapped to his and she looked both nervous and excited as he stopped in front of her. He looked down at her for a long moment and she shifted in her chair.

"Tay," he said in a low tone I hadn't heard from him before.

"Yes?" she answered in a breathless voice.

"It's time," he declared.

"For?"

He reached down and yanked her out of the chair by her shoulders. She gasped in surprise and he slammed his mouth down on hers. She froze for an instant and then groaned and threw her arms around him. They kissed like their next breath depended on it.

"Oh my damn!" I said, nudging Mal.

"Well, all right." His grin faded as the kiss between Mac and Tay turned heated with sound effects. "Whoa. That's kinda hot."

" 'Bout damn time," Burke said. "My work here is done. 'Night, all." He left without another look back at his younger brother still happily molesting Taylor Rhone.

"Um, you know what?" Mal asked me.

I ripped my eyes away from my two best

friends, who were quickly heating up from NC-17 to an R rating before our eyes. They had started groping body parts. "No, tell me what."

"They have a hell of an idea. I think I can improve on that technique, though." His eyes heated up with intensity and purpose as he stood up with me in his arms. "Which door is the bedroom?"

"And that's our cue. We're outta here," Lee said, snatching up Sugar and hotfooting for the door.

"Y'all know there's a second bedroom right behind you. Like, not even three feet away, in case you want to avoid rug burn," I called out to Taylor and Mac, who had sunk to the floor and were now horizontal while still kissing passionately. Wow, I see why they were reluctant to start; they seemed unable and unwilling to stop. I was trying to not see that particular play through to its inevitable conclusion. Way too much sharing. I couldn't stop from taking one more look. I tilted my head sideways. "He is really good at that tongue sliding thing."

Niecy shook her head and grinned at Meshach. "He's definitely thorough. You got anything in your arsenal like that?" A slow smile spread across Meschach's face. "I bet I could come up with something." They stood up in unison. "We should retire for the evening."

Niecy leaned into him. "We probably should."

"We absolutely should. See ya, bro."

Before they even crossed the threshold, I pointed to the door on the far right side of the room. "Bedroom. Now, please. Uh, Mac, Tay—if you hear me, feel free to leave or stay or, you know, whatever."

Mac lifted one hand off of Taylor's ass in acknowledgment before cupping it possessively and pulling her tighter against him. They groaned again and some dry humping commenced.

"Oh, jeez. So trying to not see that. We're out." Mal swiveled and had me inside that room with the door closed in less than four steps.

"You know, your speed on your feet is quite impressive," I complimented him.

"You think that's impressive, you haven't seen nothing yet," he promised as he settled me atop the bed.

I smiled up at him as he leaned over me. "You know what's awesome?"

"Besides us?"

I stroked my hand down his face. "No, that was what I was going to say. You and me, this: it gets better and better."

"Oh yeah." He showered tiny kisses across my face, down my neck, and across my shoulder blades. My eyes drifted shut as I floated away on the building sensation. He grasped the V-neck of my shirt and ripped it open.

My eyes flew back open as the fabric disintegrated in his hands. "Are we in a hurry?" I sat up as my bra flew across the room.

With a quick flash of a smile, he answered, "We might be. What are we doing tonight? Slow and sweet or hot and sloppy?"

"What would sweet and sloppy look like?" I joked and slithered out of the lounge pants, dropping them over the side of the bed.

He pulled me back over toward him. "Is this a challenge?"

Malachi was super competitive in all things. I knew better than to throw down a gauntlet I didn't want picked up. I rolled my eyes. "The last thing I wanted to do was get your competitive juices flowing, baller."

Wiggling his hips against me, he grinned. "Well you've definitely got some of my juices flowing, so what's it going to be?"

I reached up and helped him pull his shirt off. "I get to special-order now? Anything I want, any way I want it?"

"Whatever you want . . ." He started singing a very off-key version of a Tony! Toni! Toné! song.

"I got you singing now?" I pulled him back on top of me and traced the outline of his lips with my tongue. We took turns diving and exploring each other's mouths as our breath grew more ragged. I reached between us and unbuttoned his jeans. They were just in my way.

He pulled back to lower the zipper. He snagged a condom from the back pocket and ditched the rest. "You got me singing, dancing, testifying. You kinda got me wrapped around your finger, Carissa, you know that, right?" My breath caught in my throat as I watched him roll on the condom. I stroked him slowly, feeling him swell in my hand before he lifted my hands, kissed the palms, and placed them beside my head. "You have to know I'm yours."

I studied his expression—the serious expression—on his face. He was wide open to me, not hiding a thing. In all the years we'd spent together,

I'd never known him to just offer himself up like this. "Mal."

"You have to know how I feel about you, Ris." He stroked his hands across my face, down my arms, across my waist, and down my back. "Or do you want me to show you?"

His hands caressed my ass and thighs while his lips traveled along my jaw, crossing my shoulder and resting in the hollow between my breasts. His warm breath fired my already-heated skin and I shivered under his tender ministrations. "Sweet heaven, Mal." He reintroduced every area of my body to his lips and fingers, rubbing his body against mine when a kiss and a stroke wouldn't do. Slowly, so slowly, he unraveled me with his devotion and attention.

"Can you hear what I'm telling you?" he whispered against the crest of my breast. His thigh slid between mine and he gently spread my legs apart, pinning me beneath him. His hands cupped the backs of my thighs and tilted my pelvis open. He surged against me in a slick, electric caress. "Are you listening?"

"Mm-hmm." I undulated under him, feeling overwhelmed by the sensations and emotions he was drawing out of me. I wanted to reach for him, return the favor, tantalize him the way he mesmerized me, but I could only lie open to him. I was waiting, edgy in anticipation for him to come inside me.

"There's nothing I won't do for you. All you gotta do is ask, babe."

I bent my knees, grabbed his hips, and urged him closer. "Love me, Mal."

He slid only the tip of himself in and paused. "I do, you know."

I wriggled in impatience before it registered that he was trying to tell me something important. The intensity of his expression caught my attention. "You do what, Malachi?"

He sank all the way inside me as he answered. "I do love you, Carissa Melody Wayne." He withdrew with tantalizing deliberateness before driving back as far as he could go. "I love you." He repeated with another measured, thorough stroke. With each stroke, he whispered it again. "Carissa, I love you."

Awash with rising tides of ecstatic delight, I blinked as his words registered and took hold in my mind. My eyes opened wide and I locked eyes with him. The truth of his words was right there. "Oh my God!" I screamed as the sensations crested, flinging me into the most intense climax I'd ever experienced. I held his gaze as the tumult took him over and he shattered inside me.

The experience left me shaken and raw. It had never been like that. We'd always connected on a chemical basis, but this had been otherworldly, taking us to a place where our souls were speaking to each other. I'd be lying if I said it hadn't rattled me to my core. I had no protection against that kind of connection. When it was friendship and sex and laughs, I could keep my guard up. But this? There was no way to fight this.

Malachi Knight loved me with everything he had. I was very much afraid I felt the same way about him. As we shuddered through the aftershocks together, I tried to open my mouth and say something to respond to the intensity of his declaration.

He placed a finger over my lips. "Don't say it right now."

"You don't know what I'm going to say."

"If you're going to tell me you love me, don't say it because I said it first. If you're going to tell me something else, save it for later. Let's just have this moment." He lifted me up and we headed for the bathroom. He started running the shower and drew me inside with him. "Let's just let the night speak for itself. Tomorrow is soon enough to deal with the rest."

I leaned against him with my arms wrapped tightly around his waist as the warm water pelted us from all sides. "When did you become the mature one in this relationship?" I wondered aloud.

He kissed my temple. "Guess I grew up when neither of us was paying attention."

"I like the new Mal."

"He likes you too."

We stood in silence for a few moments before I asked a question. "So do you think Tay and Mac are still humping on the floor of the living room?"

He choked out a laugh. "Hopefully they've retired to somewhere more private. They have years of unfulfilled longing to make up for."

"Can you ever catch up on that sort of thing?"

"You can have a hell of a time trying," he offered with a grin.

"Oh yeah? You have a list of freaky things you missed out on over the past few years?"

"Oh yeah. Most definitely a list of things Carissa and I used to do and need to do again. Plus a list of things we never did and still need to do. It's a long list."

I took a step backward and dropped to my knees. "Something tells me this is on it."

His head hit the tile wall as I wrapped my hands around him and coaxed him toward my mouth. "Oh hell yeah."

27

Looks like you're useful for more than eye candy

Malachi—Saturday, August 15—7:04 p.m.

"Yessir, that sounds great," I said into the speaker-phone, my calm voice and demeanor completely at odds with how I was feeling inside. "I'm looking forward to it. Thanks for calling."

I pressed the OFF button and looked at Pierre and Carissa, the other two people in the conference room with me. Before I could fully digest it, Carissa flung herself into my arms with a shriek. "You did it, Mal! You did it!"

And that's when it sunk in. After going through a team physical and private tryout earlier today for the Houston Stars, I was back in the NFL. "It's just a one-year deal. I'll be making the league minimum for veterans. But there are a bunch of performance bonuses built in and who knows . . ."

"Who cares!?" Carissa hugged me tighter. "It's your shot. That's all you need. You're gonna be great."

"I am, aren't I?" Her enthusiasm fed mine. This was it. We'd come full circle. Once again, I was on top of the world and she was right here with me.

"Yeah, you are!" She laughed as I spun her around in a circle twice. She hopped off of me and started dancing.

"Come on!" She snapped her fingers and grinned infectiously. "You know you want to shake your ass!"

I did, I really did. I started doing a super soulful version of the Snoopy victory dance. She joined in and Pierre came around the table too.

"Let me get in here." He pulled out his iPhone and pressed a few buttons. An old school rap song started reverberating around the room. He raised his arms up and started swaying them from side to side. "Hip hop hooray, ho, hey, ho!"

The three of us were in full jam-session mode when the doors swung open. In walked Meshach, Niecy, my mom and dad, the other contestants, and the production staff.

"I guess all this booty shaking means you got your day job back," Henry teased. I picked him up and twirled him around too, before grabbing my mom up and swinging her into a dip. Meshach put his fist out for a bump. We tapped fists.

"Yep, looks like I'm a Houston Star again," I announced. I reached out and tucked Carissa by my side as I accepted congratulations. I didn't want her to slip away. She deserved to be a part of this.

Bliss came over with one of the network executives. "When are you headed to Houston?"

I glanced down at Carissa. She was looking determinedly unconcerned. "They want me to play in the home preseason opener a week from Saturday. I've got to get to the front office to sign papers and start working out with the team next week. I'll probably head out tomorrow."

"We'd like to take the show on the road for the next two weeks to close it out," Bliss announced. "We're going to follow you. You won't be competing every day, but you and Carissa are so far ahead in the point totals that the outcome isn't really a mystery at this point."

"Okay." I nodded.

"I have to start getting ready for the school year. School starts right after Labor Day. That's about three weeks from now," Carissa said quietly.

"We've talked to the administrators and they need us off campus anyway, so they are okay if you start a little late this year."

I could tell without even looking that Carissa was not feeling that at all. But to her credit, she just nodded and crossed her arms.

"We're all going to Houston?" Suzette asked with a scowl on her face.

"Yes, but we're putting you up in a rented mansion near River Oaks. No more dormitory living."

"Seriously?" XJ asked, looking excited for the first time in weeks.

"Seriously," Ren confirmed. "It wouldn't be fair for Mal to be in his house while the rest of you are in dorm rooms."

Niecy slapped me on the back. "Good going,

Blue Streak. Looks like you're useful for more than eye candy."

"Wow. Ringing endorsement. Thanks, Niecy." I smirked at her.

"We're almost at the home stretch: a few more weeks and we'll be in postproduction. As a matter of fact, we're going to go ahead and break down the sets here, so if you all want to clear out of the dorm, you can sleep in your own beds tonight. We'll fly down to Houston tomorrow night," Marcy added.

"Yes!" Jordan said, pumping his fist. Everyone was sick to death of these accommodations. Finding out we were on the home stretch of this competition was celebration worthy.

"Sounds like you guys deserve a party," Pierre said.

Again, I glanced at Carissa. She was remarkably subdued. I tapped her shoulder. "What do you think? You wanna pack up and get outta here? Just the two of us. Chat a little?"

She blinked as if surprised I suggested it. I realized that she still expected me to turn back into that self-obsessed guy who put her last and everything else first. She didn't completely trust me yet. But I was determined to change all that. Now that everything I wanted was within reach, I wouldn't settle for less. And that meant doing whatever it took to get my ring back on her finger and her last name changed to Knight.

Carissa looked around and then back at me. "We can talk later. Let's hang out tonight."

"You sure?"

"Yep."

Pierre looked back and forth between the two of us and then shook his head as if he had something to say. "So it's a party?"

"It's a party," I agreed. "Everyone's invited to my place in an hour."

"Everyone?" Bliss asked. "Cast, crew, all of us?"

We didn't hang out with the *Losing to Win* folks after hours too much. They just couldn't help being a little too interested and intrusive. But tonight was basically our last night in Belle Haven as a group; might as well do it up. "Sure, everybody's invited."

"But no cameras!" Carissa announced. "One night without sound bites, please."

"Agreed," Bliss said with a smile.

I looked around the group and realized that they all had a part in getting me back to where I wanted to be. This party would be my way of saying thank you. It was our last night together as the full cast of this season of *Losing to Win*. We would raise a glass and enjoy the night. Tomorrow was a brave new world for all of us. I met Carissa's worried look as I glanced down. "It's all going to be okay, babe. Trust me."

"I don't know, Mal. It's a lot. I'm happy for you, you know that. In fact, I'm thrilled for you, but a part of me is wondering what comes next for me. Now that we're going to Houston, I have to postpone starting my school year. It's starting to feel like my stuff is slipping away and yours is taking center stage."

"I promise you, it's not going to be like that.

Not this time. I'm listening to you, I hear you, and I want you to tell me if you're getting lost in the shuffle."

She looked into my eyes for a long charged moment. "I'm going to try."

"That's all I can ask." I took a deep breath and announced, "Your dad left town this morning."

She went still. "How do you know?"

"He came to see me while I was practicing with Coach."

"Please tell me you didn't give him any more money."

"I didn't. I wouldn't."

"What did he want?" She put her hands on her hips.

I rolled my eyes. "He gave a half-assed apology."

"For what?"

"Being Blue, I guess."

She snorted. "How'd that work out?"

"About how you'd expect. I think this was his way of giving us a heads-up that he's probably going to sell some made-up story to the tabloids."

"I expected that. He's just not a good guy." She shrugged.

"No he's not, but I am."

She nodded slowly. "I think you might be. I guess we'll see."

I exhaled. It was all starting to come together. Now I needed to make it all come true.

28

It's like we've come full circle

Carissa—Sunday, August 16—10:12 p.m.

He hadn't changed a thing in the house since I'd left. The step-down living room was the same casual but elegant blend of contemporary yet traditional pieces arranged with the slate-tiled fireplace as vantage point.

For a second, I was tempted to get maudlin. Here I sat in the living room of the house I'd sworn I'd never enter again. Exactly how and why I found myself here wasn't that big of a mystery. It was time I got real with myself; I was exactly where I wanted to be for now. No one had twisted my arm. I hadn't been backed into a corner. I'd gotten off the plane in Houston a few hours ago. When I had a choice to jump in the van with the other contestants or hop in the car to go home with Mal, I slid next to Mal without too much thought.

I was a glutton for punishment, a hopeful optimist, or a damn fool. I guess time would tell which. I had no idea what Mal and I were going to do long term. I wasn't ready to have the conversation, but I wasn't ready to walk away. The raw truth of the matter was that I wanted to be with Mal, but I didn't want to get hurt. I somehow wanted a guarantee that everything was going to work out in the end; some sort of promise that I wasn't setting myself up for a fall from which I wouldn't recover.

"So . . ." Mal said quietly from the doorway behind me.

"So," I replied, turning to look at him.

"Here we are . . . back at the scene of the crime."

I glanced around, taking note of our surroundings. I was sitting in the exact same chair I'd occupied when I gave back his ring and he was standing pretty close to where he had been when he let me leave. "Here we are."

"It's weird, though, right?" Malachi said. "You and me, in the house you basically built for us. It's like we've come full circle."

"We're smarter and wiser this time, right?" At least, I hoped that was true.

"God, I hope so." He prayed fervently.

"You and me both."

"You thinking about fleeing?" He sounded as tentative and as nervous as I felt.

The word "again" wasn't said but was inferred in the heavy silence that fell. I shook my head with a trace of a smile. "No, not gonna flee."

He took a step closer. "Carissa, do you hate being here?"

"I don't hate it. I do wonder if I know what the hell I'm doing."

"You're taking a chance; you're giving me a chance."

"A chance to do what?"

"I get a chance to redeem myself and you get a chance to see if I'm worth the trouble this time."

He had a valid point. "Okay."

Mal laughed. " 'Okay' is your fallback when you don't want to get into it. Still not ready to have that conversation?"

"Not yet. We have a little time." The show would wrap in a few weeks and by then I knew I'd have to decide what came next.

"I'm learning to be patient, Cari. But please don't think it's easy."

"I know, Mal. And I appreciate it. I appreciate the time. I just don't want to make a mistake."

"As long as you're doing what's best for you, you won't."

"Well, that's evolved of you." I was surprised.

"That's the kind of guy I am these days—evolved, Renaissance, patient." He bowed from the waist, inclining his head.

"A prince among men. All of that, huh?"

He flashed a grin. "And more. I thought you knew."

"I'm learning new things about you every day."

Suddenly, his face turned serious. "Is your boy gonna wait? Or maybe he could just give up already. 'Cause I'm not letting go without a fight and he seems like he's antsy to make a move."

Oops. I hadn't realized that Mal knew Jordy was in a waiting pattern. Then again, not a lot was secret when you hung out with the same six people almost all day every day for months. Without acknowledging what Jordy would and wouldn't wait for, I answered his question. "I'm here, Mal, so it is what it is."

He looked like he wanted to press for more information; instead he nodded. "You'll tell me if you feel like you don't want to be here?"

"Mal, I have to go back to Belle Haven at some point. My job, my house, my life is there."

"Your life is where you make it."

"Okay. The life I had before all of this started is there."

"You still want that life?"

"I don't know. I haven't decided what I want."

His eyes flared with impatience or temper, but his tone was calm when he asked, "You'll talk to me before you decide? Or at least before you go?"

"Yes. I wouldn't just disappear."

"If nothing else, I've earned the right to know what you're thinking as far as our future is concerned."

"Our future?" I wondered aloud. Then I thought to myself: when had either of us decided for sure that we had one?

He crossed his arms. "You want to pretend we don't have a chance at one?"

"I don't want to pretend anything."

"Good," he snapped.

"Good."

"Are you coming to my practice tomorrow?" he asked hesitantly. And that was another new thing making me wonder if Mal really had changed for the better. Back in the day, he would have assumed that I was going to be there and been irritated if he even had to ask.

"I'll be there right after morning workout. You excited?"

He unfolded his arms and eagerly sat on the sofa beside my chair. His face lit up with anticipation like a child on Christmas Eve. "Ris, I'm so pumped. I can't believe I'm here, you're here, we're here, and I get to play football tomorrow. It feels like a dream. For the first time in a long time, I'm actually nervous."

"What are you nervous about?"

"This is Malachi 2.0, Ris. I've rebooted everything. This life I want is falling into place; it's all so close I can taste it."

This *was* Malachi 2.0. The old version thought he was invincible, unbeatable, and infallible. This one worried that it was all too good to be true. "I'm right here."

He expelled a breath. "Amen for that. As for the football part? I think I've got the new system down, the schemes and the packages. But I feel like all eyes are on me. Normally, I'm okay with that. God, I hope I don't screw up."

I grabbed his hands, which he had clasped together. "You're not going to screw up. You were born to play this game. This is what you do. And you do it best when the pressure is high. You've got this."

"I have to admit, I'm feeling abundantly blessed. How many people truly get a do-over? I keep wondering if there isn't some karmic bounce back still waiting to kick my ass."

"Whatever you've been through these past few years, it's done. You're back where you're supposed to be and it's all good. It's your world, Mal."

He shook his head. "It's our world. Ours."

I could tell he needed reassurance. I couldn't withhold it because I was conflicted. "You're right. You're not alone. It's you and me. But you're the one who's going to light it up tomorrow. You're going to be amazing."

He closed his eyes and bent his head. He squeezed my hands tighter. Tugging me up and over to him, he wrapped both arms around me, pulling me tight. "You can't imagine what it means to hear you say that."

I hugged him back just as tightly. "Don't ever doubt that I believe in you. No matter what happens between us, I respect what you do out on the field and I know you can be one of the best . . . still. When you go out there tomorrow, you go out there knowing that you've earned your chance. Take it and be great."

His voice was low and raspy when he responded. "God, I love you, girl."

I drew in a quick breath and exhaled. No way was I touching that right now. He was emotional, there was a lot going on in his head, and now wasn't the time. I shifted and trailed a series of kisses along his neck. "C'mon, Big Baller. Let's get to bed, you've got a big day tomorrow. You need your beauty sleep."

"I need a little something more than that," he growled as I wrapped my legs and arms around him.

"Oh, I think that can be arranged."

29

Sorry, you can't have it all

Carissa—Sunday, August 22—12:20 p.m.

I released the breath I didn't know I was holding and jumped to my feet. "Yes! Woo-hoo!" I turned to high-five Mac and Taylor only to find them in yet another lip lock. "You two take the phrase 'making up for lost time' to all flavors of extreme." I turned back to the field in time to see Malachi do some sort of dance before pointing the ball in my direction. Damned if my grin didn't spread a little wider. I never got over the pride of seeing him excel out there.

We were at Mal's preseason football game. It was early in the first quarter and Mal had just scored a touchdown, putting the Stars up by fourteen points. In addition to most of the cast and crew of *Losing to Win*, a large group of friends and family had come to Houston to watch. I was seated down in the players' wives section in between my mom and Mal's mom. Taylor and Mac were behind me. Everyone else was up in one of the booths.

"Smile, baby, you're on the Jumbotron thingy." Eloise elbowed me in the ribs.

I flashed my pageant smile and waved before blowing a kiss to the camera. Might as well give them what they wanted. The camera panned down to Mal watching me on the Jumbotron and he blew a kiss back and got immediately teased by his teammates. The game was being shown on the same network as *Losing to Win*, so I was positive that little exchange would be broadcast out hundreds of times.

I sat back with a smile.

"Girl, give in already," Taylor said.

I twisted around in my seat. "Oh, look who came up for air."

She and Mac stared back at me with zero chagrin. None. Those two. Once they decided to cross the line from friends to lovers, it was full steam ahead and no looking back. I didn't think they'd spent a night apart since Girls' Night In at the Idlewild. I rolled my eyes at the two of them.

"Whatevs. What are you talking about?"

Taylor smirked. "Just go head on and admit that Mal is your man, you two are back in love . . ."

"If you ever fell out . . ." Mac added.

"And that your happily ever after is just around the corner."

I shook my head in denial. "My life is in Belle Haven."

"Your man is in Houston," Eloise stated.

"He's not my man!" I protested. "Or at least, he won't be for long."

At this Valentine stepped in. "Child, what are you talking about?"

"I'm sorry, Mrs. Knight, but this is how it starts. It's all fun and football and freak—um, fondness and then it goes to hell."

"What goes to hell?"

"Our relationship. Sooner or later, it's not enough for Mal and he turns mean and I turn clingy and then it falls apart."

Eloise said. "You make it sound like a pattern. It happened once. Years ago, when neither of you knew what you were doing."

"Yeah, but—I want to teach, I want to finish renovating my house, I don't want to be the trophy of a football player." Uncomfortable silence fell since I was literally sitting in the middle of the football trophy club.

Valentine dropped her voice. "Girl, you are doing the most. Who says you can't teach, who says you can't finish the house. You have a car, airplane tickets, no chains trapping you in the attic. Do you? And you can't be a trophy if you don't let someone treat you like a trophy. You hear me?"

"Yes, ma'am."

"Cari, you know all those times I told you that you could have it all?" my mom asked.

"Yeah."

"That's some bull. Sorry, you can't have it all."

"What?! Mom!"

"Sorry, baby, I wanted you to feel empowered, but you're old enough to know the truth. The truth is that we are not Superwoman. We can only be great at a few things at a time. Now you have to decide what you want to be great at. You can pick two or three things but not everything."

Taylor fell back in her seat with her mouth dropped open. "Why doesn't anyone tell us these things?"

Valentine patted her on the thigh. "You girls only hear what you want anyway. Eloise is telling the truth. Now, I was a doctor's wife, a teacher, a mother, and I sat on the city council. Some days I was a great wife. Some years I was a great mother. Most of the time I was good teacher and I had my moments on the city council. But I wasn't going to give up the wife and mother part. Everything else could suffer but not those, understand."

"I can't have it all and I have to decide what I want."

"Basically." Eloise nodded.

"I just don't know." I shook my head. I guess it was time for me to take Dr. Julie up on her suggestion that I figure out what my happily ever after was supposed to look like.

"Whatever you decide, don't be all year about it," Valentine said. "My son deserves to have somebody by his side who will stick it out when it's all lights and glitter like today and when it all comes to an end."

Something in her tone made me frown. "I'm there for him."

"You weren't when he needed you. When he got hurt, he needed you. But you were hurt so you let him suffer alone. Now, you both were young and mistakes were made, but I expect more from you, Carissa. Don't let me down."

I noticed my mom nodding along. "Et tu, Mother?"

"Truth is the truth no matter who's telling it."

"Aw, girl, just give in. It's easier in the long run," Taylor said as Mac slipped an arm around her and kissed her forehead.

"You two make me sick," I teased with a grin.

"Hater in the house," Mac sang.

The crowd roared around us and I swung back around to see Malachi streaking down the sideline for a thirty-yard run. "He looks good out there today."

"That's my boy." Valentine beamed proudly.

"That's my man," I corrected her with a smile. Now, what was I going to do with him?

30

What would that look like

"So." Dr. Julie peered at us over the top of her glasses. "Last session. Give me a few words to describe how you feel?" The cameras swung toward us and awaited our answers.

"Tired," I said baldly.

"Over it." Carissa nodded.

"Hungry." We'd stayed up watching movies last night and then overslept and had to race here to make it on time.

"Starving!"

"Is 'red ta go' considered a word?" I asked.

"Only in Louisiana, babe." Carissa patted my hand.

We were in Dr. Julie's makeshift office at the host hotel for *Losing to Win*. When they announced that we had to attend a wrap-up session with the life coach, everyone groaned. This was the only time both Carissa and I could come in due to my practice and travel schedule. We were limping into the last part of the show and we were more than ready to wrap it up—though wrapping it up meant discussing what came next and that was an area where Carissa was dragging her heels.

Dr. Julie started talking about setting continuous achievable life goals and I held in a snort of laughter. She wouldn't find two more goal-oriented people than we were. I tuned out the rest of Dr. Julie's lecture and allowed my eyes to wander along Carissa's frame. Though I doubted she'd find it so, I thought it was funny that she was dressed in a T-shirt and wide-leg pants and had her hair pulled back so that her outfit and hair were similar to how she'd looked when the show ambushed her a few months ago. But this time her clothes fit and flattered. Her skin was glowing with good health. Her smile was wide and genuine. Her chin was lifted at a jaunty tilt and her eyes were bright. The time had restored more than her shape. She was back to being Carissa Wayne.

Her hair bounced as her head swung toward me. "Malachi, are you listening?" she asked me.

"No. No, I'm not." I shrugged.

She smirked. "What are you doing? Daydreaming?"

Dr. Julie smiled. "He's looking at you, dear. He hasn't taken his eyes off you for the past ten minutes."

"Oh, really?" She quirked a brow.

"Tell me, Malachi," Dr. Julie probed. "When you look at Carissa, what do you see?"

Finally, a question I liked. "I see beauty and

strength, intelligence and charm. But I always saw that in her."

"What's different about what you see now than what you saw a few months ago?"

"Now I see the future; before, I only saw the past."

Carissa blinked and her eyes went wide.

Dr. Julie asked her, "A future with Malachi . . . What would that look like, Carissa?"

She looked completely panicked. "I don't know, I haven't—I don't . . . I'm not sure."

"You haven't thought about it at all?" Dr. Julie asked incredulously.

I watched her squirm her way to an answer. "I didn't say that. I'm just not ready to decide what the long-term future is going to look like."

"Hmm. That seems selfish." I was glad Dr. Julie said it because I was surely thinking it.

"I beg your pardon?"

"You do realize your decisions affect other people? There's Mal, the place where you work, the kids you teach, your family and friends, and let's not get into Jordan."

"No, let's not," I agreed hastily. The thought that dude was lurking just around the corner waiting for me to mess up so he could swoop in remained a thorn in my side.

"I do understand I'm not an island anymore. Thank you, Dr. Julie," Carissa said sharply.

In an instant, my patience snapped. "I guess I don't know what more I can do to prove that I'm worth your time and trust. Have I let you down once this summer?"

She jumped a little at my question. "No."

"Have I ignored you, flirted with random women, or made anyone or anything else a higher priority than you?"

"No," she answered in a small voice.

"So please tell me, educate me, teach me—what's it gonna take?"

"I don't know. Time, maybe?"

"Maybe?"

"Well, you're putting me on the spot, Mal."

"Putting YOU on the spot? I'm on the spot. I'm on the hot seat every damn day. I've got reporters asking me about you. I have teammates teasing me. I have your friends and family plus my friends and family warning me to do right by you. Telling me to do the right thing. I'm trying to do the right thing. What are you trying to do?"

"I'm just trying to live!" She flung her arms up.

"Wow. If I said that to you, you'd call me selfish and tell me I hadn't changed."

"What's your point?"

"My point is maybe it's time you owned up to your part in the soap opera of Carissa and Mal, don't you think?"

"What did *I* do?"

"Well, I can't make a relationship work alone and I can't break a relationship alone. But I can't read your mind, Cari. I couldn't then and I can't now. If I'm not doing what you want, giving you what you need, if you're upset or feel mistreated, you have to say something and speak it plain. Don't wait until it gets unbearable and then bounce." I sat back in the chair and crossed my arms, belatedly wishing I hadn't said all of that with cameras rolling.

"So you're mad."

"I'm frustrated."

"You're still sitting here."

"Right, you're the one who leaves when she's upset. I stick."

She winced. "Oh. Direct hit. I guess I never apologized for that."

"For what?"

"Bailing and stealing your new car. And not coming back when you got hurt. That was tacky of me."

"It was."

She got up and slid into my lap. "I'm not perfect either."

"Oh yeah?" I mocked her and looped my arms around her waist.

"But I'm still here. I'm here with you."

"That's not going to be enough for long."

"I understand." She kissed my cheek.

I turned toward Dr. Julie. "Are we done?"

She chuckled. "You two do a better job of counseling each other than I could. Stay like that. Be open with each other and remember that there's a reason you've been in each other's orbit for all these years."

We both blinked at her because she lost us with that orbit comment.

Dr. Julie stood up and extended a hand. "It's been a pleasure working with both of you. I expect to hear great things about you in the future."

We shook her hand and exited without a single look back.

"As an apology for jacking your Benz, how

about I buy you breakfast?" Carissa joked and took my hand in hers.

"This better be a hell of a breakfast."

"Are you really still mad about it?"

"Do you think if I was mad about it I would've paid it off?"

"Good point. Then you can buy *me* breakfast."

I shook my head. "Always so high maintenance." We were cutting through the lobby when Niecy and Meshach got off the elevator.

"Who's buying breakfast?" Niecy asked.

Carissa raised her hand. "I have a car note to pay off."

"What?" They looked at her in confusion as we laughed.

"Everybody order the lobster omelet," I teased. "That's all I have to say about that."

31

This I know for sure

"**M**an, you were lighting it up out there today."
Coach Haines slapped me on the shoulder as we
jogged into the tunnel toward the locker room.

"Thanks, Coach!" I grinned and high-fived a
fan hanging over the edge of the stadium seating.
We'd just finished our last preseason game. If I do
say so myself, we beat the hell out of Cleveland. I
had over one hundred receiving yards in the first
half alone, scoring two touchdowns before they
told me I was done for the day. The final score was
41–13.

In fact, the past two preseason games had been
monster games for me. I'd never felt better out
there. The routes just seemed to open up for me. I
was bouncing back from hits. The quarterback was
young but talented, with an eye for picking apart
defenses. He was a second-year guy out of USC, his

spirals were some of the best I'd seen, and he knew how to get the ball into a tight pocket.

We'd been taking some extra time to practice together and were already getting into a rhythm that made us tough to stop if we had the ball in our hands. I liked the chemistry of the team. There were no underachieving showboats, and everybody believed that with the talent and the depth we had on the roster, this team could go deep into the playoffs. With some teams, you just had that feeling that excellence was the standard. It was the best possible situation for me.

As long as I stayed healthy and kept my head in the game, all things were possible. A year ago I couldn't and wouldn't have dreamed that everything would fall into place. I had Carissa waiting just outside, I had teammates I believed in. I had everything back that I loved.

"Blue Streak, what are you trying to prove out there?" Kenny, my offensive tackle, broke into my thoughts as he caught up to me by the lockers. "Damn, we know you're back and better than before. Quit making the rest of us look bad."

"Just trying to earn my pay," I said before adding with a grin, "But I can't help it if you young slackers can't keep up." At thirty-three years of age, I was considered one of the old heads in the locker room. This game was the first one where the coaches decided to start me over the young wideout, Ossie Wallace. Wallace was drafted in the first round. Though I felt a twinge about snatching the youngster's spot from him, it was best he learned about competition at this level early in his career. No matter your draft rank, no one was going to give you anything out on the field. You had to fight for it, earn it, and take it.

"Well, you're earning it," Coach Haines announced. "And you'll be the starter, our number-one receiver on opening day. Ossie will learn a lot under you."

Yes! I thought, holding back the fist pump I longed to do. Instead I smiled modestly before saying, "Feels good to be back. I won't let you down."

"You've made a believer out of me," the receivers coach seconded. I nodded and drew the jersey over my head.

"I appreciate that, Coach."

"Before we let the reporters in, let me say a few words," Coach Haines announced. "Great win out there. Great effort for everyone: offense, defense, and special teams. It's rare that we can put together a team this solid. We play like this the rest of the year and we'll be unstoppable. I don't know about you guys, but I could use a big pretty ring for this finger." He held up his hand. "Who's with me? Stars on three. 1 – 2 – 3 . . ."

"Stars!" we all chanted.

"One last thing . . . Game ball goes to the guy who, if he keeps up at this pace, will be comeback player of the year. Malachi Knight." He handed the game ball to me.

I grabbed it and raised it up. "Thanks, guys. You can't imagine what this means to me. Couldn't have imagined a better group of men to welcome me back to the league."

"All right, Hollywood—don't tear up on us now," Isaac, a defensive back who was still on the team from a few years back, called out, and everyone laughed.

"Ah, why I gotta be Hollywood?" I protested with good humor.

Just then the locker-room doors opened and a slew of reporters came in. "Malachi, how do you feel after today's win?" the first one called out.

"We saw Carissa outside, she's looking good," another shouted at me.

"Have you finished filming the last segment of *Losing to Win*?" And another joined in.

"And that's why you gotta be Hollywood," Isaac pointed out.

I shrugged it off. What could I say? The spotlight was definitely shining brightest on me right now. I raised the ball back up. "Thanks again, fellas." Then I held up one finger to the reporters. "Give me one second, guys." I hurried over to my locker and pulled out my phone. I had learned my lesson about keeping Carissa waiting on me. Quickly, I sent her a text. Swamped with reporters. Wanna wait or meet me at home? I pressed SEND.

Pierre's coming in. I'll be at restaurant when you finish up. She answered.

I'm starving, order me a steak!

Excuse me, Baller. You gotta keep in field shape. I'll order you the salmon and you'll like it. She added a smiley face.

We had one last weigh-in for *Losing to Win*. We were so far ahead in the points it was almost impossible for us to lose at this point, but we weren't taking any chances. *Whatever you say, ma'am.*

Damn right. She sent back, causing me to chuckle to myself. I looked up to find the press corps grinning at me.

The on-field reporter from the NFL Network held out her mic. "Whenever you're ready, Mal."

Pierre walked in and came over. "Good game, 84."

"I didn't suck." I smirked at him before turning to face the reporters and take questions.

It was forty-five minutes, a shower, and what seemed like a million repetitive questions later that I tightened the knot on my tie and climbed behind the wheel while Pierre slid in beside me. I locked the doors and started the car.

"I have news," he announced in a calm voice.

"Yeah?" Pierre was dramatic and liked to tell things in his own good time.

"Nike called."

I slammed on the brakes in the middle of reversing and swiveled my head in his direction. "What?!"

"And they aren't the only ones. We got over a dozen nibbles looking to sign Mal Knight to endorsement deals."

"Really? Already? I haven't even played a regular season game yet." Things were happening so fast, and this time, I was determined not to let it go to my head. I had to admit to being flattered, though.

"Keep driving, I'm hungry. Anyway, I guess Corporate America likes what they see. And everybody loves a triumphant comeback story."

"Is that what I am? A comeback story?"

"Man, c'mon. You were the epitome of done, sitting on the sofa packing on pounds. You were a few years away from a 'whatever happened to that guy' segment on ESPN. Look at you now."

"I guess so."

"Have you taken a second to let it sink in?"

I could admit to Pierre that I was a little bit dazed. You make a plan, you work toward the goal, and it's hard to recognize when you've arrived. "A little bit. Carissa and I were talking about it a few weeks ago. It's hard to believe we are here. Again."

"It's different this time, right?"

"Oh, definitely. Everything is just a bit sweeter the second time around."

"Your profile with the show and now with your performance on the field—the sky is the limit. We should be able to write our own ticket after this year."

"Wow. It's happening so fast."

"Isn't this what you wanted?"

"It was. It is. Just feels like something's missing."

"What? Carissa's here, you're back. We're about to get paid. Life is good."

"Is she really here, though? Like, all in?" I caught myself voicing the question that had been circling in my mind for a few weeks.

"What do you mean? You don't think she's in it

for the long haul? That doesn't sound like Carissa Wayne."

"Tell me about it. The woman who has every area of her life planned and color coordinated is being deliberately vague. I can't nail her down. Every time I try to talk about the future, she shuts down or changes the subject."

"Well, that's . . ." Pierre paused.

"Awkward?" I suggested.

" 'Troublesome' was the word I was going with."

"Frustrating," I amended.

"It's ironic, really." Pierre shrugged.

"How so?"

"Well, here you are with the world at your feet and the one thing you really want is the one thing you're not sure you can have. Irony."

"Yeah." My lips twisted. "Thanks for sharing that."

"You're welcome. But what's the rush? You two have all the time in the world."

"You would think so, wouldn't you? But I'm feeling kind of urgent. I hate to go all sensitive, P. The truth is, I want that commitment, I want her locked down. We've come too far for me to lose her now."

"You don't really think you're gonna lose her to Jordan, do you? She doesn't seem all that into him from what I've seen."

"Yeah, I don't know. He's the safe bet. He gets a woman like Carissa, he'll never do anything to mess it up. I can't make that guarantee. Shit, I'm not perfect."

"Oh, this I know. I gotta say, though, I don't think Jordan wins in the end. I just don't."

"I don't want to lose to anything or anybody."

"Then sit her down and force her to talk about it."

I sent him an incredulous look. "Are you kidding me? Ah . . . no. Imposing my will upon her is what sent her running to the next state last time. This time, she's gotta come to it on her own. When she decides what she wants, I'll be here hoping it's me."

"Whoa, look at you."

"What?" I took my eyes off the road once more to slide him an irritated glance.

"You're all new, Malachi. Sensitive and shit. Let me see if I can get you a Hallmark commercial or Kleenex."

"I told Carissa I was Malachi 2.0," I admitted.

"Damn, Dr. Phil, wanna hug it out?"

"Kiss my ass."

He snorted. "And just like that, the real Malachi Knight's back."

It was the perfect time to pull up outside the restaurant; Pierre's snarky witticisms were on my nerves. I tossed my keys to the valet and strode inside. I caught sight of Carissa right away. She was wearing the amazing red dress we'd bought in New Orleans. Niecy and Shach were sitting with her. When she saw me heading her way, her face lit up and she looked relieved. My girl still didn't 100 percent trust me. But I figured a lifetime of doing the right thing by her would fix that soon enough.

A few people tried to stop me on my way to her, but I grinned and waved and kept moving. Reaching the table, I leaned down and kissed her. "Greetings, Carissa Wayne."

"Hey, Rock Star." She grinned. "Good game today."

"He was all right," Pierre teased and sat down.

"Stop it." She swatted his arm. "My man rocked."

That was all I needed to hear to make my day. One positive word from her and I felt like Superman. I dropped into the booth beside her and slid my arm around her. "I did all right, didn't I?"

"So much so that you deserve a treat."

"Oh yeah?" I raked my eyes across the bare skin showing.

Shach laughed. "Think with a different body part, bro, your lascivious intentions are showing."

"Can you blame a brother?" I stroked my hand down Carissa's arm; her skin was incredibly soft.

She shivered under my touch and beamed. "Behave, Malachi. Here it is."

A waiter walked up carrying sizzling platters of food. He slid a huge dish in front of me. "Good evening, Mr. Knight, I understand you prefer your steak medium well."

I looked down at the perfectly grilled ribeye swimming in butter on the plate and almost teared up. Life was damn good. "You're a good woman, Carissa."

"Best believe it." She met my eyes.

"Oh, I absolutely do." Tearing my gaze from hers, I picked up my knife and fork. "I'm about to commit a crime on this plate. Are we being filmed tonight?"

Niecy shook her head. "They're waiting for us at a restaurant across town. We totally gave them the slip."

"Good people, let's eat."

32

Tell us, how do you feel?

Carissa—Thursday, September 10—7:42 p.m.

"With a combined weight loss of close to one hundred pounds and our highest point total ever, the winners of this year's *Losing to Win* are Carissa Wayne and Malachi Knight. Tell us, how do you feel?" Jim asked gleefully. We were in the grand ballroom of the Westin Galleria in Houston taping the show's finale. There was not one of us who wasn't ready to be over and done with this show. I was in a clingy peacock blue tank dress that I would not wear again after tonight. It was great that I fit in the size 6, but that didn't mean I wanted to showcase all the goods. I preferred to dress with a little more mystery. The five-inch stilettos were a no-go as well. They were silver and sparkly and cute but hurt like hell. I was never one to sacrifice comfort for cute. Mal was in a black suit that emphasized the broad expanse of his shoulders and the taper down to his waist. He shifted closer and gave me a look indicating that it was my turn to talk.

Since we were finally nearing the end, I was able to dial up the good-humored smile one more time. "I feel great, Jim, really terrific. Every day has been a monumental struggle, but I can truly say it's all been worth it in the end," I responded graciously. It was easy to be gracious now that the experience was over.

Honestly, the whole television part of it was a giant pain in the ass. The lack of privacy, the intrusion into and disruption of day-to-day living, the pseudocelebrity status? Hated it. But working out, spending time with people I liked (Suzette excluded), and getting paid for it? That part turned out okay. Even though I had dreaded reconnecting with Malachi, finally putting the past in the past was worth it as well.

"Mal, what about you?"

He grinned widely. "What can I tell you, Jim? This show has given me back the things and people that are important to me. I feel great." I made sure to keep my face neutral.

"You're the starting receiver for the Houston Stars. What are your immediate plans?"

"Play football, see if I can talk a certain lady into spending more time with me, and maybe eat a burger. Not necessarily in that order."

Just then, they brought out a gigantic paper check with our names on it. Confetti and balloons fell from the ceiling, and Mal and I struck a pose holding the million-dollar check.

"What are you going to do with the money?" Jim asked, being intrusive for hopefully the last time.

Mal and I had discussed this so our answer was prepared. "After helping out a few folks in Belle Haven, we'll be opening up the Wayne-Knight foundation," Mal supplied. "The purpose of the foundation is to reach out to teens who want the opportunity to go on to a facility of higher education. We're going to provide counseling and activities and scholarship opportunities."

Jim looked stunned. "Wow, that's impressive."

I offered up another smile. "Well, we both believe in giving back. Community activism has long been a goal of ours."

"Any other projects, maybe of a more personal nature, that you want to tell us about?" Jim prompted.

Mal leveled a hard stare his direction. "Nothing we'd care to share with the viewing public at this time."

"You know I had to try." Jim tried for an innocent look.

"Yes. We know," I responded.

"All right, then." He went back into glitzy announcer-speak. "Great season! Best of luck to you two and all of our contestants. Until next year, you have been watching *Losing to Win*! Good night, everybody!"

"And cut!" Bliss called out. "That's a wrap. We'll get everybody back together for a reunion show later in the year or in January, depending on schedules. It's been our best season ever!"

I was a wreck. I hadn't slept well last night. I

unclipped the microphone and handed Malachi the giant check. We'd already deposited the real one into an account.

"Carissa, can we have a moment?" Bliss asked.

I nodded as Jordan also called out, "Can I see you for a minute or two as well?"

Oh. Okay, then. Mal folded his arms and looked at me. His expression very clearly asked, "What are you going to do?"

Well, this was it. I exhaled a shaky breath. I had to make decisions about the future right now. I had put it off and ducked it and avoided questions and hints and probes for months. It was time to pay the piper. In my mind, I still flip-flopped. Take a chance on Jordy or stick with Mal? Houston or Belle Haven? Was staying with Mal a move forward or a step back? Would I eventually feel for Jordy what I knew was there with Mal? *Come on, Carissa, choose already!* My internal dialogue was going a mile a minute.

"Bliss, can you give me a few minutes?" Without waiting for a response, I turned to Mal. "See you at home in a little while." I took a step toward Jordan. "Come walk with me for a sec, Jordy." I paused at the sound of Malachi's voice calling my name.

"I'll be waiting," he announced with significant snap to his voice before exiting in the opposite direction.

There was a small hospitality suite set up as a dressing room on the right side of the ballroom. I ushered Jordy into it and shut the door behind us. So this was it. Lead with my head or my heart? Play it smart or go for broke? What did I want my life to be?

"What's it going to be, Carissa?" Jordan asked without preamble.

"What's next for you? Where are you headed?" I countered.

"I've been wanting to get back to New Orleans for a while. When my marriage fell apart, I started putting some feelers out. I've been offered a partnership in a program to counsel at-risk kids in New Orleans. With or without you, I'm headed back there."

"Then I guess I'll see you next weekend when I come visit." The words coming out of my mouth surprised me.

"As . . . a friend?" he probed.

"As a friend who'd like to be more."

His face lit up. "Really? You're leaving Mal?"

That was what I didn't want. I didn't want it to be a Jordy versus Mal thing. It was about what was best for me. I wanted a good guy that I could trust and build something with. Someone who would always put me first and have my back no matter what. To my way of thinking, it was just a matter of time before the fame and the glam life transformed Mal into that guy I left before. I was cutting my losses before that happened. I couldn't put myself at risk like that. Not again. If it all fell apart, I wasn't sure I could put the pieces back together again. Maybe I was running scared, but I was running to where I knew I'd be safe. "What I'm doing is exploring an opportunity for a relationship with you."

He stared at me insistently seeking clarification. "But no Mal."

"No Mal," I repeated.

"You haven't told him yet," Jordan observed.

"I have not. But I will tonight. I'll head back to Belle Haven right after."

Jordan tugged me into his arms. "I've been patient, but damn, I wanted this day to come."

"You've been extraordinarily patient and understanding," I murmured as I hugged him back. "And I appreciate it."

He pressed a kiss on my forehead before sliding his lips along my jaw to land on my lips. With a murmur, he parted my lips with his tongue and kissed me deeply. Okay, it didn't stir me. It was nice, but I didn't feel the sizzle.

Carissa, I told myself, *sizzle is what got you burned before.* Passion can grow. But I'd be lying if I said that kiss didn't make me feel a little bit guilty. Like I was cheating. I shook off the feeling, squeezed his hands, and stepped back. "I'll see you this weekend. I've got to go."

"I'll be waiting," he promised. He was the second man in the last half hour to say as much. It gave me pause. I waited for a feeling of calm, a validation that I was doing the right thing to settle over me. It didn't come. Instead, I squeezed his hand and went to look for Bliss.

I caught up with the production team a few doors down. Pushing the door open, I made my announcement bluntly. "Hey, guys. I'm not doing the new show."

"Why not?" Marcy pressed.

"Flat out, I don't want to. It's not my thing. I

appreciate the offer and the opportunity, but I'm done."

Ren looked as though he wanted to argue, but Bliss put her hand on his arm. "If you ever change your mind, especially if you and Mal end up together, let us know. Even if it's just to do a wedding show. Really, we'd front the whole thing. Just think about it. You two were ratings gold."

I didn't want to burst her bubble. "Well, thank you, I'll bear that in mind. Safe travels to you all. It's been quite the experience working with you." I headed back into the hallway to find my purse. I ran into Niecy first.

"What did you just do?" she asked angrily.

"Why?" I took a step back.

"I know you. I know that look on your face. It says I've done something stupid and now I'm conflicted." She stared me down, waiting for my answer.

This was the blessing and curse with good friends. They knew you even when you didn't want them to. I sighed. "I might be somewhat conflicted. I just did either the smartest or dumbest thing ever."

She literally slammed her hands on her hips and stomped her foot. "Oh Lord, Carissa. Don't tell me you're giving Jordy a chance? I love Jordan, I do. I've spent all summer wondering why a guy like that is willing to wait for a woman who is so clearly meant for someone else. If I thought you could give Jordan what he deserves, I'd back you 100 percent. But this right here is some next-level bullshit." Meshach stepped into the hallway and she waved him away. "Cari, don't do this."

"Don't you think I should try with Jordy?" I wondered.

"Sure. In another lifetime, maybe, when you don't already have the perfect damn lifemate wrapped around your finger. Jesus, Carissa! What are you doing with your life?"

That stung. I really thought she'd applaud my decision. It was the smart thing to do, after all. "Ouch. I thought I was being smart this time."

"Who gives a shit about smart or stupid when it comes to love?" She was borderline screaming at me. "You either love Mal or you don't."

"Um . . ." I couldn't think with all the swirling noise in my head.

"Girl, do not play games right now. Do you or do you not love Malachi Knight?"

"Dammit, of course I do. He is the love of my freakin' life!" I admitted. "But . . ."

"But what? You're in love with Mal, but you're going to try Jordy on for size? How is that fair to either one of them?"

I argued, "What about me? I want to put me first this time."

She rolled her eyes. "I'm sorry. I do not understand. What is it about being with the man you love in a gorgeous home you designed, running the foundation you've always dreamed of that equates to not putting yourself first? Please define this concept for me."

Niecy was really heated with me. Listening to her did cause me to second-guess my thinking. "I just thought . . ."

"You didn't think, you ran scared. That's not

the Carissa Wayne I know. And if you did have a thought rattling around in that mind of yours, maybe you thought that you owed Mal a little payback for how things went last go-round and this was your chance to get it. You went and got all thin and successful and now another man, a great man, wants you. So now you can say, 'Take that, Mal Knight!' "

"That's not how it is," I claimed, weakly wondering if that wasn't a little part of what it was.

"Is that what's going on here, Carissa? Am I the rebound guy to make your ex know what he's missing?" Jordan asked softly from behind me. Niecy whistled low and disappeared behind a door. I hadn't even realized Jordan was still in the building.

I pivoted slowly. "Jordy . . ."

He put his hands up. "Never mind. I overheard you say that you still love Mal. You called him the love of your life. Were you hoping that falling in love with me would help you fall out of love with him?"

"That's really not what I was thinking." But damned if I could explain at that moment exactly how I thought this would all work out.

"I don't want to convince a woman—you especially—to fall in love with me. I had one woman leave because she thought I wasn't what she wanted. I don't need to go through that again. I won't go through that again. I don't want to be with you looking over my shoulder for the next Malachi Knight sighting, wondering if that time will be the inevitable time when he takes you away from me. I'm not going to be that guy."

"I wouldn't do that to you, Jordy. If we're to-gether, it would be you and me," I protested.

"You wouldn't want to do it to me, but I think we both know that in the end, Mal is the guy you're going to be with. He's the guy you're sup-posed to be with, apparently. I knew this, but I had to try. You know this, but you won't admit it for whatever reason. Either way, I definitely don't want to be the guy you chose because you thought I was the safe pick. I want to be the one who brings a sparkle to your eyes when you enter the room; I want your breath to catch when I step near. I want to be the only one who makes you feel that way. I deserve to be the love of someone's life."

In that instant, I got it. And I felt more than a little ashamed for what I had almost done to this nice guy who did nothing wrong but want to be with me. I flung my arms around him and squeezed. "I'm so sorry, Jordy. You don't know how much I really want you to be that guy." It would be so much easier if I was head over heels in love with Jordy. But of course, I couldn't do things the easy way.

Jordan sighed and returned my hug, adding a platonic little pat on my shoulder. "I'm torn be-tween being really, really flattered and really in-sulted."

I laughed and kissed his cheek. "Be flattered. I've loved Mal Knight all of my adult life and the only guy I have ever thought about replacing him with is you."

He gave a rueful grin and backed away. "I'll take that as my consolation prize. A part of me

knew this is how it was going to end. Be well,
Carissa Wayne."

"You do the same, Jordan Little." I felt even
worse that he was so damn nice about it.

With a last wave good-bye, I turned back toward the ballroom to resume the search for my
purse. Niecy fell into step beside me. "Um, hey,
girl. You're going to need to hurry on home. You
got some explaining to do to your man."

"What, why?" How did Mal already know what
happened?

"Meshach dropped dime on ya. Sorry. I tried to
stop him and he didn't get the whole story; his
eavesdropping abilities aren't as good as mine. He's
been on the phone to Mal three times already."

"Dammit!" I gave her a one-armed hug and
sped up. "I gotta go. You heading to New Orleans?"

"We're stopping in Belle Haven first, but yeah,
New Orleans after that," she declared happily. I
was glad it looked like things were working out for
Meshach and Niecy. Now I had to go repair my
own relationship I had foolishly endangered.

"So happy for you, and thank you for talking
some sense into my thick head."

"I'll send you a bill and thanks, girl. Where are
you going to be?" she queried.

"I'll let you know when I figure it out." Dropping all pretenses, I spied my purse, scooped it up,
and ran like hell for the parking garage. I needed
to get home. To Mal.

33

I would've been the beggingest, pleadingest man you ever saw

Malachi—Thursday, September 10—9:07 p.m.

"**M**al?" Carissa called out as she came in through the garage door. I mentally prepared myself for what was coming next. Deliberately I shifted on the sofa so I looked casual and calm when she entered the room.

"I'm in here," I called out and picked up my iPad. *Just stay calm, Mal,* I told myself. *Whatever she says, you can handle it. You've handled worse. You lost her before, you could survive it again.* I shook my head and exhaled as she walked in the room. "Hey."

She paused tentatively inside the door. "Meshach called you?"

"He did," I replied tonelessly.

"Do I want to know what he told you?"

Suddenly I was out of patience. "Just tell me what you have to say, Carissa."

"Promise me you won't get mad?"

I laughed shortly. "I absolutely cannot make that promise."

She took a short step forward. "Promise me you'll hear me out."

"That I can do."

"I really thought . . . I'm really scared . . . The thing that has me worried is . . ."

Now I was worried. Carissa did not stutter. I set the iPad down and pushed to an upright position, focusing all my attention on her.

"My thought was—what if I go all in with Mal and he breaks my heart again?"

"What if you break mine again?"

"Again?" she asked in confusion.

"You broke mine when you left."

"You broke mine way before that."

I nodded. "So you've said."

"I don't think you get what that night did to me."

"The night you left?"

"The night you belittled me, ignored me, and treated me like a bothersome groupie for the last time."

"Again, I apologize. I do know I acted like a dick, but no, I didn't realize it felt that way to you. I never meant to make you feel that way."

"Okay. But understand that I vowed not to let anyone make me feel that way again. Ever."

There was nothing I could say to take back that night or the ones like it that had come before so I just clasped my hands. "I can't take it back. I can only apologize and promise to do better. Your feelings in that regard are understandable."

She continued. "My fear was and still is that all

of this"—she gestured to the house; the television coincidently was tuned to the NFL Network where they were showing my last touchdown—"is going to go to your head. I'm afraid you'll lose your way and I'll get shifted to the back. Don't get me wrong; you've been great this summer and these past few months. It's been great. But I don't want to live in your shadow, Mal."

"I don't want you to. I never did. I just sucked at juggling priorities and making sure we were on the same page. I did a piss-poor job of keeping my eyes on what's really important, but that's never going to happen again, Ris."

"It's not?"

"It's not," I reiterated firmly. "I'm not that guy. I lost everything. Everything that really mattered to me. I would have given up the house, the cars, the bank accounts to get you back."

"What about football? Would you give up football to get me back?" she said in a voice a little above a whisper.

My breath whooshed out and I considered my words carefully before I spoke. I knew that whatever I said next would determine our future. "If it came down to either football or you? I'd choose you. I won't pretend it wouldn't be hard as hell, but for you, I would do it. Do you want me to do it? I can walk away and we can run the foundation together. We've got money in the bank; I've got a few things lined up. We can call a press conference and be packed up and in Belle Haven in three days' time."

"I wouldn't ask you to do that." She launched herself at me and I caught her close. "I love you too much to ask that of you. I love you, Mal—football, fame, and all. I can't pretend that I'd prefer we weren't so high profile right now. I hate this part of the game, the fans and the fame, but football is what you love and this comes with you. I want you complete when you're with me."

"Am I with you?"

"You're with me."

"And you love me?"

"I never stopped."

The vice grip that had been squeezing my heart loosened and things inside of me shifted from frightened to content. "What took you so long to tell me?"

"I couldn't. If I said it, it was real."

"What about Jordan?" I asked.

She pulled back to meet my gaze. "I won't lie to you. I told him I'd give you up and try with him."

I winced. "I hope he knows you lied to him."

"He called me on it before I had to take it back. We parted as friends."

"Um-hmm. Distant friends who rarely see each other. Did you really think I would let you go that easily?"

Her eyes widened. "What would you have done?"

I shifted her closer to me. "Made both of your lives a holy hell. Every off day I had I would have been at your spot pleading 'please, baby; baby, please.' Every interview I would have been begging and singing, 'Until you come back to me, that's what I'm gonna do.' Girl, I would've been the beggingest, pleadingest man you ever saw."

She dissolved into giggles. "Thank God we're spared that."

"I was terrified you were coming over here tonight to tell me you were leaving me for him."

"I almost did," she admitted in a small voice.

"That cuts." That cut to the bone. I came that close to losing her.

"But I came to my senses. I'm here, Mal. I'm here to stay."

"What about Belle Haven?"

"Mac can finish working on the house, especially since I need to expand the master suite to fit a certain pro baller."

"Damn right. A brother needs some closet space."

She rolled her eyes. "When I checked in with the administrators at Havenwood, it's pretty clear they are okay with offering the substitute teacher my full-time position. Apparently, I've become more of a disruption than a guiding force."

"I don't want you to give up teaching if you love it," I protested.

"Give up teaching high schoolers at a private school? I think I'll survive the loss. I'd rather concentrate on getting the foundation up and running here and in Belle Haven. That's the real kind of mentoring and teaching I want to do. I want to reach the kids we can help the most. There are teenagers hungry for education everywhere. We can show kids that education is a chance for a better life."

"Or we can teach them sports," I teased.

"Ri-ight because so many kids make it to the pros from Belle Haven, Louisiana. But you know, it might not be a bad idea to do a summer workshop combining our interests, either here or in Belle Haven." Her eyes lit up talking about it.

"Sports and Shakespeare might actually be cool."

"We'll make it so." She hugged me tighter.

I nodded and stroked my hand up and down her back. "We'll split our time. Off season in Belle Haven, season here in Houston for however much longer I play."

"So we'll be here a while, then."

"Ris?"

"Yeah?"

"Can I ask you something?"

"Yeah."

"Marry me?" I held my breath and waited for her answer.

After a beat or two, she asked. "Really?"

"Really. After the season, let's go somewhere tropical."

"Belize?"

"Why Belize?"

"Why not?"

"Why not indeed?" I reached into a drawer on the coffee table and pulled out a small box. I saw the expression on her face. With an inward grin, I opened the lid and turned it toward her.

"Oh!" She exclaimed as her eyes lit up and she reached for the ring.

"You thought I'd give you the same ring? You hated that thing," I teased her. This was a three-carat, brilliant-cut sapphire surrounded with round diamonds. Much more her style.

She held out her finger.

"Is that a yes?"

"That's a yes. I love it."

"And me?"

"And you too."

I slid the ring onto her finger. "This is it, woman. You and me. We're done being stupid with each other."

"This is it. You're stuck with me even if I gain forty pounds, cut off all my hair, and develop an addiction to chocolate truffles."

"You're already addicted to chocolate truffles and I liked you with the extra cushion."

"Mal," she protested.

"I did! More bounce to the ounce." I grinned.

"You're so nasty."

"You like me that way."

"I love you that way."

"Then that's all we need."

Epilogue

We won so much more

"Somehow, when you said we needed to get a workout in this afternoon, I had envisioned something a lot sexier than this," I huffed and raised the arms on the butterfly machine over my head. We were in the gym of the JW Marriott Ihilani Resort and Spa in Kapolei near Honolulu, Hawaii. Malachi walked over and looked at the settings.

"Come on, lightweight, you can do better than that. You were up to eighty pounds on this thing before."

"Yeah, that was before you had me lying around sipping champagne and eating cake," I complained.

"That was one day and I told you it was not necessary for the bride to go back for seconds."

"That cake was like ambrosia, though."

"The cake was my choice, if you recall," he bragged.

"I recall. So we're back around to where it's your fault I'm out of shape."

"First, you are nowhere close to out of shape. I don't think you've gained a pound. And I've done a pretty forensic analysis of your body. But sure, baby. Put the blame on my broad chiseled shoulders, they can take it."

Jerk. He did look amazing. I adjusted the weight and puffed harder through two more reps. "Arrogance does not become you." I swished past him to the leg press.

"But this six pack does. I gotta keep my bedroom physique." He patted his stomach and laughed as I glared at him.

He hopped onto the treadmill and broke into a jog immediately. If he wasn't mine, I'd truly dislike him.

"Before you get too carried away over there, we have to do one last thing tonight."

"Only one?" he said silkily.

I smiled back. "Only one suitable for public viewing."

"What is it? Commercial, interview, shoot?"

"Photo shoot."

"You're almost done with the legs, you got glutes and abs, and we'll go."

I frowned. "What's wrong with my glutes?"

"Not a damn thing. As a matter of fact, if you want to cut this short, we can slide upstairs so I can show my appreciation right quick."

"I don't know. I don't want to keep you from getting your twenty minutes of cardio in."

"You doubt your ability to keep my heart rate up for twenty minutes?"

I hopped off the machine. "You know what; I'll get that heart rate and a few other parts up and pumping. Let's go, player."

It gave me joy to see him almost trip in his haste to leave the treadmill and follow me. I put a little extra sway to my hips for his benefit.

"Oh, we're starting on that heart rate right now, huh?"

"You know it."

"Carissa! Mal! One more, over here," the photographers called out as we attempted to stroll casually along the beach in front of the hotel. To the left of the random photographers were the crew members from the network.

"This is your fault," I muttered as we turned, smiled, posed.

"Your idea." He leaned down and nuzzled my neck.

"How do you figure?" I asked and stretched up on tiptoe to graze his lips with a kiss.

"You knew when you mentioned that the network would foot the bill for this wedding if we agreed to let them film the whole event that I was going to be all in."

"Cheap ass," I teased.

"Hell yeah. The league was already paying to send us here for the Pro Bowl. Moving the wedding from Belize to Hawaii and having someone else pick up the tab was a no-brainer."

"Yet here we are again on display for all the world to see."

We clasped hands and strolled slowly, pretending like we didn't have a slew of cameras aimed at us.

"Woman, did we not fly your fam and mine out here for free?"

"We did."

"Did we not feed two hundred people grilled lobster for free?"

"We did."

He picked me up and swung me around. "Are we not Mr. and Mrs. Malachi Knight?"

I flung my head back and chortled with glee. "We are!"

"There you go."

I got the signal from Bliss that they had enough footage for what they needed. Mal set me back on my feet and we headed in the opposite direction of the cameras. "If only you hadn't won the Super Bowl and the Super Bowl MVP and the Comeback Player of the Year award. Damn overachiever."

"Yeah, sorry I didn't suck."

"All that success made this a complete circus."

"You know how I do."

"Bringing the contestants over and combining the reunion show for *Losing to Win* was a smart idea too. A pain in the ass, but a smart idea."

He nodded. "Even Suzette was pleasant for once."

"Free trip to Hawaii? Damn right she put a smile on her face and showed up. So who's next, do you think? Tay and Mac? Shach and Niecy? Sugar and Lee? Even Jordy showed up with a cute woman on his arm."

"I wouldn't bet against any of them," Mal shared as we quickstepped through the lobby toward the elevators. We slid inside and smiled at each other.

"It's funny," I started.

"What's funny?"

"The show that I dreaded doing? That I hated the very idea of? Turned out all right."

He nodded. "Did a lot of good for a lot of people. We've got the foundation up and running. Belle Haven is actually a tourist spot. A bunch of friends got hooked up. Pretty much win-win. Especially since we did win."

I rolled my eyes at him. "We won the show, yes."

"We won so much more." He pulled me close as the doors opened onto our floor.

I walked backward toward our suite. "C'mon, Mr. Knight. Now that we've satisfied the cameras, let's get some honeymooning on."

"Whatever you say, Mrs. Knight."

"Now that's what I like to hear." I slid the DO NOT DISTURB sign on the handle and let the door swing shut behind us.

Don't miss

Best Kept Secrets

The explosive first book in the Chesterton
Scandals series by Shelly Ellis.
On sale in September 2015!

Chapter 1

Leila Hawkins paused as she mounted the last concrete step in front of the double doors of the First Good Samaritan Baptist Church—one of the oldest and largest churches in Chesterton, Virginia, her hometown. Nestled on Broadleaf Avenue across the street from rustic Macon Park, the house of worship had hosted many a baptism, funeral, and nuptial inside its brick walls in the one hundred and some odd years of its existence. And since 1968, a stark white sign had sat along its exterior, highlighting a Bible verse chosen by the honorable reverend, or the assistant pastor when the reverend was ill or on vacation. Leila stepped aside to let a couple pass as she squinted at that sign, which hung a foot away from the doors and several feet above her head.

A FOOL GIVES FULL VENT TO HIS ANGER, BUT A WISE

MAN KEEPS HIMSELF UNDER CONTROL, the sign read in big bold letters. PROVERBS 29:11.

Her eyebrows furrowed.

What the hell . . .

Was someone reading her mind?

Who cares if they are?

She grabbed one of the church's stainless-steel door handles.

She was on a mission today and she wasn't going to be deterred from it. She was giving "full vent" to her anger, whether any celestial being liked it or not. Leila was crashing this hifalutin wedding, and only lightning bolts or locusts would keep her away!

She walked into the vestibule, then tugged a heavy wooden door open, preparing herself to be met by a hundred stares, finger pointing, and indignation the instant she stepped inside the sanctuary.

"Hey! You're not supposed to be here!" she waited for someone to shout at her.

Instead, she was greeted by a light melody played by a string quartet and the polite chatter of the two hundred and some odd guests who were taking their seats in the velvet-cushioned pews.

No one stared at her. Hell, they barely seemed to notice her!

The tenseness in her shoulders instantly relaxed. Her white-knuckled grip on her satin clutch loosened. She reminded herself that she was walking into a wedding, not a gladiator pit.

"You're here to talk to Evan," a voice in her head cautioned her. "Not to fight with him. Remember?"

*That's right. I'm just here to talk to him, to have a
conversation with an old friend.*

And if Evan chose not to be polite or listen to
her, then and *only then* would she go off on him.

She looked around her.

The sanctuary was filled with splashes of pink
and lavender, which Leila remembered were the
bride's favorite colors. Roses, hydrangeas, freesias,
and lilacs decorated the pulpit and pews, filling
the space with their alluring scent. Ribbons and ivy
garland were draped over anything and everything, and free-standing candelabras were along
each aisle and by the stained-glass windows.

Leila felt an overwhelming sense of déjà vu.
She hadn't set foot in this church since her own
wedding day ten years ago. As she gazed around
her, all the memories of that day came rushing
back like a tsunami: the anticipation and nervous-
ness she had felt as she waited for the church doors
to open, the happiness she had experienced when
she'd seen her handsome groom waiting for her at
the end of the aisle, and the overwhelming sadness
that had washed over her when she had looked at
the wedding guests and had not seen her then best
friend, Evan, among their friendly faces.

But she had known Evan wouldn't come to her
wedding. Stubborn Evan Murdoch had told her in
the plainest way possible that there was no way he
would stand by and pretend that he was happy
about her nuptials.

"That son of a bitch is going to break your
heart," Evan had warned her over the phone all
those years ago when she'd made one last-ditch
effort to ask him to come to the wedding. "He's

going to drag you down. And when he does, don't come crying to me."

Leila wasn't sure what had made her angrier: that Evan had given her that dire, bitter prediction on the eve of her wedding—or that his prediction had come true. But today she would have to put aside all that resentment and anger if she was going to get Evan to do what she needed him to do for her mother. Her mother . . . a proud woman who had juggled multiple jobs and saved every dime she had for decades to gather the money to put Leila through school and give her a reasonably happy life. Leila had tried to repay her by purchasing her a two-bedroom bungalow in a middle-class neighborhood where they still held summer block parties, where neighbors still waved and said hello. But now Leila's mother would lose her home in a few months without Evan's help.

Leila's grip on her purse tightened again.

She'd argue. She'd beg. She'd do what she had to do to get Evan to listen to her.

For Ma's sake, she thought.

"Bride or groom?" someone asked, yanking Leila from her thoughts.

"What?" Leila asked.

She turned to find an usher leaning toward her. An officious-looking woman stood behind him with the kind of pinched face reserved for those who waited at the counter at the DMV and dentists' offices. A clipboard covered with several stacks of paper was in her hands. The woman discreetly whispered something into her headset while the usher continued to gaze at Leila expectantly.

"Are you with the bride or groom?" He gestured toward the pews. "On which side would you like to be seated?"

That was a tricky question. The bride hadn't invited Leila to the wedding; neither had the groom. But Leila certainly knew the bride better. Paulette Murdoch, Evan's sister, was someone Leila had once considered a friend—almost a little sister.

"Umm . . . uh, bride . . . I-I guess," Leila finally answered.

They noticed her hesitation and exchanged a look that Leila couldn't decipher. The woman behind the usher whispered into her headset again and waited a beat.

What? Leila thought with panic. *What did I do wrong?*

The woman stepped forward, plastering on a smile that seemed more forced than friendly.

"I'm sorry. Would you mind giving me your name?"

"Uh . . . why?"

"I just want to make sure you're seated in the proper area." The woman then pulled out a pen and pointed down at the stack of papers. Leila could see several names listed along with check marks next to each of them.

You've gotta be kidding me, Leila thought.

They actually had a guest list for the church! What did they think? Someone was going to sneak into the wedding?

"You are sneaking into Paulette's wedding!" the voice in her head chastised.

But still, this was ridiculous! Leila wondered if the guest list had been Evan's idea.

Wouldn't want the unwashed masses to wander in off the street, would we? Leila thought sarcastically. *Wouldn't want the poor people to stink up the place! Only the best and the brightest for the M&Ms!*

M&Ms or Marvelous Murdochs . . . People had been muttering and snickering over that nickname for decades around Chesterton, using it to derogatorily refer to the Murdochs—one of the most wealthy, respected, and (some said) stuck-up families in town. Of course that was better than their old nickname, the "High Yella Murdochs." That name had faded once the Murdochs became more equal opportunity and let a few darker folks like Evan's mom into the family.

"Well, my . . ." Leila paused, wondering how she was going to get out of this one. She most certainly wasn't on the list. "My name is . . . my name is, uh—"

"Leila! Leila, over here!" someone called to her. Leila turned to find her childhood friend Colleen waving wildly. Colleen sat in one of the pews toward the front of the church.

Saved by the bell!

"Come on, girl!" Colleen shouted, still grinning. "Sit by me!"

"I guess my 'proper area' is up there, then?" Leila asked.

The usher laughed while the woman with the clipboard continued to scrutinize her, not looking remotely amused.

"Go right ahead," he said, waving Leila forward.

She walked down the center aisle to Colleen. As she did so, she ran her hands across the front of her pale yellow dress. It was an old ensemble that she had thrown on at the last minute after raiding her closet. She hadn't worn it in years, certainly not since she had given birth to her daughter. It felt a little tight and she worried that it wasn't very flattering. The ill-fitting dress only added to her already heightened anxiety.

"I haven't seen you in ages, girl! I didn't know you'd be at Paulette's wedding," Colleen cried, removing her heavy leather purse from the pew and plopping it onto her ample lap. She shifted over, causing an elderly woman beside her to glance at her annoyance. Colleen then adjusted the wide brim of her sequin- and feather-decorated royal purple hat. "I saw you come in, but you didn't notice me waving at you. What were you thinking about, staring off into space like that?"

Leila pursed her lips as she took the seat nearest to the center aisle. "Just took a little trip down memory lane, that's all."

"*Memory lane?*" Colleen frowned in confusion. Suddenly, her brown eyes widened. "Oh, I forgot! This is the church where you got married too, isn't it?"

Leila nodded.

"Ten years ago last month! Girl, I remember," Colleen continued. "It was a beautiful day, wasn't it? And you had looked so pretty in your gown." She patted Leila's hand in consolation. "I'm so sorry to hear about you and Brad, by the way."

"Don't be sorry," Leila assured.

I'm certainly not, she thought.

Not only had Brad broken her heart, like Evan had predicted, but that man also had put her through so much pain during the course of their marriage—between the lies, philandering, his get-rich-quick schemes, and his all-around bullshit—that he was lucky she hadn't thrown her wedding ring down the garbage disposal in outrage. Instead, she had pawned it to pay for a hatchback she'd purchased for her move from San Diego back to Chesterton. She'd had to get a new car after her Mercedes-Benz was repo'd thanks to Brad neglecting to mention that he hadn't made any payments in four months.

"So it *is* final then?" Colleen asked. "It's over between you two?"

"Almost. The divorce should be finalized in a few months, I guess."

Leila certainly hoped it would be. But frankly, it was no telling with Brad. He had been dragging his feet on the divorce proceedings, saying that his focus was instead on his criminal case. He faced charges for fraud and money laundering because he and his partners had bilked several wealthy clients in Southern California out of more than twenty million dollars with some elaborate Ponzi scheme.

Thanks to Brad, his lawyer, and the California court system, Leila's life was still in limbo. She felt like she was *still* swimming her way out of the whirlpool Brad kept sucking her into.

"Well, I'm glad you came back here," Colleen said. "We missed you. I know I certainly did. I'm sorry your divorce is the reason why you came, but . . . you tried your best, right?"

Leila nodded then turned away to stare at the front of the church, wishing desperately that

Colleen would drop the topic. She didn't want to think about Brad right now. She had enough on her plate today.

"You put up with more than most wives would," Colleen continued, oblivious to Leila's growing discomfort. "It's a wonder you lasted as long as it did. I know I wouldn't have!"

Leila's smile tightened.

"All that lying and cheating—and now that pyramid-scheme nonsense! That man has dragged you through the mud, Leila. Right on through it!" Colleen shook her head ruefully. "Girl, I would have taken a frying pan to the back of that man's head *years* ago!"

It was bad enough to have a wreck of a marriage, to find out that you were sharing a bed every night with a liar and a hustler. But it was ten times worse knowing that everyone in town also knew— and Chesterton was a town that loved its gossip. She was sure her failed marriage and Brad's criminal charges had been gossip du jour in every beauty salon, church gathering, and coffee shop in Chesterton for months!

Of course, Evan had discovered the truth first, but he hadn't needed the town gossips to tell him. He had figured it out himself. He had seen through the varnish and spotted the shoddy workmanship underneath. He had seen the *real* Brad back when she met the smooth-talking Casanova her junior year in college. Though Brad had blinded Leila with his sweet talk, worldliness, and charm, Evan had called him on his bullshit. But she had been too naïve and lovesick at the time to listen to her then best friend. She wished now that she had. It could have spared her a lot of disappointment, agony, and heartbreak in the long run. It could have spared her from severing ties with Evan and the humiliation she was suffering today.

"The flowers are beautiful," Leila said with a false cheeriness, trying to change the subject from Brad. She looked around her again, taking it all in.

Paulette Murdoch was probably deliriously happy with how the decorations had turned out. The décor fit her to a T.

"I knew everything would be this nice though," Leila said. "Paulette's dad never spared an expense, *especially* when it came to his little girl. I've been away for a while, but even I remember that much."

Colleen shook her head and leaned toward Leila's ear. "Not her father, honey," she whispered. "All this was arranged while he was sick in the hospital and after he died seven months ago. It's Evan who dished out the money for this wedding. He controls the purse strings now!"

Of course he does, Leila thought sullenly. Evan controlled everything. He held all the cards, which was why she was here today.

The last note of the melody the string quartet had been playing ended and the violins started to play *Canon in D Major*. The chatter in the sanctuary ceased as the church doors opened. The groom and his six groomsmen strolled toward the front of the church, near the pulpit, in single-breasted tuxedos with pink calla lilies pinned to their lapels.

The groom was a handsome man. He stood at six feet, had ebony-hued skin, and wide shoulders. *Just Paulette's type*, Leila thought, remembering when Evan's little sister had described her ideal man more than a decade ago as Leila painted the teen girl's toenails.

Leila watched as the bridesmaids began the processional. They were all wearing satin gowns of various designs, but in the same shade of lavender. They clutched bouquets of hydrangea, freesias, and roses. The adorable ring bearer and the flower girl made their way down the center aisle next. The little girl reminded Leila of her own daughter, Isabel.

Suddenly, the music changed again. This time it was Vivaldi's *Spring*. Everyone took their cue and rose from the pews in anticipation of the bride's entrance.

Seconds later, Paulette stood in the church doorway, and she took Leila's breath away.

Leila couldn't believe this was the same unassuming teenager she had last seen ten years ago. This woman was beautiful and regal. Her long, dark glossy hair cascaded over her bare burnt-copper-toned shoulders. Her curvy figure was accentuated by the mermaid cut of her strapless wedding gown, which was decorated with Swarovski crystals and lace. A cathedral-length veil trailed behind her dramatically.

Paulette looked so beautiful, so stunning, so absolutely—

Perfect, Leila thought as she stared at her in awe.

And holding Paulette's satin-gloved hand was Evan. Being the new family patriarch, it only seemed right that Evan would give the bride away today. Judging from the grin on his strikingly handsome face, he seemed proud and happy to play the fatherly role.

Evan hadn't aged much in the past decade, but he certainly looked more handsome and distinguished than Leila remembered. He had the same coppery skin as his sister and was even taller than the groom. The glasses he'd often worn during childhood were gone. Leila was happy to see he had finally given them up for good. She had always thought he had the most soulful dark eyes that shouldn't be hidden behind thick, plastic lenses.

As the brother and sister walked down the center aisle toward the altar, a lump formed in Leila's throat. Her heart ached a little. This was the man whom she had once called her best friend. Once, they had been so close. She had been able to turn to Evan in her darkest moments, to confess to him her worst fears. Now he wouldn't even return her emails or phone calls. He hadn't met her daughter. He had gotten married five years ago and she had found out about it months later. She hadn't even met his wife!

Leila stared at the front pew, looking at the faces of the folks who sat there, wondering if his wife was among them.

She and Evan were practically strangers now. What the hell had happened to them?

Time . . . distance . . . silence, she thought.

But they could still make it right, she told herself, filling up with the warmth of the moment. They could put the past behind them. They could make amends. The guy standing in front of her didn't seem petty or angry. Maybe she had just misunderstood him. Maybe they just misunderstood each other. Once she told Evan why she needed his help, he would listen. She knew he would!

As Paulette and Evan drew closer, Leila grinned at the bride, whose loving gaze was focused solely on her husband-to-be.

Meanwhile, Evan's eyes drifted to the wedding guests. He nodded at a few in greeting. Finally, he noticed Leila standing in the pews near the center aisle.

"Hey, Magoo," she mouthed before giving him a timid wave.

Magoo. It was the nickname she had given him back when they were kids. Whenever he hadn't worn his glasses, he had squinted like the cartoon character, Mr. Magoo. His nickname for her had been "Bugs" after Bugs Bunny, thanks to her bucked rabbit teeth, which had thankfully been corrected over time by a good set of braces.

When Leila waved at him as he walked past, Evan did a double take. Leila watched, deflated, as his broad smile disappeared. His face abruptly hardened and his jaw tightened. The dark eyes that she had once admired now snapped back toward the front of the church. Evan looked more than irritated at seeing her standing there in the church pew. He looked downright furious.

The warm, mushy feeling that had swelled inside of her abruptly dissolved. Her cheeks flushed with heat. Her heart began to thud wildly in her chest again.

"There goes that fantasy," the voice in her head scoffed.

She should have known it wouldn't be easy. Evan was obviously still cross at her and even more so now that she had sneaked into his sister's wedding.

Fine, she thought angrily. *Be that way, Evan.*

But she wasn't giving up. She was still going to find a way to talk to him today—or yell at him or plead with him, whatever was required. She would find a way to plead her mother's case.